T0278316

THREADS

OF US

THREADS
OF US

A Novel

CHRISTIE HAVEY SMITH

GREENLEAF
BOOK GROUP PRESS

This is a work of fiction. All characters, businesses, organizations, locations, landmarks, legends, and events are either a product of the author's imagination or are used fictitiously. Any resemblance to actual persons, living or dead, is entirely coincidental.

Published by Greenleaf Book Group Press
Austin, Texas
www.gbgpress.com

Distributed by Greenleaf Book Group

For ordering information or special discounts for bulk purchases, please contact Greenleaf Book Group at PO Box 91869, Austin, TX 78709, 512.891.6100.

Design and composition by Greenleaf Book Group and Kim Lance
Cover design by Greenleaf Book Group and Kim Lance

Publisher's Cataloging-in-Publication data is available.

Print ISBN: 979-8-88645-239-6

eBook ISBN: 979-8-88645-240-2

To offset the number of trees consumed in the printing of our books, Greenleaf donates a portion of the proceeds from each printing to the Arbor Day Foundation. Greenleaf Book Group has replaced over 50,000 trees since 2007.

Printed in the United States of America on acid-free paper

24 25 26 27 28 29 30 31   10 9 8 7 6 5 4 3 2 1

First Edition

For anyone who has ever gotten lost.
And for Adeline. This is for you.

PART ONE

To know where you are going, you first have to
know where you have come from.

—INUIT PROVERB

Everything is held together with stories.
That is all that is holding us together.
Stories and compassion.

—BARRY LOPEZ

PROLOGUE

GRACIE

OCTOBER 2014

A regular person does not run from the last terrible bit of her father's funeral. Only someone who has lost basic coping skills or gone a touch mad would do such a thing. A regular person would, at the very least, maintain the most primitive ability to just hold her chin up for twenty more minutes. But as it turns out, I am not a regular person.

The day had begun with a small gathering of family at Chicago's Lakeside Funeral Home followed by a lovely service at the church. My body had been squeezed by distant relatives, my face clasped by countless pairs of hands, and by the time Aunt Flora and I stepped out of the black town car in front of the cemetery, my shield of emotional composure was deteriorating. I watched in a daze as cars parked one by one in the synchronized choreography of a funeral procession, and when I saw a cousin who had flown all the way from London bobbling toward me from across the parking lot, I ducked my head and followed a stream of black clothing into the gravesite chapel.

My mouth was dry from hours without so much as a stick of gum. I didn't remember being quite so parched when Grandmama Marie died or dear Aunt Hazel. Funerals are strangely dehydrating, but I had handled those sad occasions far more heroically than this one. I found a large peppermint candy rolling around in the bottom of my handbag—miraculously still in its plastic wrapper—and had just popped it into my mouth when I saw Mrs. Dearborn approach.

"You look wonderful, dear," she said, patting my arm with faint affection. "The spitting image of your father." We both hailed from Surrey in the UK but had not seen each other in years.

I lodged the oversized mint into one cheek, then the other, and offered a nearly incomprehensible "Thank you."

That's when Mr. Dearborn charged over to join our conversation. "I'm sorry. Your father was a great man," he said. "You gave a strong eulogy today. In fact, you remind me of him."

"Exactly what I was just saying," Mrs. Dearborn echoed. "Such poise."

I smiled politely and fiddled with my necklace, the string of pearls that had once been my mother's, thinking that might be the end of our exchange. It was not.

"The news must have come as quite a shock," Mrs. Dearborn went on. She kindly extended her thoughts on the difficulty of sudden deaths while I tried to assess whether I might be able to chew the mint without breaking a tooth. I had a talent for humiliating myself in unconventional ways, but certainly I should've been able to conceal this power on such a vulnerable occasion.

Reaching into my bag, I searched for the tissue I'd used earlier to blot my mascara. When I'd scraped every corner and found nothing that could relieve me of the enormous candy, Mr. Dearborn pulled a handkerchief from his breast pocket and gallantly held it out to me.

I had managed to keep a level head all afternoon, but this was the moment I thought I might cry. I forced a smile and accepted the awkward gift, then tried to disguise the transfer of the mint to the handkerchief. After a minute of panic wondering if I should give it back—*absolutely not*—I was free to resume holding my head high. I would let the Dearborns see the likeness of their late friend, all the while wishing that I could just disappear. I would let them see poise, not the twenty-six-year-old woman who was desperate for a glass of water—parched from treading through grief as if it were an Olympic sport, albeit far less dazzling than synchronized swimming or water polo.

"Had you seen him recently?" Mrs. Dearborn asked.

"I was supposed to see him just the next morning," I heard myself say. "There was something he wanted to talk to me about."

"Such a shame."

It *was* a shame. A shame of the highest order. I had lost my father very unexpectedly. It could also be said that I had lost him many years before when I lost myself. Our relationship had been impaired ever since. Now I was left to wonder what he meant to say to me and what I was to make of the things he'd left behind.

The reverend made a move to still the murmuring crowd. "Now, be in touch if you need anything," Mr. Dearborn said. "I hope you keep that chin up."

"But of course, you will," Mrs. Dearborn said. "You are your father's daughter, after all. A fine young lady."

Fine young lady. The words pounded in my head, and the beads of sweat that had trimmed my hairline for hours fell into a trickle of skin-born tears. I swiped my forehead with the back of my hand, not wanting anyone to notice that I was coming undone. But suddenly, my whole body felt heavy with clarity. I was *not* a fine young lady. I was a bloody mess, an imposter modeling a look of bravery when inside I felt as though I was going down in battle.

To the Dearborns, I said, "Thank you very much."

To myself I muttered, *you're not fine.*

That's when the panic ignited like fire in my belly and rose into a flush on my face. My breath became shallow as if a two-ton weight had been placed on my chest. Adrenaline fizzed through me in a rush of heat and made my muscles feel as though they were swelling against my bones. My heart pounded, my blood sugar dropped, and as I struggled for oxygenation, I debated my options. Would I stand there and fight against my body's distress, cling to the low likelihood of shattering into pieces? Or would I run, flee the whole unbearable scene?

I glanced around the room. Did I even know these people? I tried to look away from the sea of strange faces; still, I felt every sympathetic gaze. Everyone could see that David Wilder's daughter was nothing short of a disaster—a one-hundred-and-eight-pound weakling unraveling before their eyes. I forced air into my lungs, then out again, and when the reverend had successfully captured the attention of the room, I made my exit. I slipped out the chapel door and stepped onto the lawn that laced the paved road to the gravesite.

It was autumn in Chicago. The air was infused with an earthy aroma, and a mist hung high in the sky. I wobbled on the damp sod in heeled shoes, trying to catch my breath, and lifted my face to the sun. I imagined it would refract the light in my watery eyes and transform them from hazel-gray into brilliant emerald. "The irrepressible green of sadness," my father once said after I'd been crying. I'm not sure if anyone else had ever seen my eyes change in color. Such details have a way of vanishing before anyone can understand the story.

I knew a few things about vanishing acts. My father had perpetually moved around the globe, leaving one city for the next. As a result, there was very little evidence of my childhood. Even if there had been a steady landscape where I could have planted a time capsule, I'm not sure what I would have put inside it. My first pair of dance shoes perhaps, old mix tapes, or the photograph my father took outside Highclere Castle when I was five. The photo had sat in a sterling frame for a time, fostering a memory. It was a portrait of me striding across a gravel footpath with a toy sword in one outstretched hand. Rogue twists of hair framed fierce delight on my face, as if I were prepared to protect earth, body, or soul with nothing more than a five-dollar gift shop item and a sparkle in my eye.

For some reason, this is the image that came to me as I tried to collect myself outside the chapel. I wondered where the photo in the sterling frame had gone and wished I had found a way to bury mementos instead of memories.

Wrenching one heel from the lawn and then the other, I stumbled toward the road in my tailored skirt. I pulled my cell phone from my bag and lifted it this way and that, hoping for a signal, for a ride—an escape route of any kind.

"Gracie," came a deep voice. Startled, I turned. Beau Griffin, my father's building contractor, stood on the grass behind me. "I'm so sorry for your loss," he said with a rare genuineness. "I don't mean to disturb. I saw you step out, and I just wanted to see if you were okay." He stuffed his hands into his pockets and looked up to where I still held my phone to the sky. "What are we doing out here?"

Though he was only slightly older than me, in that desperate moment, Beau Griffin reminded me of one of the mature oak trees clustered there on the lawn. Tall, rugged, gentle—a strength into which I could perhaps lean without too much bother. I lowered my phone. "I'm trying to get a signal. To order a car. Do you have a signal?"

"Well, I have a car. Do you need a ride?"

I nodded vigorously.

"No problem." He glanced over his shoulder. "But do you want to go back in there first?"

I imagined all those people stopping to look at me, David Wilder's resilient daughter, and the ground swayed below me. He extended a steady hand, but I shifted away. "If you don't mind, I'd just like to go."

We started in the direction of the parking lot. He had to hurry to keep pace. "It was a nice service," he said. "Never seen that many carnations before."

"Aunt Flora thought that was better than going for the roses."

"I think carnations are totally underrated."

I squinted up at him, doubtful, but his face was sincere. "I always thought funerals were supposed to reflect the person who died. One last celebration in their honor before getting them on to their final resting place. But I'm not sure there has been much of my dad in this day. There should have been roses. There should have been a soprano singing Puccini at the church. And Aunt Flora is serving chocolate cake at the luncheon. He didn't even like chocolate cake."

"Too rich."

"Exactly." He stopped walking, prompting me to do the same. I peered up at Beau Griffin and into a halo of sunlight. "His ashes shouldn't even be here," I said. "They should be buried in Surrey with my mum."

One corner of his mouth curled up tentatively. "You know, Gracie, I think funerals are for getting the people who are grieving wherever it is *they* need to go."

"You do?"

He moved toward one of the parked cars. We had passed a row of silent sedans, coupes, and SUVs in every shade of gray, but he unlocked the passenger door to a brilliant blue classic convertible. I'm not a car person, but it was glorious.

"Is this yours?" I asked.

"It's a Ford Falcon," he said, more self-conscious than proud of the unlikely getaway car. "You ready?"

I hoped he wouldn't notice my eyes turning emerald as I slid into the refuge of the passenger seat, trying not to choke on emotion.

The Falcon's white canvas top was secured in place, but the windows were down when we pulled out onto the pavement. Waves of dark hair lifted from my face while I watched the cemetery disappear in the side mirror. I was a thousand miles away from accepting that this—running and numbing and avoiding—does not, in fact, work. The burden of heartache cannot be lifted on a fleeting autumn breeze and left behind in a pile of oak leaves. And answers do not materialize on the horizon simply because one wishes them to appear.

———

But answers do come. Not scripted in longhand or printed tidily in black ink, but they come. Understanding arises like a memory or photograph unfolding from where it was long ago tucked away. It arises when the warrior child recalls that she's not made of poise and pearls; when she decides she's had quite enough of running and bravely strides back out into the fray, knowing she can feel everything and not fall to pieces.

I just wasn't ready yet.

GRACIE

EIGHT DAYS EARLIER

"Hold your breath and you'll nosedive," my copilot yelled into his headset, seemingly unfazed as the plane pulled sideways. "This happens with a single-engine aircraft; propellers spin clockwise, and we roll left." I adjusted my control inputs, but the torque of the plane intensified, throwing us into a spin. We were falling headfirst, with a deep length of blue the only thing in sight. "Shit!" my copilot yelled, this time in a far more pressing tone. "That's not sky, Gracie, that's Lake Michigan! Come on. Do something. Pull up!" I grabbed hard on the yoke but could not get the nose of the plane to pitch upward. Our momentum only increased. I could not take in air. Then there was darkness.

I was damp with sweat when I awoke.

This was the day I was to revive my career with a singular act—like a trapeze artist midair, hoping to catch a singular bar. So I suppose it was fitting to start the morning by tumbling through the sky. A parachute would have been nice, though. Free-falling into oblivion was not the subtext I'd envisioned for this critical moment. Certainly, it was not going to help my fear of flying. I reasoned that my dream was nothing more than classic anxiety—perfectly ordinary. Although, as I pulled myself from a tangle of sheets and put my feet on solid ground, I did find it peculiar that my copilot had my father's face.

I had recently taken a fall of a different sort when I was dismissed from my position with Boden Contemporary Dance. Thankfully, one of my former teachers from Juilliard had invited me to dance in the Contemporary Choreographer's Showcase, an event hosted by Garza Dance Company. Olivia Garza, my idol since I was a girl, had danced with New York City Ballet before returning to her roots in Chicago and starting a company of her own. Now she was recruiting new dancers. I had rehearsed for weeks, and like that audacious acrobat, placed my hopes and dreams on a single catch—today's performance.

I fumbled around in the dark for a warm pullover and made a dash for the thermostat in the living room. The front window and its yawning metal frame were to blame for the chill in the air, but they were also responsible for the splendid peek-a-boo view of Lake Michigan. This morning the water was rough, and the trees that lined the city street below bent west with gusts of wind. A marathon of gold and crimson leaves blew by the window, letting fate carry them, as I imagine we all must. I stretched my arms above my head until I heard my back crack, then went to get ready.

I was sitting on the yellow tile countertop in the kitchen finishing a bowl of bran flakes when my flatmate's curvy figure appeared in the doorframe. Ana's dark hair was piled neatly on top of her head, and she already had her bag slung over one arm. "Today's the big day," she sang as she went for the coffeepot.

I shut my eyes against the thought. "It's colossal. Wait until you see the choreography. Hardest I've been given in years."

"Please, you're like a prodigy," she said while filling a travel mug with smells of hazelnut and cream. "And I've never seen you prepare more for a performance. You're ready."

In the seven years I'd known Ana, she'd never been anything but honest. Still, I had self-doubts. "You really think so?"

"I'm telling you, honey. Just go out there today and do what you know how to do. And don't fuck up."

"Ha! No pressure." I hopped off the counter, my Converse low-tops squeaking against the floor.

"Hang on," she said, taking a step closer to me. "You've been pulling at your eyebrows again."

"Damn. I know." I stooped to catch my reflection in the chrome toaster. "I don't know why I do that. There's nothing left but scraggly bits."

"Hold still." She fished a brow pencil from her bag and went to work skillfully filling them in. "That should do it, but keep this," she said, handing me the pencil. "I've got to go."

"Thanks, Ana. I'll walk out with you."

"Where are you headed?" she asked as I followed her across the floral rug in the living room to the front door.

"I'm meeting Mark for an early coffee."

"He's coming to the show, right?"

"I think so."

"You think so?" She turned to face me, her naturally thick brows lifting suspiciously. "Does Mark know how important today is to you?"

"Yes. He's been really supportive. Just busy with work," I said, opening the door to the building corridor.

She tilted her head, her eyes softening. "I don't know, G. I'm not sure I see it."

"See what?" I scooted her into the hall so I could lock up.

"This thing with Mark. I mean, is he the person you tell all your stories to?"

"I don't know. Is that the relationship measuring stick now?"

She tapped the elevator button with a knuckle. "It's a part of intimacy."

"Right, but that can evolve over time. It's not like we have to dive all the way in from the start to know if we're a good match."

She hit the button a second time. The building was old and the elevator, slow. "You've been together for nine months."

"And you and Tess for almost a year, and it's not like you're talking about long-term plans."

"That's not—" She stopped herself.

"What? Not true?"

"We should take the stairs."

"Ana, what are you not telling me?" I asked as we began our descent down the four flights, my voice echoing in the lofty stairwell.

"It's your big day," she reminded me. "We should be talking about the showcase."

But once we were on the pale travertine floor of the lobby, she turned to me and conceded with a sigh. "Tess asked me to move in with her. Before the first of the month. I'm so sorry, G. I've been wanting to tell you, but with everything you have going on—"

"This is great!" I said, my voice possibly raising an octave too high.

"Yeah?" Her big brown eyes searched my face as I tried to hide my disappointment. It's not that I thought she'd be my flatmate forever. I just hadn't allowed myself to imagine her ever leaving.

"Of course," I said. "It's exciting!"

"I don't want to bail on you with the rent and everything, honey. But Tess is the one. I mean, I've never been so happy."

"Yes! You should move in with Tess."

She pulled me in for a hug that can only be described as an affection-ate mugging. After what felt like several minutes, she set me in front of her. "Okay, time for your big day."

I lifted my chin with a plucky can-do spirit. "I got this."

"Hell yeah, you do. And I've got my tickets right here." She pulled them from her bag and slid them into her cleavage for safekeeping. "Fifth row center, baby!" she added before shimmying out the door.

Ana headed south for the Magnificent Mile where she would take the early shift waiting tables at an upscale bistro, and after attending my performance that afternoon, she would finish her day playing upright bass in a local jazz club until two a.m. I headed east, wishing I had thought to bring an umbrella.

It had been a balmy start to October. One might have confused it for spring if it hadn't been for the orange foliage and the absence of bees in the park. Now temperatures had dropped, and clouds were threatening rain. People left apartment buildings in groups the size of elevator cars and tangled with the winds as they scattered up the street. By the time I could see the spot where I was to meet Mark, winds were blowing up skirts all over town. I pulled a red scarf from my bag and fixed it on my head as drops of rain started pelting the pavement. "Some weather," a woman said to me as we forged into the crosswalk. I readily agreed and followed the wind into the Dollop coffee shop.

The room buzzed with caffeine-infused activity. I pulled my scarf down around my shoulders and looked for a seat. A man with loads of teeth nodded at me and then at the empty chair at his table. I smiled timidly and instead chose one of the two empty stools by the window— prime coffee-shop real estate and a fine spot to wait for Mark.

In the time that Mark and I had been together, he'd passed the bar exam and become an associate at Stetson and Lawrey. His schedule was demanding, and though I didn't mind the nonchalance of a quick morning coffee, I'd pinned my hopes on him being able to attend my performance that afternoon.

Rain beat against the glass pane as he came pushing through the door. "What a jam to get out this morning," he said, shaking out his coat and draping it over the stool beside me. "The office called while I was trying to leave, and then everyone in the whole damn city decided to get on the El." He leaned over, his face softening into a kiss. "Hi, gorgeous."

I palmed his cheeks to dry the rain. "You've been burning the candle at both ends."

"I don't do anything halfway." He paused. "Are you wearing a cape?"

I touched the red fabric loosely knotted around my neck and gave him a winning smile. "It's a rain cape. All the fashion this season."

"Sexy," he said, clearly amused. "I'll put in an order. The usual?"

"Yes, thank you." I watched Mark step away to order a cup of tea for me and a large coffee, extra hot, for him. He looked smart in his navy suit and tie. There was something about his stature then that reminded me of a marble column. It might have been the gleaming fabric of his suit or his confident posture. Whatever it was, I now wondered if I looked as tousled as I felt. I returned my scarf to my bag and fidgeted with my burgundy cardigan, but the cotton weave resisted tidying.

Mark strode back over, a cup in each hand and a cluster of white square napkins wedged between two fingers. "Did you get my message?" He took a sip of his drink and then plunked his cup down hard, grimacing with the burn of hot coffee. He certainly didn't do anything by halves.

"When did you call?"

"This morning. But your phone went straight to voicemail. Is it off?"

I pulled my phone from my bag and saw that the battery was dead. "Shit. I must have forgotten to charge it last night. With everything on my mind, I didn't even think to check."

"Busy day?" he asked. And I knew that he'd forgotten. How had he *forgotten*?

"Oh, just the showcase," I said with mild sarcasm.

His surprise was earnest. "My God, that's today? Shit! I have to be in court at eleven and again at two. I don't know how I'd get down there in time."

This all hit a little hard. Less so the not-going part; more so the forgetting part. I understood that Mark had a lot on his mind, but it seemed I hadn't made the cut. I was off the mind, so to speak. I tend to be cheerful in undesirable circumstances. When waiting forty minutes in the cold for a bus that doesn't come, or saddling up for that mammogram my doctor ordered to be sure the lump was nothing more than a pocket of fluid, I push on with a smile. Genuine positivity in the face of discomfort—a coping mechanism, I expect. Survival by the cheeriest. But that morning in the café, my goodwill toward objectionable situations was in short supply. I might have even given Mark a salty look when he said, "My God, that's today?" I didn't mean to lay on a guilt trip or anything; I was simply hoping for a different outcome.

"Do you have to attend both appointments?" I asked. "Maybe one of the other associates—"

But he was quick in his defense, pithy as ever. "It has to be me, Gracie. I can't just step away midday. You've seen how hard I'm working." It was true. We'd both been working hard. He sighed loudly. The couple sitting beside us might have glanced over. "You know I'd be there if I could. I feel terrible that you're disappointed."

Weirdly, now *I* felt guilty. For feeling disappointed, I suppose. "It's okay," I assured him.

After a resolving moment, Mark said, "How about I take you to that little patisserie that you love later tonight? We can gorge ourselves on chocolate croissants, get post-performance fat and happy, and you can tell me every perfect detail."

I smiled at the suggestion and gave his arm a squeeze in a show of forgiveness. "I have dinner plans with my father, but I can meet you afterward."

Mark inclined his head, perhaps recalling this detail, which I was sure I'd already shared. My father's career was in the global marketplace. He traveled thirty-five weeks of the year to New York, Singapore, London, or Hong Kong. He'd spent most of this year doing business in Madrid, but today, I was his destination.

"You nervous?" Mark asked. "Performing in front of Olivia Garza?" His eyes widened with excitement.

"Yes! Exhaustion has been the closest I've come to relaxing for weeks."

"I'm with you there." His phone buzzed from inside his pocket. He pulled it out and asked if I'd mind excusing him for just a minute. I raised my cup in a salute as he took leave briefly, stepping outside under the shallow shelter of the marquee.

I passed the time the way I always did, by people-watching. A dozen customers were casually queuing up, waiting for mochas and lattes. I

jiggled my foot to the tune of idle chatter, the espresso machine sputtering in a soprano key, and the rain prattling a rhythm against the
windows. A woman at a small table tenderly fed her toddler rice cereal
from a purple spoon while the child repetitively thumped the table with
happy hands. An elderly man methodically unfolded his newspaper, the
pages rustling quietly underneath it all. The day itself was unfolding,
splendid and ordinary, completely unaware of my jittering foot and the
butterflies beating noisily inside me.

———

My au pair Madame Bisset had taught me about the butterflies. She
had a way of making nervousness sound delightful and exciting. "It's just
little *papillons*," she would say. "Nothing that can hurt you, *ma chérie*."
Madame Bisset moved with my father and me from Paris to Montreal
the year I turned nine. She packed only one bag, her avocado-green hard
case containing floral dresses and novels with covers picturing dramatic
women with mounds of hair. Madame Bisset had a pile of hair herself
in striking auburn, and she always wore bright red lipstick, which would
crinkle into a pucker on her lips when she was quietly thinking. Her
voice was light, and she could make it small enough to speak for my
dolls or the mice that scampered across the attic rafters on warm nights.
By day, we followed the ducks around the pond and the tourists through
the park. Like the tourists, we wondered and wandered and dreamed.

Madame Bisset was as steady as the heat wave of my summer in
Paris, and she stayed with me for six solid years after, from Montreal to
Rome. I had many childhoods, but those years eclipsed them all. She
made it possible not to feel the subtle but ever-present ache for my
mother, who was taken by a cancer that traveled from breast to bone
undetected during the year she nursed me.

Before the care of Madame Bisset, I lived in Zurich for fourteen
months under the watchful eyes of Miss Landenberger, a no-nonsense

woman with a unibrow and no patience at bedtime. Prior to Landen-berger, I was cared for by Nanny Odili for two years in Singapore. And before all of them, there was the very Irish and magnificently freckled Nanny Tracey, who I simply called Tutu. She was with me in England after my mother passed. She saw me through my fifth birthday and the move to Singapore before moving back to Ireland, where she said she needed to go about the business of growing old.

My final au pair who bridged the gap of time between Madame Bisset and adulthood was an American to whom I kept no emotional ties. By then I knew not to truly love anything that could leave.

Madame Bisset used to say, "*Aide-toi et le ciel t'aidera.*" Heaven helps those who help themselves. "People will come in and out of your life, Gracie darling; you must find your own direction." She did her best to help a compliant and nervous young girl know her own heart and calm her own mind.

One evening on the way home from the shops, when the sky was thick with clouds and darkness fell like a blanket before the sun had fully set, a panic grew in my chest. I squeezed Madame Bisset's hand as my body rattled with apprehension. "We need a taxi. It's too dark," I insisted.

But she did not bat an eyelash at my demands. "What's the matter with the dark?" she asked innocently. I didn't dignify the question with an answer. It seemed perfectly obvious to me that the dark was where ominous creatures lurked.

"Find your feet," she said, and I obediently left my anxious mind and looked to the ground. "Now find the music."

"There isn't any music," I argued. I could only hear the traffic on the street, a car horn, a police whistle.

"There's music everywhere. Find the rhythm of something outside yourself and move to that instead of your anxious thoughts."

It sounded like a game, so I loosened my grip on Madame Bisset and let my feet find a metrical stride to the rhythm of the street noise. After we'd danced the three blocks home, Madame Bisset's ruby red mouth bowed like a curl of ribbon. "You have a song in here too," she said, pointing to where my heart thumped gleefully in my chest. "You must learn to listen for it. This is how you will find your way."

I tilted my head, confused.

"You are not the nervous butterflies, Gracie darling; they will come and go. You are the music that will get you further than up the street—that will take you all the way. Do you understand?" I don't suppose I fully grasped Madame Bisset's loving words that night, but I wanted to become the music and dance.

By my ninth birthday, my only wish was to go to the ballet. My father bought two tickets to Les Grands Ballets Canadiens de Montréal. Madame Bisset dressed me in a silver skirt and clapped when I twirled the fabric into a halo of silk at my waist. When I stepped into the theater and saw the grand stage for the first time, I was overcome with excitement.

The ballet that had come to town was *Coppélia*. I was entranced with the female ballerina perched on a high balcony, and her pursuer, Franz, who fell in love with her though he did not know she was merely the doll of a mad scientist. The lead was danced by the most elegant woman I had ever seen, Olivia Garza. She was luminous, with almond-colored skin, and her feet skimmed the floor with elegance and energy. Her performance was so extraordinary that I could barely take in the other dancers.

She was music.

By the end of the ballet, I knew I would become a dancer like Olivia Garza. I told my father, "One day I will perform on a big stage like this one."

His eyes crinkled. "Maybe one day you will."

Seventeen years later, I had risen to meet the expectations of the world around me and found much success. But I had failed to meet the most basic expectation I had held for myself: *Find your own direction.* I could follow intricate choreography, but I could no longer find my way in the dark. I could hear the music of the outside world, but I could no longer trust what I found within myself. The echoes of Madame Bisset's voice sang in my memory: "It's just little *papillons*. Nothing that can hurt you, *ma chérie*."

———

Thunder rumbled in the distance as Mark reentered the coffee shop. "Sorry about that," he said when he took his seat. "I just can't miss a beat on this case. It's huge." He dragged out the vowel in *huge* for emphasis.

"A tough one to sort out?" I asked.

"No, we have a solid strategy in place. I just mean that it could be huge for my career."

I was genuinely proud of him, but as Mark went on to explain the nature of his appointments that afternoon, my mind clung to the word *huge* with curiosity. No matter what I'd accomplished in my short life, I did not think I had done anything huge, exactly. Necessary, yes; exciting, of course; regrettable, to be sure; but never positively huge. I was wondering if I should measure my day, assess its weight and volume, when I heard Mark take an audible sip of his coffee. "I really am sorry I'll miss your show," he said, swigging down the last of it.

"It will be one hell of a performance," I said brightly.

"Will someone record it?"

I promised to ask, careful to disclaim, "Of course, I'm just in the one piece."

"A lot to sift through for two minutes," he reasoned.

"Right. Four minutes, but yes." I hoped minutes were not the measurement for the size of one's day. I smoothed my paper napkin into a rectangle, carefully matching the corners, then asked, "What did it say? Your voicemail this morning."

"Oh, that I'd like for you to come with me to an event next Saturday. It's a black-tie kind of thing, so I wanted to give you a heads-up. You'll need a dress. It's just a bunch of attorneys, but hopefully you won't be too bored." He gave me a wink.

"Yes. Of course. Sounds lovely."

"Thanks, Gracie." His phone buzzed again, and he glanced down at it. "Shit. I've got to take this."

"Go. Really. I have a full morning anyway. I'll see you tonight."

"Thanks for being a champ about this. I know you'll do great."

"Knock wood," I said, rapping my knuckles on the countertop.

He kissed me as he rose from his chair. "This is Mark," he spoke into the phone.

"Good luck," I called out. *You too*, he mouthed silently before breezing out the door.

Once he'd gone, I watched people file out of the café and make their way into the morning. Others entered from the street, swinging through the glass door, shaking rain from their clothes before greeting friends. I watched as back and forth the world entered and exited through the swinging door, the movement fanning the flutter of the *papillons* inside me and the rhythm of my anxious right foot. Nerves were typical before a big performance, but it seemed something else was stirring in me. I wondered what Madame Bisset would have said about it. She'd likely have tilted her head to one side, pursed her red lips together, and quietly asked, "What do *you* imagine it is, Gracie darling?"

GRIFFIN

It had been a long time since I'd put on a shirt with a collar. I pulled an old J. Crew out of the back of my closet and the ironing board from where it was collecting dust in the basement. I showered, trimmed my beard down to something a little fuller than stubble, and even spritzed some cologne. By the time I surveyed the results in the bureau mirror, I hardly recognized myself. This was a far cry from my typical T-shirt and jeans, but it was what the day called for.

I grabbed my jacket and walked down Hudson Street toward the Brown Line train. It was the long way around, an old divergence. I still lived within the eight-block radius that had hosted my childhood. The red brick and green ivy buildings were like old relatives, and that morning it felt like the city itself was watching me.

Construction workers stood under an awning staring up at the rain and cursing the misleading weather report. I could see where they'd been pouring asphalt into hairline cracks in the road, last efforts before the first snowfall. I always found the process satisfying to watch. It reminded me of a documentary I saw once on the art of gold repair in Japan called *kintsugi*—repairing broken ceramics, historic pieces, and heirlooms by pouring liquid gold into the seams. I stepped between raindrops and over veins in the newly glued pavement, steering clear of the still-tacky areas.

Liquid gold did not flow through my part of town, but its history wasn't unlike a variety of broken pieces having been fused together. Families with long lineage, diverse with stories of searching and surviving, had settled here and created a new kind of history—one with cracks and imperfections, but also stability and pride. My father was second-generation Irish and my mother first-generation Brazilian. Their stories, like all their neighbors and friends, were harbored in the old brick and ivy. I practically nodded with reverence when I passed. Each structure seemed to know the secrets of the men and women who had built them and kept them. They knew the footsteps of those who had come and gone. I could almost see how arguments had splintered the plaster, how insane laughter had filtered through the wooden surfaces, and just out of reach were accounts of the children who were raised and the elderly who were buried—their stories had seeped into the foundation. I'd spent my working life in construction repairing historic buildings. I was pretty sure the city itself knew all my secrets.

There was one building in my neighborhood that seemed to understand more than any other what a person can endure in the search for happiness. I turned my back to the wind and humbly faced its towering presence. Its lower windows were boarded up and its door was bolted shut in silence. Old Fidelis and I had both hit a run of bad luck, but for a long time this relic had been a beacon. Erected as St. Christopher's Church in 1850, it was one of the few buildings to survive the Great Chicago Fire of 1871. Sometime after, it was given the nickname *Fidelis*, a Latin word meaning "faithful and true." During World War II, the old stone lady supervised neighborhood black-out drills, and in 1968, she stood tall as civil unrest assailed the city. For those who looked up, Fidelis remained a symbol of unbeatable courage. Then in 1972, a businessman named Carl Abrams bought the dilapidated church, reinforced it with steel beams, and converted the three-story structure into office lofts to be inhabited by ordinary CPAs and chiropractors. Despite its new commercial function (and the irreverent renaming: the Abrams Building), Abrams upheld tradition and allowed the community to access its massive stone arch.

I learned about the local legend before I could talk. Grandparents tell their grandchildren to believe in the healing arch of Fidelis, and sooner or later those children grow to taste some kind of trouble and meander in with a loss or a fear to give over to the wall. They write their hardships down on small scraps of paper and wedge them between the gaps in the stones, hoping the holy house will heal their pain. Abrams respected its significance within the community and allowed visitors to drift in and out of the lobby during business hours. But parents and grandparents say it was never the same.

Fidelis was my favorite spot in the city. As a kid, my mom would take me there after school and let me eat my snack on the bench that faced the front entrance. She remembered Fidelis from her own youth when it was still a church and she could attend Sunday service before her shift in the women's section of Marshall Field's department store. The only Fidelis I knew was the one with Abrams's placard nailed into the brick, but that wasn't what I saw when I stood beneath it. I saw its immense cathedral window and impressive spire. I memorized every etching in the stonework above the Corinthian columns. I knew it all by heart. I was going to become an architect. I was going to design a building that could match its strength and character. Anyway, I was going to try.

I was eleven years old the summer Jimmy Valasco dared me to steal a paper from the arch. A bunch of us kids from Little League were trading baseball cards on the steps of the building, when Valasco noticed that I was more interested in Fidelis than his Ozzie Guillén rookie card. I was sure that Valasco was the kind of guy who would drown kittens for fun, and I looked to my best friend Daryl Cooper for an out. Cooper, who had discovered his dad's weight-lifting set and had prematurely formed biceps under his dark skin, was my only chance at keeping Valasco from tormenting me for life. But Cooper was ascending in the social order of our neighborhood, and after assessing the dare, he said that he didn't see the harm in it. That sealed the deal.

I opened the heavy oak doors of Fidelis to commit a crime, a cultural misdemeanor. The air inside the soaring atrium was cold. I surveyed the massive arc of stone trimmed with crumpled paper, checked to be sure that no one was watching me, then snatched one of the papers from the wall and ran.

When I held my prize up to Valasco, he laughed as if it wasn't a big deal. But when I got home and opened the thin, aged message, I knew it was in fact a very big deal. The perfect cursive script read: *I cannot have a baby. I will never have a child. Please receive my anguish.* I didn't know much about babies not being born when I was eleven, but I believed that I'd stolen a woman's chance to heal. The idea of it has haunted my life. Fidelis would tell you if it could. It knows the whole story.

⁓

My train car was full. I squeezed between a woman in a business suit and a man with an oversized energy drink longer than I liked before getting off at Chicago Avenue. Even with the shaving and the ironing, I still had an hour before my appointment with David Wilder. Enough time for a routine visit to Oakview Assisted Living.

Teddy was already in the lobby when I arrived. He grabbed my shoulders a little harder than usual when I pulled him in for a hug. My little brother was not as tall or as broad as me in build, but what he lacked in size he made up for with genuine enthusiasm. I knew from the size of his greeting that he was concerned about me. "How's it going, man?" he asked.

"Good," I lied. "They down yet?"

Teddy shook his head and led the way to a small table in the corner of the dining hall. The room smelled like oatmeal and antiseptic. "You all set for your meeting?" Teddy asked.

"I better be. I got all my chips on this one."

"It'll go great, brother. You deserve this." That was questionable, but I was grateful for the kindness.

David Wilder had called me to bid on a project, the details of which I did not yet know. I had been his contractor on the remodeling of his foyer a few years back, and his kitchen more recently. But I hadn't been getting very many jobs lately, and I never count on a paycheck until I have cash in my hand.

"You making ends meet this month?" I asked my little brother.

"Sure. How about you?"

"Don't worry about me," I insisted while pouring orange juice from a plastic pitcher into two small paper cups. "Keeping my nose—"

"To the grindstone," we said in unison. A lesson of hard work deeply ingrained.

But the truth was, the old adage had been more of a literal deface-ment. My wife, Keira, had recently left me. My business, Griffin Custom Homes, was on the outs, and my life's plans were too. I was a lost dog short of a country song.

Teddy poured another round of OJ. "What do you say we meet up with Cooper tonight and grab some dinner? He's investigating a new case, but said he'd be free around six. We can celebrate your big meet-ing and try those hot wings that Coop says could bring a corpse back to life." I could only say yes. My little brother hadn't quit on me, even though I was the corpse in this scenario who would have preferred to just drink a six-pack of beer on the couch.

Everybody gets kicked in the teeth a few times. Only twice had I been knocked down hard enough to place an appeal in the stone arch of Fidelis. The first time, I was thirteen. I'd felt the seams of the stones for a lonely gap that could hold these words: *Please bring my mother back. I need her. Thank you, Beau Griffin.*

My mother was diagnosed with early onset Alzheimer's a month before my fifteenth birthday, but I knew that something was wrong long before that. At first it was only little things, like forgetting words, confusing directions, or losing track of what day it was. She and Pop must have tried to ignore it for some time. Maybe they avoided it like I did the study in our house on Park Avenue—the room where she lit a fire in the fireplace on a winter night, using Sunday's newspaper as kindling, before wandering off to bed. The wood had been very dry that winter, and a spark must have caught the nearby newspaper pages. The smoke alarm woke us. Pop used a fire extinguisher on the ignited carpet and a smoldering wall while Mom demanded to know who had been playing with matches. Pop's tears were as desperate as Mom's need for an explanation. Or at least that's how I remember it. After that, I found ways to dodge the study completely, walking the extra distance around through the kitchen to reach the front door. I downplayed my cautious maneuvers through the house, pretending that running the long way around was only a game. But I would never really be rid of the trouble that happened in there. It wasn't mine to do away with. It belonged to the house on Park Avenue.

Mom moved into Oakview Assisted Living before I graduated from high school. Pop spent nearly every day there, and with his nights he tended to our old house. Then, last summer, I hitched a trailer to the back of my pickup and helped move Pop into the nursing home too. When we went to see Mom in the memory care unit, she thought Pop was the building manager come to fix the window that didn't open. By some miracle, she was still alive, but she didn't know us. I wasn't sure Fidelis had any power at all, but that didn't stop me from going to the wall a second time shortly after I moved Pop into the nursing home. That sad little message read: *I've destroyed everything. Please help me make it right. I'm so sorry. B.G.*

"What time's your interview?" Pop was asking, all business, as he wheeled Mom's chair into the patch of sunlight next to Teddy at the table. Mom's gray hair was pulled back, accentuating her hollowed cheekbones.

I recalled Pop saying on her seventieth birthday that she'd earned every one of those gray hairs. Pop had already toasted eighty and looked thinner up top by the day. I visited Oakview several times a week, but there were moments when I almost couldn't recognize those two fragile people as my parents.

"It's not for an hour, Pop. Plenty of time," I assured him. I got up to greet my mother. She was calm and approachable that morning, but her eyes told me that I was something new. She patted my face with her cold palm. I would have done anything to have just a couple of minutes with the woman I used to know. The woman who spoke fluent English and Portuguese, who sang when she cooked and laughed with her whole body. I would have told her all that had happened, and she would have helped me make sense of it. Instead, I smiled into the vacant face before me and offered her some orange juice.

"You can't rely on the train schedule," Pop said. "You should give yourself thirty minutes to get there."

"It's just up the block," Teddy said in my defense.

Pop peered down his round, reddened nose. I could see the indentation where his glasses had been. He never skipped reading Mom the morning paper. She may not have known what year it was, but Pop made sure she was up to speed on global politics and the old neighborhood. "You don't want to blow this, Son."

"I don't plan to blow it, Pop."

"That's a good lad," he said, as he'd said so many times before. It didn't matter that I was thirty. I could just as well have been ten. "And if this doesn't work out, I have a friend in commercial renovation. Bob Kelly. I'm sure he'd hire you. I'd just have to make a call."

"I have my own company, Pop," I reminded him between clenched teeth. "I don't need to take a job with Bob Kelly."

"It's good to have options when work is slow," he said, then quickly changed the subject. "Did you hear that your cousin Jack is getting married? Met a gal at a charity benefit."

I nodded and took a bite of oatmeal.

"She's a real gem, Jack says. The kind that will be in it for the long haul."

"Pop . . ." Teddy said cautiously.

"What?" he postured. "It's nice to remember there are good people out there. Willing to commit and work through things."

I dropped my spoon into my bowl with a clank. "You going to make this about Keira at every breakfast?"

"I just don't understand what the hell happened there."

That was because I had never tried to explain it to him. "Sometimes you just have to let people go, Pop." I jammed another spoonful of oatmeal into my mouth to keep from saying anything more.

I ate quickly, then squatted down in front of Mom and told her, "I hope it's a good day."

Her deep brown eyes seemed almost lucid then, as if for just a second she recognized something. She leaned in a little closer and said in a voice I'm sure only I could hear, "One moment begets the next."

The hairs on the back of my neck stood on end. Were these words surfacing at random? Like a song lyric that got repeated, lingered, and was now lifting from the void? I called Mom's confusion "the void" because it felt like an empty hallway, no more in the present than the past, where a person sits until they're allowed to peek through the door into the land of the living. I used to sit in the hallway of the house on Park Avenue listening through the bedroom door to Mom crying until she'd get wise and say, "Go on, Beau. I'm fine." I'm sure everyone knows some kind of empty hallway. But Mom spent most of her time in hers. And I couldn't be sure if the words she spoke then were random or if she was peeking through the door, having found a way to say something when all other words were lost. I couldn't be sure, but there was something in her eyes that gave me reason to think that she was speaking to *me*. And then she said it again and touched my cheek with her fragile hand. "One moment begets the next."

The train car was only half full when I boarded. I took a seat in the back and propped my head against the chilled window, letting the cold spread down the side of my face.

People had worse things to deal with than me. If the world were full of stone archways that could unburden human pain, they'd all be full. But that morning my burden felt particularly heavy. As the old El train and I gasped into the station, I hoped my meeting with Mr. Wilder would help me turn things around.

3

GRACIE

It had been Ana who suggested I try therapy. Shortly after I lost my position with Boden Dance—when I was still walking around the apartment like a zombie in pajamas—she took me by the shoulders and said, "It's time." She handed me a piece of paper with a phone number and the name Dr. Dionne Peck scribbled in blue ink. I tried to protest, telling her I was fine, that I just needed a few more days to get my head around it. It was just a job. But Ana and I both knew it wasn't just my job that had been pulled out from under me. Dance was my identity, formed by decades of training. Getting sacked from a prestigious dance company at age twenty-six was not unlike receiving a devastating prognosis from a doctor. I could be finished. And this was the rut that finally pitched me into therapy, into the soft mauve-colored chair in Dr. Peck's downtown office. I'd been at it for nearly four months but was only just getting the hang of it.

As I wound my way through her building the morning of the show-case, I wondered if it might have been poor planning to see her before my performance. I had no interest in talking about Mark and his not coming to the show. I needed to put that behind me. But I was still curious about the dream I'd had that morning and wondered what Dr. Peck would have to say about it.

"You were falling from the sky," she echoed, after I'd relayed the details.

"Just a classic anxiety dream, right? Before a big day?"

"Possibly. It could be the weight of the performance or your father coming to see you. Dreams can also reveal insight or fear."

"I'm afraid of flying," I explained, thinking that might be a plausible explanation. "The idea of being squeezed into a steel tube and launched into a storm forty thousand feet above ground is, well, terrifying. I spent my childhood in airplanes but now limit my time outside the States to rare visits with relatives in England, made possible by a *large* sedative to get me through the eight-hour flight."

"That's completely understandable," Dr. Peck said without pause, and I felt strangely validated. "Have you had any other vivid dreams lately, Gracie?"

I had opened this door, so I would walk through. "Yes. A couple of weeks ago."

Her dark coils of hair sprang to life as she nodded for me to go on.

"I was a bear being hunted in the woods. I was caught and tied down, then stared up the barrel of a shotgun."

"How awful."

I pulled balls of burgundy fuzz from my cardigan, not wanting to remember how very awful it was.

"Fascinating that you took the form of a bear," she said.

"Well, I am fierce." I glanced up with a wry grin.

She returned my smile. "Did you recognize the hunter?"

"No, he was a faceless sort of man."

Dr. Peck leaned forward. "Gracie, you've been under a lot of stress. Certainly, that could be what your dreams are about. It's also possible that we need to address the trauma, talk through what happened, so that it doesn't *hunt* you."

When I first met Dr. Peck and gave her a brief history of my life, I intentionally skimmed over one part in particular. Now, it seemed, I wasn't going to be able to dodge it so easily.

"Some things have to be worked through before we can truly let them go," she said.

I wondered if Dr. Peck knew about this from personal experience. She breathed like someone who didn't take oxygen for granted. Many times, I'd thought to ask her about her own story, but therapy was not a two-way street.

"Is it possible that at some level you don't want to let the pain go?" she asked.

"No," I said straight away. Also, maybe. Truly, I'm a puzzle.

For the most part, I thought I was terrific at letting go. After my mother died, my father and I flew around like common swifts, rarely landing on anything with staying power. Letting go seemed as much the problem as the goal.

"I may have some anxiety," I told Dr. Peck, "some considerable pressures and dizzying thoughts, even some trouble sleeping and bad dreams . . ." I could hear how long the list was getting, so I got right to the point. "I'm just not sure I'm interested in diving back into the past," I said as politely as I could. It was bold of me to think I could circumvent the way in which therapy actually works. But it felt as though I'd once been bitten by a large, hateful spider and was now being asked to address the ordeal by inviting it to come back and crawl all over me. I just couldn't see how this would be helpful.

Dr. Peck was a patient woman. "I understand the desire to want to rationalize your way forward," she said. "But in my experience, you cannot make sense of the irrational, cruel actions of others with rational thinking."

I thought about that for a moment.

"Gracie, healing is not a linear process. Nor is growth. It's a cycle of moving deeper. Of investigating your feelings and allowing them to take you back to where they began so you might begin to understand them. Just give it some thought," she urged. "These things take time."

"Absolutely. Thank you. I will give it some real thought," I promised.

"Now, why don't we talk about what's happening *today*."

"*Today*," I glanced at my watch, "in less than an hour, I will meet my father, we will go to the theater, and hopefully, I will knock everyone's socks off." I smiled nervously.

I had not seen my father since a scorching day in July. He'd taken me to lunch, and I'd asked him what he thought about me spending a few months unemployed, preparing a singular piece that could possibly determine the fate of my entire career. He only sighed and said that it was up to me. I worried that he'd given up on me. David Wilder always had an opinion about my future. Then in August, I received his note. It came on one of his trademark red-rimmed note cards, in his distinct script:

> *Grace Marie, I would like to attend your performance at the Harris Theater in October. There is something important I want to discuss with you over dinner afterwards. I have high hopes for you. Until then, Dad.*

I didn't tell Dr. Peck that I kept the note card on a corner of my dresser the way one might a prize ribbon, and nearly every time I saw it, my eyes stung with the suggestion of tears.

I did tell her, "My father is taking me to dinner after the show. There's something he wants to talk to me about."

Her face lit with interest. "This could also be an opportunity for you to say some of the things *you've* been wanting to say."

I nodded, though I had no intention of talking to my father about the choices I'd made that ruined everything between us. Not today anyway. "I just hope he'll be proud," I said.

"More important, I hope that today you will be incredibly proud of yourself. You've worked hard for this."

"Thank you. I just wish I could get Kyle Boden's voice out of my head, telling me that I'm shit."

"Did he really say that before he let you go?"

"Well, no. I'm paraphrasing. I believe his exact words were . . ." I dropped my voice into a lower register to imitate the haughty nature of my former boss. "I just put you in the center of a spectacular piece about beauty and heartache. And you gave me a perfectly executed performance with *zero* emotion. I've found your replacement, and she starts Monday." I'd nailed the intonation, but as I watched the wheels whirl in Dr. Peck's mind, suddenly I wasn't sure I wanted to unpack this particular nightmare.

"Do you think he made an unfair assessment of that performance, Gracie?"

I wanted to shout *yes* and rant about the injustice. But I could not. "Contemporary dance is . . . emotional," I explained. "And . . . well, sometimes art mirrors life in uncomfortable ways."

"*That* is a powerful revelation," Dr. Peck said. "Art can mirror life in all kinds of ways. Might I add that life can also influence art. It might be worth exploring how your experiences could fuel your creative process. Tell me, what is it you want to be able to show up there on stage?"

It was an incredibly thoughtful question. The only trouble was, I didn't know how to answer it.

4

GRIFFIN

Despite the amount of work I'd already done for David Wilder, I'd only met him a handful of times. Our dealings were largely handled over the phone. With both the foyer and the kitchen, we met at the start so I could bid and lay out plans. Mr. Wilder always seemed to know what he wanted and rarely wavered with decisions. If there were details that he didn't care about, he would say as much, leaving me to my devices. He was formal and didn't engage in small talk. There were never any comments like *great weather we're having* or *hope you have a terrific weekend*. No bullshit of any kind. He got right down to brass tacks with directions, paperwork, and a handshake.

"I want the woodwork to look like it always belonged. This building is over one hundred years old, and I'd like to give it back its pride," he'd said when we first met about the foyer.

"Of course," I'd agreed, noting how the beams did sag in places and how the crown molding was cracked and showing its age. I asked him, "Would you like me to also build out the entrance to the living room? Widen the doorframe and give it more of an open concept?"

He'd appeared confused, like I'd just changed the subject. "I fit through the doorway just fine," was his answer. And that was the end of that.

After that first meeting, Mr. Wilder would check in by phone from wherever he was doing business. He'd email signed change orders and occasionally request progress photos in exchange for progress payments, which were delivered via Mr. Brockwell—Mr. Wilder's personal attorney and something of a consigliere. When the project was complete, I always got a handwritten thank-you note delivered to my business address in a red envelope. The first note that came took me by surprise. Contractors don't typically get formal thank-yous. When the second envelope came after the completion of the kitchen, I was so damn proud that I hung it on my fridge. The Wilder kitchen was a beauty. I had crafted the cabinetry myself, which was stunning alongside marble waterfall countertops and a black Viking range. I sent a thank-you note of my own after that project to Neil Katz, the client who had referred me to Mr. Wilder in the first place. I'd done a complete restoration of Katz's Lincoln Park brownstone a few years before, and he'd been happy with how it turned out. I'd been especially pleased with the casing we'd built around the oversized navy-blue front door. Major curb appeal.

I didn't know what Mr. Wilder's next project would be, but I was hoping for a big job. Camilla, his housekeeper, pointed down the dimly lit hallway. The den door stood open like an entrance to another dimension, with light pouring through from the other side. "Please wait in there, Mr. Griffin," she instructed in a voice as pointed as her nose before hurrying back into the kitchen. I glanced around to admire the trim work I'd built in the foyer before starting in the direction of the den. The hallway was lit by picture lights that illuminated framed photographs taken of elegant poses and flawless smiles. They weren't anything like the photos that had hung in my childhood home on Park Avenue. I'd grown up with a less artistic arrangement, which included typical school portraits and shots of Teddy and me fishing with Pop. We'd since sold the old house, but I could still picture the wooden frame with the photo that told the story of how I'd gotten a tooth knocked out by Bobby Long's hockey stick the summer of '92, and another that showed me squeezing Teddy so hard under the Christmas tree that I might have made him cry. Mr. Wilder's gallery didn't reveal any real moments from what I could tell. But one frame caught my eye. It held a shot of a beautiful girl with dark hair who I guessed was the daughter he'd mentioned once or twice. She was standing in front of an old stone theater, somewhere in Europe maybe, wearing a fitted black top and what I thought might be a ballerina's skirt. She was glancing over her shoulder, her expression distant, as if she'd been caught off guard by the camera. This picture made the rest of the posed photographs—portraits, travel, and golf—look almost artificial, the kinds of pictures we hang to remind ourselves that we're happy. I was all too familiar with those kinds of self-deceptions. I'd created a phony gallery of my own over the last few years with Keira. I'd framed only the good moments and hung them above the stairs in our brownstone. I hadn't wanted to see the fading smiles.

I slowly made my way toward the end of the hall, passing a half bath before reaching the French doors to Mr. Wilder's personal office. The doors had been left open, so I took a step inside and glanced around. It was a sunny room gleaming with dark wood. An oversized desk held piles of paper flanked by a green desk lamp and a large world globe. The walls were a deep blue and displayed half a dozen paintings. I couldn't say what most of them looked like. There was just one that caught my attention: a colorful abstract portrait of a young woman at a window done in oil and framed in gold. I didn't see a lot of art in those days. I didn't own a single print and rarely took the time to stop by the Art Institute, even when relatives were in from out of town. But there had been a time when art meant something to me, back when I was enthralled with architecture and history and my great big plans for creating some art of my own in this world. So, I suppose it could have just been the recollection of a long-lost passion that had me lingering there, bending toward the painting with interest. And then I heard a voice say, "Hello."

I spun around and there she was, the girl from the photograph. She was slightly younger than me, with a slender build and a beautiful heart-shaped face. Her eyes, shy and brilliant, held mine until I could find words. Words of any kind. I finally landed on "Hi."

"I don't think we've met," she said, extending a delicate hand, which I quickly took in my large, sweaty palm. "I'm Gracie Wilder." Her accent was English but more relaxed than her father's.

"Griffin. Mr. Wilder's contractor."

"Oh, yes. You did the kitchen. It's beautiful!" Her eyes glittered up at me, a kaleidoscope of grays, blues, and greens.

"Thank you." I bobbed my head in gratitude and left an unfortunate gap of silence.

"So, is he here?"

"Mr. Wilder? No, not yet." I gestured loosely to the painting as I fumbled with an explanation. "This caught my eye, and I sort of wandered in."

"That one is my favorite too. It's a little sad, and I guess I like that about it." She smiled, maybe self-consciously, and glanced back toward the hall.

I wanted to say something worthwhile so she wouldn't leave or vanish into thin air. "Well, I don't know. Do you really think it's sad?" I paused to gather some confidence and inspect the painting more closely. "You might be underestimating its meaning here."

She sounded uncertain. "Do you think?"

"Maybe this woman is just waiting for something."

"Waiting for something that's not coming?" she asked in earnest. "Is that why we see the contrast of light and shadows and her fist closed against the window?"

I was out of my depth; that was clear from the start. But I was committed. "Maybe," I stalled, "but see how her face is pointed toward the light? It's like she's coming through something. And the fist, well, that could be a sign of strength. In fact, I'd go as far as to say that this is a portrait of empowerment, not defeat."

Her lips parted before she spoke. "Well, that's an incredibly positive interpretation."

No one was more surprised than me.

Then she added, without a hint of mockery, "Especially since the title of the painting is *The Forgotten One*."

I stifled a laugh. "That *is* sad."

A smile broke across her face. "A bit."

"I think I'll stick to carpentry."

"No, there's an artist in you, Griffin the contractor."

"I only took Art History 101 in college. To impress a girl."

"How'd that work out?"

"Unimpressively. What about you? You an artist?"

"Well, I'm brilliant at stick figures."

"Is that right?"

"Yeah, I can draw them doing things: walking the dog, answering the phone." She animated this with mechanical arm movements.

"They should be up here," I said, pointing to the office walls.

She beamed. "They should."

My cheeks ached from the unusual smiling. The whole room felt relaxed now—not the stiff, formal space I had first walked into.

"Well, I'm sorry my father is running late," she said. "But come on, I'll walk you into the den."

I watched her walk across the hall. Or maybe she floated; I could hardly tell. The den was the size of my living and dining rooms put together. It had two seating areas, and a large window was flanked with heavy velvet drapes. Gracie peered down onto the street below, maybe expecting a car to be pulling up in front of the building. "So, is Griffin your first name or surname?" she asked after a moment. "Or maybe it's an only. Are you the Bono of home repair?"

"Last name. Beau Griffin."

She turned toward me, her hair backlit in the morning glow, and I could see her eyes glisten with recognition. She stepped closer, her smile fading. "Oh, I didn't put it together. I'm so sorry. I read about your accident in the paper. Are you . . . okay?"

Shit. I had hoped to skip this part. I was always hoping to skip this part. I squinted into the bright daylight framing her silhouette, then glanced away. "Well, have you seen the other guy? I'm not the one who got banged up." Humor really is a weak defense mechanism.

"I've been by the Fidelis building," she said, reverently. "I've seen it. And evidently you are just as strong." She perched on the arm of a dark green wingback chair. "It's amazing you didn't get . . . well, really hurt. I can't even imagine it."

But I could. I replayed the horrible scene in my mind several times a day. There was no unseeing it. The boy in the street. My foot slamming on the brake pedal. My pickup jumping the sidewalk. Seeing that I was headed for a collision with Fidelis, with no way of stopping it. The impact of my truck shattering the twelve-foot window. The flames that burst. The backlash. The press. The community. Angry Mr. Abrams. The endless fallout.

"There was someone in the street; I had to swerve," I said, trying to avoid the empathy written all over Gracie's face. She must have sensed as much because she relaxed her posture.

"I'm glad you're okay," she said. "That's what matters. The rest will get sorted out. People make a big deal out of nothing, really. It's just a bunch of stones."

"Really old and meaningful stones," I pointed out, "but I appreciate it."

I took a seat on the sofa across from her, and she leaned in, curious. "Maybe you could be the one to fix it?"

That would require someone to let me *near* it. "Oh, well, that's not really my thing," I explained. "My work is mostly residential."

Her face was sincere. "Someone will fix it eventually. Soon it will be old news. What has it been, a couple of months?"

"Six."

"Right. Well, somebody is sure to bang up something soon enough and take the attention off you. I could help if you'd like. Maybe go break some windows in the public library or something?"

Whatever tension I'd been holding in came out as laughter. "You know, I could have used you six months ago for some positive PR."

She grinned. "I'm not even convinced that stone archway is all that powerful."

"You've put a paper in the wall?"

"Once, when I was about sixteen. I wrote desperately with teen angst, *'Help me to be strong. Help me to be great.'* And, well . . ." she swiped a hand through the air as if presenting herself. "Not so great."

"You're a dancer?" It was an easy guess based on the picture in the hallway and the way she moved across a room.

"An out-of-work one, but yes. Contemporary, jazz, ballet." She walked again to the window. "Honestly, if I'm not meant to have a thriving career on stage, I would rather just fade into the wallpaper, a bother to no one. Least of all my father." She glanced over at me. "I don't know why I just told you that. Sorry."

But I could relate. "I'm beginning to think success is really just coping well with disappointment."

"You don't really believe that. You just convinced me not to see defeat hanging on the wall in the other room."

"Yeah, I have no idea where that came from. I'm intimate with defeat."

"You've had a tough go of things."

"I'm getting my ducks in a row."

She absentmindedly fiddled with her hair. "Someone recently told me that you can't go about solving irrational problems with rational solutions. What do you think of that? Do you think that's true?"

Her question hung in the air for a moment, too thick with thoughtfulness to just evaporate. "That's the most rational thing I've heard in a long time," I finally said. My life had been a succession of absurd events, and I had not been able to repair a single one with a rational solution.

"Yeah. Well, maybe life will surprise us." Her eyes met mine for a gentle, halting moment. Then she glanced at the clock on the wall. "I better get on." She pulled a piece of paper from the pocket of her sweater and placed it in my hand. "Will you do me a favor? When he gets here, will you give him this?"

I saw that I was holding a ticket to a performance. "And if he doesn't show?"

"Scratch paper." She smiled, and before I could fully get to my feet, she left the room in one fluid movement. She called back through the door, "Best of luck, Beau Griffin."

But luck was something saved for lost pennies and four-leaf clovers; not simple men like me. The big meeting never came to fruition. Twenty minutes after Gracie had gone, Camilla walked into the room, her face as white as a sheet, to say: "I'm so sorry. I just got word that Mr. Wilder will not be coming. It seems he . . . is dead."

5

GRACIE

The rain had stopped, but wind still howled through the streets. I hurried down Michigan Avenue in a flurry of commuters, wondering if Griffin was meeting with my father and explaining in his low and steady voice that I'd come with the ticket to the showcase. The idea of it calmed me briefly. But by the time the Harris Theater came into view, my nerves were again frayed. I sprang through the intersection and past a middle-aged woman playing the blues on a timeworn guitar. She nodded a greeting as I moved toward the large glass entrance of the theater on a breeze of minor notes.

The green room was already wild with activity. I knew this room well, and all the other ones like it. A theater green room was a place where seams and nerves unraveled, where sequins and tempers popped. I tried to find a section of counter where I could lay out my makeup without tangling with someone else's hairpins. I had finished my hair and was ready to get dressed, when one of the other dancers screamed at the sight of a broken shoulder strap. As the seamstress and the stage manager descended, I slipped into the black shiny fabric of my costume and out the green room door. That's why the production assistant couldn't find me. I was side stage in a dimly lit corner. She didn't spot me until it was nearly curtain time.

"Gracie!" she said, relieved. "I've been looking everywhere for you. Someone in tickets took down a message for you. Said it was urgent." She placed a folded piece of paper in my hand and scurried off, having completed her mission.

Urgent messages did not typically come my way. I reasoned that the production assistant was just being theatrical in tune with backstage culture. I stared at the delicately folded paper between my fingers, imagining it was a note from my father saying, *Gracie dear, so sorry I'm running late.* The idea of it only triggered further anxiety. I quickly shoved the feelings down and the message into my bra for later. Whatever it was, it could wait until after this possibly life-altering performance.

I peered through the small gap between the curtain and the framing of the stage and saw that the house was nearly full. Hundreds of people had come to see choreographers from around the world showcase their work, but two seats toward the front sat empty. They were the seats next to Ana and Tess that I'd reserved for Mark and my father. I tried to remind myself of why I was there. Today I was dancing for Olivia Garza. She was the one I needed to impress. There would be no point in all this preparation if she did not truly see me. My heart continued to beat rapidly. The *papillons* felt like baby tigers. Luckily, I could still hear Madame Bisset's voice in the recesses of my mind, how she would whisper to me from the wings, "Gracie darling, when you dance, you make magic."

Then it was my cue. I lurched forward from the darkness and onto the stage, five other dancers with me. We slid across scuffed floorboards into bright lights with the thumping rhythm of the music driving us. I had rehearsed until every move had become polished and deliberate. I flexed bare feet and shattered streams of dust held in the spotlights with powerful extensions. The choreography for this piece was dark, foreboding. I leapt into the air and was taken into the arms of a male dancer. He lifted me high above his head like a freshly slayed animal before throwing me across the stage. I landed lightly and pirouetted into the spotlight for my solo. While the five dancers behind me crept low and sprung high in unity, I extended one leg high behind my head into a perfectly poised arabesque. The muscles in my legs twitched as I readied for the next steps, but through the shadowy light that lay across the audience, I thought I might have seen a distinguished-looking gentleman with salt-and-pepper hair sitting forward in his seat. Had my father arrived for the performance after all? Or was the light just playing tricks?

I quickly refocused and moved into the next series of lifts, powerfully alighting to the floor. I felt strong and sure as I executed each formidable eight-count.

When we fixed our bodies into stillness with the final note of music, the audience exploded with applause. I took my bow, the curtain fell, and all went black.

I was in the lobby hugging Ana and Tess goodbye when I spotted Olivia Garza across the crowd. Once she caught sight of me, she excused herself from her conversation and crossed the room.

I sucked in a breath and straightened my back.

"Gracie Wilder?" she said, extending a hand.

I exhaled and took her hand far too enthusiastically. "A pleasure to meet you, Ms. Garza."

"That was an interesting performance. You make even the most difficult choreography appear effortless and energized. You've clearly had impeccable training." For a moment, my heart wanted to leap out of my chest. Then she added, "But I cannot figure out why the performance didn't really move me. Do you have any ideas?"

My blood ran cold as I tried to speak. "Perhaps I didn't push myself quite hard enough at the crescendo."

"I'm not sure you really unlocked the true anguish of the piece."

I was mortified, completely crestfallen. "I will absolutely consider that, Ms. Garza."

"Please do," she said. "I think you have a lot of untapped potential."

She began to walk away, and I heard myself call out, "Wait!"

I flooded with panic and froze. Had I just yelled a demand at Olivia Garza?

She turned around and waited expectantly for me to say something. I stammered. "I'd . . . I'd like to dance for you again. I'm better than that performance, and if you'd be willing to give me the opportunity, I'd like to show you."

She looked as surprised by my candor as I was. "Why?" she asked.

"Because . . . you're the reason I'm here."

Her face softened with modesty. "How old are you? Twenty-five?"

"Twenty-six," I said faintly. Age was against me. Most of her dancers were under twenty-two. I stood motionless as she seemed to consider all that I'd said.

Finally, she spoke. "My dancers go on to be celebrated choreographers, you know. Have long careers. I'll be making decisions in a few weeks for additions to the company."

I figured I had nothing left to lose. I gulped and said, "My schedule is very flexible."

She glanced around the room, clearly amused by our dialogue. "Okay. In three weeks," she said. "Thursday. Here. Four o'clock sharp. I'm confident you won't waste my time."

"Certainly. Thank you, Ms. Garza."

Once she'd waltzed off, I ran out of the theater and let the cold air assail my lungs. She was taking a chance on me. I'd have to invent an epic solo. This realization nearly pulled me to the ground. I managed to hail the first taxi that approached and climb into its concealment. "Where to?" the driver asked. Then I remembered the message still tucked into my bra. I pulled it out and unfolded it.

Your Aunt Flora called. You need to go to your father's house right away.

I gave the driver my father's address and tried to ignore the thumping inside my chest.

———

I was out of breath when I reached my father's door and keyed my way inside. "Hello?" I called out into the quiet.

"In here," a male voice sang from down the hall.

Mr. Brockwell, my father's personal attorney and longtime friend, was sitting on the sofa in the den. Next to him was my father's sister, Flora. She wore a gray angora turtleneck that seemed to be consuming her petite face, and Mr. Brockwell sat only as upright as a weary man in a necktie is capable.

"What's going on? Is my dad here?" I dropped my bag in the doorway and waited for someone to say something.

"Grace Marie," my Aunt Flora began, her voice low and wobbly, "your father . . . has died, dear." The room fell silent, though I may have heard the earth crack. "Last night around nine o'clock, he was struck by a car while crossing the street in front of the Waldorf Astoria in New York. He had internal bleeding and did not make it through surgery."

"But that's impossible," I countered.

They waited while I worked to postulate an alternate reality.

"At nine o'clock, he would be through with dinner. He'd have retired to his room, as he's always done. He'd be on his way to bed, not leaving the hotel."

"Maybe he was popping out to the shop?" Aunt Flora offered weakly.

Mr. Brockwell stood. "I'm so sorry. I don't know where he was going."

"Then we don't have the right information," I insisted. "There must be a mistake." Mr. Brockwell inched a chair closer to me, hoping I might sit. But I could not move. I could only try to explain away the new, sharp pain in my chest with plausible misunderstandings. "He always kept to a plan—you know that. And he had plans to get up very early this morning and fly home. He'd arranged it many weeks ago. There was something he wanted to talk to me about." My voice caught in my throat.

Mr. Brockwell walked over and helped me into the chair. "I know this is hard," he reasoned. "I'm sure the doctors did all they could. Perhaps if you listen to his message, that would help. Apparently, he tried us both from the hospital. I didn't pick up his voicemail until early this morning."

Tears pooled in my eyes. "I didn't charge my cell phone last night," I said in a doleful whisper.

Mr. Brockwell put a reassuring hand on my shoulder before returning to the sofa. He spoke slowly. "Grace Marie, I know this is happening fast, but there are just a few matters to address. I will be spending the next several days gathering the particulars of the will. You have a trust, which you'll receive in parts after age thirty. But I was able to gather from your father's message that he has something for you now. He instructed me to pick this up from his office right away, and I went this morning." Mr. Brockwell lifted something off the floor. It was a large cigar box decorated with gold sequins and blue satin ribbon. I remembered giving it as a Father's Day gift decades ago. "He said that he was sending you an email from the hospital related to this."

We were all silent for a moment, staring at the bedazzled cigar box. Finally, I reached with a trembling hand and took it from Mr. Brockwell. Aunt Flora pursed her lips and twisted her rings, waiting impatiently to see what I had been given. I wished that she would cry, or offer me a consoling hand, or get the world to stop spinning so fast, but she was not equipped to do so.

I removed the lid from the box, and for a moment, the world stopped turning. There, resting quietly, was a bronze key and a fabric blackbird with red-tipped feathers and crystal wings.

I gently picked up the bird and with it came a tender, bitter-sweet memory.

It was the night of my ninth birthday. My father and I were walking home from the ballet through Old Montreal when we came upon a local artisan in front of her shop. She wore her white hair in a tight bun at the back of her head, leaving her deep-set eyes center stage on a long, weathered face. She was trying to entice pedestrians into the shop with a display of stone figures and silk birds. The birds were no bigger than a sparrow and had tiny crystals stitched into each wing. Bright blue ones, red ones, others as yellow as canaries. I didn't know what a person might do with such a gift. Perhaps hang one in a well-lit window or perch one on a cozy shelf. Still, I was captivated by the silk creatures. I dragged my father closer so I could stroke the feathered tail of the red-winged blackbird and examine its jade-green eyes.

"Come along," he said, eager to get home. "I've got an early flight." But I remained motionless watching the crystals catch the light of the streetlamps.

"The blackbird is one of the most bountiful birds in North America," the old woman said. I looked up in surprise. "*Familier, mais très spécial,*" she emphasized with crisp intonation while placing the small treasure in my hands to further examine. "The blackbird is a bird of promise, an intelligent creature that can guide you when you are lost. Its enchanting song will lift you toward the light." It felt as though she wasn't just speaking of folklore, but rather that she was speaking directly to me.

"How can a bird do all that?" I asked.

She smiled, though her lips never moved.

"Grace Marie, it's time to go," my father said. He took the bird from my hands and handed it back to the shopkeeper.

"May I please have the bird, Daddy?" The request shot out of me before I could consider a more agreeable approach.

"You have no need for such things."

I whined, but he was not moved. "Come along," he said, taking my hand firmly in his.

I looked back at the old woman. She stood under the streetlamp, holding me with her gaze as my father towed me up the street.

———

Seventeen years later, I sat in my father's house with the blackbird in my hands.

"What's it for?" Aunt Flora asked.

"I don't know," I said, choking back emotion I'd locked deeply away. "I haven't seen it since I was nine years old."

6

ÉLOÏSE

The polished onyx sculpture of the dancing bear might have seemed a clearer choice for a girl who'd just come from the ballet, but Gracie picked up the blackbird. My mother noticed. "It chose her," she said that night, pulling a blanket over her lap by the fire. She took a black ink pen to a sheet of paper and lovingly scrolled: *The Blackbird*.

"Which story is this again?" I asked while stoking the embers of my little fireplace with an iron prod.

My mother's family lineage was indigenous to Quebec. Our ancestors came from the shores of Ungava Bay. My mother both feared and adored her ancestors, often dreaming of them calling to her from kayaks in the St. Lawrence River, where fresh water runs north through Montreal and mixes with the salty sea. Where she said Ungava Inuit spirits fish.

My mother said she was born of fire, of creativity and a yearning for purpose. When her ancestors would come for her, she believed her time in this world would be snuffed out. It was her job to make them happy so they would not come for her too soon.

Ungava Inuit have many stories that have been orally passed down. Some, my mother said, had been told to her by her great-grandmother,

her Ananaksaq, when she was only as tall as the mounds of snow that lined the cottage where she lived. Ananaksaq was as intimidating as some of the stories she told, my mother once said. But she and the stories were respected. My mother knew to listen closely, even as a toddler when language was something new. She heard the stories for a long time.

When my mother's parents passed on to the next world, she began to dream new stories, stories she'd never been told. She believed that these were given to her from her parents, who had gained new wisdom in death.

The story of the red-winged blackbird is one such dream that came with vivid colors. My mother said that she awoke from this dream feeling afire with light. She said she spent three days wrapping herself in the images and then got to work making art and symbolic figures into which she painted the story. She said that this was her responsibility. To see the story and help others to see it too.

I could hear the stories, but I wasn't sure I could see them. I was not naturally passionate about the path of my ancestors the way my mother had always been. And so that night by the fire, I asked her to clarify for me which story belonged to the blackbird.

"The fox runs from the Amarok," she reminded me. "Losing her companion, the blackbird. Losing her way, losing her spirit."

I vaguely remembered how it went. "What if this girl you saw today never returns to the shop?" I asked.

"I believe she will, and she may need this story."

When she said this, she didn't mean that she thought the child needed a new book to read. She believed that these stories could change people's lives the way they had shaped hers.

I did not think stories could mean something to someone who did not understand where they came from. Like a fairy tale, it seemed that there was little to gain other than proof of darkness and light. Sometime after I'd put my dolls into a brown box in the attic and entered middle school, I lost interest in the world my mother spoke of. "I know the ending," I would remind her before she could get to it, and she would sigh and shake her head in disappointment. But what I didn't understand was that the stories had already formed me. They had smoothed and set the shape of my knowing. I would later come to find myself confronted with a path of darkness—the car I was not to get into, the sidewalk that was lurking with more than shadows—and I would recognize the story that would play out and know not to proceed. I learned to honor my ancestors with my listening, to my mother and then to myself. But I did not practice the telling of their stories.

A week after my mother wrote out the story of the blackbird by the fire, a young girl came into my mother's shop accompanied by a beautiful woman in a blue dress. I was behind the counter reviewing the sales log when the bell rang on the door. "How may I help you?" I asked my guests.

The woman gestured for the child to answer. "I'm here about the birds," she said.

"I heard that there was a young lady interested in the blackbird. Is that you?"

She mirrored my amazement.

I reached under the counter and pulled out the thin paper book that my mother had bound by string. "This is a gift," I said, walking over and placing it in her hand. "My mother wrote down the story, hoping you might return. And as she suspected, here you are."

The child politely thanked me and asked, "But can the blackbird really guide someone?"

I hesitated and lowered my voice, unsure if these things should be spoken about loudly. "In a matter of speaking, yes. You just need to know what you're looking for."

7

GRACIE

"Are you going to listen to the message?" Aunt Flora was asking.

Mr. Brockwell had gone, and she had already made a few calls about funeral arrangements. I hadn't moved from the green chair in my father's den.

"Grace Marie?" Aunt Flora tried again.

I looked up to where she was standing in the half-light that trickled in from the window. Orange hues painted her face. "October really is the bravest month, don't you think so, Aunt Flora?"

"What's that?" she asked, as if she'd simply been unable to hear me in the deafening silence of the room.

"October," I went on. "It's like a long and certain sunset. A golden hour that stretches out for weeks, telling of what is leaving. The trees outside are mid-performance in a vibrant show of death while people just walk on by, oblivious."

"I think it might help if you played his message, dear," she said and then puttered from the room.

Before he left, Mr. Brockwell had lent me a cell phone charger. My phone now sat on the console table, charging in clear view. I found some courage and slowly pulled myself from the chair. My legs felt as though they were full of sand as I walked over, picked it up, and powered it on.

I had two voicemails. One from Mark. And one from Dad.

I sucked in a deep breath and touched his name: *Dad*. I did not exhale or dare to breathe again until I'd heard every word he spoke. His voice was hoarse with pain but resolute with willpower.

> *Gracie, dear. I'm in the hospital. There was an accident.*
> *Please reach out right away. I'm having—I'm having the*
> *nurse help me write you a letter. That I will email. It—it will*
> *explain everything. There is much to explain. I'm in New York*
> *Presbyterian Hospital. I'll be waiting for your call. I'm sorry*
> *about this. Your performance.*

The message abruptly ended, and I gasped. Of all the calls ever made, why had I missed this one? He'd been waiting to hear back from me. And now he was gone? I thought I might be sick, that emotion would violently purge its way out of me. I grabbed a glass of water that Aunt Flora had left on the coffee table and spilled most of it down my shirt as I tried to drink.

Maybe if I could find his email, I could make sense of what was happening.

I paced the Persian rug and frantically flicked through my phone. There were several new messages in my inbox, and I scanned the list in search of the name David Wilder. But I found nothing. I spent twenty minutes sorting through old accounts, changing passwords, checking junk mail, searching and scouring the internet, but to no avail. There simply wasn't an email from my father.

Was it possible that this could all have been a mistake? What if he was still awaiting my call? If I tried to ring him, would I find that he was very much alive? He might answer and complain about how rumors are spun. *There must be another David Wilder in the hospital,* he'd say. *I was*

released last night, and I'm arriving in Chicago today. I'm sorry I'm late.
And I'd laugh with relief and say, *You had me worried!*

The thought of it made me crazy, so I rang the hospital in New York.
I was transferred four times only to learn that they did indeed operate
on my father, that he had not made it through surgery, and that they
could page the doctor to ring me back at a later hour. But they would
not otherwise disclose the names of their personnel or put me on the
line with the nurse who had helped my father with anything, let alone
an email. The swine that was operating the front desk wouldn't budge.
I all but screamed and told her to bugger off.

It was a dead end, and it seemed to broaden the gap between my father
and me.

For a long time, there had been a distance between us—an expanse
carved out by misadventure, miles, and miscommunication. We had
flashes of connection, like a shared laugh over an ironic T-shirt, excitement over a Beatles song coming on the radio, or a flower in bloom that
reminded him of my mother. But these moments were fleeting. And
now the distance between us had spread out into infinite space. There
was no way to reach out, as he had asked me to do in his voicemail, or
to call and say, *but wait, you can't go, there's still so much to talk about.* And
there *was* still so much I needed to talk to him about.

I fell back into the green chair with a thump and gazed at the
leather seat sitting empty on the opposite side of the coffee table. His
favorite chair.

I narrowed my eyes until I could see my eyelashes and summoned
the image of him sitting across from me. His casual attire of khaki
pants and a button-down shirt; his salt-and-pepper hair and dark-
rimmed glasses.

The last time I'd seen him sitting there, he'd only just gotten the
glasses. It was several months before, when I still had my job at Boden.
He'd asked about how I was getting on with rehearsals, then offered
me fettuccini for lunch. I had already eaten and felt a little guilty for

declining the fettuccini. I cheerfully changed the subject, telling him that I liked his bold new look.

He touched a finger to the center of his glasses with a crooked grin. "Do you?"

"Yes. Very smart. Very Colin Firth," I said.

He chuckled. "They help me see, anyway. Which reminds me, have you read about the new exhibit on ancient Egypt at the Field Museum? There was an article about it in the *Tribune* yesterday. It made me think of you." He picked up a single page of newspaper from the coffee table, one that had been intentionally set aside. "You were once rather interested in this particular history, weren't you? Around age twelve maybe, when you studied the ancient pyramids in school?" But it wasn't a question. He was only being polite. I had tried to create elaborate hieroglyphics on my bedroom wall.

I may have pushed those days into a far corner in my mind, but my father had not. He hesitantly handed me the newspaper page, and I smoothed the thin, delicate sheet in my lap.

"Wait until you see, Gracie dear." He went on to explain a recent excavation that unearthed relics from five thousand years ago.

But now, as I blinked away the memory and let my eyes rest on the empty chair, what stirred up feelings far deeper than ancient treasures were simply his words: *It made me think of you.*

8

COOPER

I was sitting on the desk in my makeshift office at Stetson and Lawrey, eating half of yesterday's ham sandwich, when Gracie Wilder appeared in the doorway. The skin across her forehead was puckered in waves. Her cheeks were not pink from the cool weather; they were pale cream—the counterpart to my coffee-colored complexion. I was listening to Mark Schaffer go on about the case I'd been hired to investigate. He was an excessively groomed young associate who had yet to earn my respect. I had met Gracie a few weeks before in that same doorway, but even if you had never laid eyes on this girl, you wouldn't have needed a detective to tell you that something was off. Mark, however, did not seem to pick up on the grave expression on her face.

He led with, "Gracie, I thought we were meeting later tonight," and moved to put an arm around her.

But she turned into him stiffly. "My father died," she said. I watched Mark slowly grip his arms around her. "Oh my God! How?"

"There was an accident."

"I'll tell Stetson I'm leaving. I'll take you home." Mark glanced at me. "Sorry, Cooper, I . . ."

"Not a problem," I said, swallowing back day-old bread and putting down my sandwich. "Daryl Cooper," I said to Gracie when he'd gone. In case she'd forgotten my name. I offered her my deepest condolences. Then a chair and a glass of water. She declined both. "You must be in shock. You doing okay?" I asked. "I don't mean to pry."

"No. It's a good question," she said. Her eyes drifted around the room like she might be in search of the answer. They landed on the giant corkboard behind the desk where red nylon thread was strung between half a dozen pushpins. "What's this?" she asked after what felt like several minutes.

I rubbed the stubble on my chin. "Oh, that's just evidence. Every new file on a case gets a pin and a tab."

She stepped closer to examine the small labels tacked down by each pin. "And the thread?"

"I'm just connecting the dots . . . how one thing leads to another."

Our conversation began as a necessary distraction in a somber moment. But I might have known, even then, that a line was being drawn between Gracie and me.

She examined the strands woven through the pins. They looped and crossed over each other—intertwined. The labels were plain and said only things like *Simmons/Polinski meeting NY*, *Simmons/Gower meeting Chicago*, *Stock Trade February 2*, and so on. "Your system is not straight-forward," she said.

"No. But I guess it's how I think."

"Do you always find what you're looking for?" she asked, stepping back and taking in a wider view.

"Pretty much. I mean, I don't do homicide cases or anything so glamorous, but I can make a dollar out of fifteen cents on any civil inves-tigation, corporate case, or personal predicament."

"One length of thread at a time."

"That's right." We were quiet for a moment. Gracie shifted away, as if distracted. The only sounds were distant phones ringing out at reception and a copy machine humming down the hall. I glanced at my watch. It was a Tag Heuer with an oversized face. The minute hand was clicking toward five o'clock. "Are you sure I can't get you some water?"

"Do you ever think that we're just . . ."

I waited.

"At the mercy of other people's actions on a daily basis?"

I couldn't begin to understand what it must have been like for her. Standing there trying to make sense of the circumstances that had led to her father dying in a sudden accident. But I could not think of a softer answer. "Well, yes."

She was gazing out the window now, seeming to stare at nothing in particular. "We don't have much control over our lives. Not much at all."

It was hard to argue her point. I found the rules of cause and effect to practically govern life. Some things we can predict, like calling a pocket in a game of pool. But most days we can't see what's coming. I leaned against the desk, careful to move my limp sandwich out of the way. "But we aren't just passive participants in all this," I said, gesturing to what lay beyond the window. "We get up each day, put our head into the wind, and find out that we're also powerful beyond belief."

I had hoped this would be an uplifting speech. Something of the you-can-handle-anything variety. But her brow was still knit tight. "Things end. And we're powerless to do anything about it," she said.

What Gracie Wilder needed in that moment was something that I was sure a million other people in Chicago could have delivered better than me. But there she was, standing in front of *my* desk. "You're not powerless," I said. "Everyone, everything, has its own kind of power."

I really believed this to be true. I was a longtime science buff, and I'd been paying attention to how it was modeled all the time. Like how the dust from the Sahara Desert travels more than three thousand miles across the Atlantic Ocean to fertilize the Amazon rainforest with the phosphorus necessary for plant growth. The Amazon then produces twenty billion metric tons of water. Which flows upward and collects into an invisible river flowing through the sky. When this cloud stream hits the Andes Mountains, it becomes rain, pouring nutrients into the Pacific Ocean that feed the diatoms—those single-celled algae that create fifty percent of the oxygen we breathe. Diatoms need nutrients, and when they aren't fed, they turn to dust. And it all starts again.

The way I saw it, everything was a part of some kind of causal chain. Especially us.

"But is it just us humans fumbling around?" Gracie asked the blur of activity on the street outside. "All chance and happenstance?"

I tracked human idiocy on a daily basis, so I'm sure my expression was sympathetic when she turned to face me.

"I always believed that it was more," she said. "That there was another hand in it. *Meaning* of some kind. Like an invisible thread keeping everything together. But I don't know. Terrible things happen, and it doesn't add up. It just doesn't." She took a step closer to me, and I could see her pupils quivering. "I don't know what my dad meant to say to me. He sent me an email before he died, a letter that's meant to explain what he left behind. But I can't find it. I've searched my accounts; even accounts I haven't used in years."

"There are things you can do to retrieve digital information."

"I'm told that his company is getting his briefcase with his laptop from the hospital. They mean to protect confidential information."

"You'll find it. Everything ends up somewhere."

"Maybe you could help?" she asked.

"Sure," I shrugged, "just let me know."

Mark came back into the room in quick steps. "Tomorrow then, Cooper. We'll go over findings at eight. Did you get the report back from the NYPD? I have concerns about—"

I cut him off with a wave of hand. "Tomorrow."

And Mark whisked Gracie out the door.

———

I showed up at the Ale House at five thirty. There was a flyer tacked to the window outside. It was a notice that the 150th anniversary celebration of Fidelis had been postponed indefinitely. As if the plywood on the windows wasn't reminder enough. I tore the paper from the glass and stuffed it in my pocket before going inside.

The place was full of regulars. A sea of blue jeans and dark wool sweaters; folks who practically blended into the wooden tables and bar tops. But there was a guy seated in front of the tap in a blue collared shirt that stood out. He was a portrait of misery, not too unlike one of the many colorful painted portraits that hung on the dark paneled walls of the pub. At second glance, I saw that the civilian shirt had Griffin stuffed inside it. I straightened my retro Hawks hat that I was rarely without during hockey season and clapped a greeting onto his back. He stood so I could pull him in for a hug. I quickly got the scoop on the meeting that didn't happen with David Wilder, knowing the punch line before it came. "He's dead," my buddy told me in disbelief as he swigged down a black and tan.

I told Griffin how I'd heard the news an hour before from Wilder's daughter Gracie, explaining her connection to Mark Schaffer at Stetson and Lawrey.

"I met Gracie just this morning," Griffin explained, and we each remarked on how strange it was for both of us to run into her the day her dad died. "I was waiting for him when Gracie stopped in," Griffin went on. "I don't even know what job he wanted me to bid on. And I have nothing else lined up."

"There'll be more jobs. Maybe you should go to Wilder's funeral. He might have some friends in need of a contractor."

The comment was slightly irreverent, and as far as I could tell, Griffin blew right by it. He went on, saying he couldn't figure out why Wilder had called him for a job in the first place. "Hadn't he seen the news, or did he travel too much to catch wind of the thing? I mean, why would he still trust me after all that had been written in the paper?" Griffin asked the bottom of his glass.

"Maybe Wilder didn't care what had been written about you in the paper. Maybe he ignored the headlines and just saw the truth," I suggested.

"Well, then he was the only one." Griffin lifted his empty glass to cue the bartender. "And as far as I know, Fidelis could get torn down to the ground tomorrow."

"Nah. It's under review," I said impulsively and then bit my tongue.

"Tell me you didn't go down to City Hall again."

I waved away his reaction. "It's fine. It's just that the building is going through a review process with the historic division and safety departments, and the clerk at the desk didn't know up from down, so I'm not clear if—"

"Stop. Seriously," he said. "I don't want your fingerprints on this one, okay? You'll fuck it up." This stung, but I didn't let it show.

The news headlines that had tarnished Griffin's reputation around town were about a guy who went off the deep end and drove his car into an architectural gem, destroying history and hopes within the community. Griffin hadn't been quick to defend himself, but I did every chance I got. That was *not* his story.

Here's what really happened. One night in late April, Griffin had a few of us guys over for drinks out on the porch. Halfway into that evening, Griffin mentioned that things with Keira had gone south. They'd been having problems for a while, but now she was pushing him away. The bottle of whiskey only had one shot left in it when I had the brilliant notion that I should check it out. That's the problem with being an investigator; I can hardly turn off the mental process of pulling something apart until there's an answer. It's like a compulsory itch. I figured, worst-case scenario, some guy was screwing my buddy's wife. I knew everyone that Kiera knew; we'd been kids together. Maybe I could put a stop to it.

Griffin laughed. "Oh yeah, you do that, Coop." I ignored his sarcasm. In retrospect, I wish I took things more lightly, but I wanted to get to the bottom of it. I would have done anything for Griffin. He's the closest thing I've ever had to a brother.

It only took me a couple of hours the next morning, but the minute I had the information, I wished I didn't. I pulled at my collar for an hour, then finally picked up the phone. You gotta call a thing a thing.

"Coop, what's up?" Griffin answered. I hesitated. "Whatever it is you think you know, I *don't* want to know. This is not how I'm going to fix things with Keira."

He had a fair point, but I wasn't sure I could let it go. My pits were sweating through my shirt. "Griffin, you need to talk to her. See if she's okay. See if she wants the same things that you want. And if she doesn't, you need to ask yourself if you can be okay with that."

"Come on, man." He sounded tired, like he just wanted the whole subject to be dropped and his problems with it.

"I hate to see you living in the dark. I'd rather you have the whole truth." I was going to hang up then.

"What truth?" he finally said.

I took a deep breath, hung my head, and slowly said into the phone, "Maybe Keira has been distant because she . . . recently terminated a pregnancy. I'm sorry. Talk to her. See what's going on. I'm sure you guys can figure it out."

I don't think he said anything after that. The call dropped. I felt terrible. What had begun as a casual inquiry had evolved into a great infraction. I tried to think positively. Maybe Griffin would understand the reason for Keira's secret. But I knew that all Griffin ever wanted was to build buildings and a family. Coach a youth hockey team and camp out in the backyard on the weekends like we did as kids.

The next morning Griffin's questions spilled out over Sunday break-fast. He told Keira that he knew what she'd been through. Keira, reeling from the realization that he (we) had violated her privacy, explained that she had miscarried at eight weeks and needed to have a procedure. "I didn't tell you about the pregnancy because I was scared," she told him. "We're not happy." She explained that while he'd been dividing his time between construction projects and Oakview Assisted Living, she'd been dreaming about the future. And this wasn't what she wanted anymore.

On that cold April morning, Keira told Griffin that she wanted a divorce. She packed her bags, loaded her car, and left him in a haze of grief and confusion.

Griffin, who by the way was as sober as a judge, got into his pickup to go for a drive. Sitting at home in his empty house was too painful. He sped down the same few blocks on North Wells that he'd driven down hundreds of times before. Right as he was about to drive through the intersection in front of the Abrams Building—his revered Fidelis—a bird flew headlong into his windshield, splattering blood and feathers across the glass. This made it difficult for Griffin to see that Mike Willinski, a local teenager, was skateboarding through the middle of the intersection. Griffin's foot was already on the brake when he saw Willinski, but at the speed he was going, his only choice was to swerve out of the way to avoid hitting the boy. He yanked the steering wheel hard to the right and pressed the brake into the floor. His truck reeled up onto the sidewalk, wood and tools flying out the back, and finally came to a stop as it hit the side of Fidelis. The collision shattered a gigantic stained-glass window and absurdly upset the gas line to the office kitchen. The front of the truck crumbled upon impact, but Griffin managed to escape before flames burst. Thankfully, no one had been on the truck's path, tenants were out-of-office, and the building only burned for twelve minutes. But that was enough time for severe harm to be done. Griffin's insurance would cover the damages, but his life would go up in smoke. It was *his* Great Chicago Fire. The building was vacated, offices were moved, shattered windows and waterlogged doors were boarded up, and old Mr. Abrams was up in arms. The repairs would be expensive, and it would be a long time before the insurance money came through.

Abrams threatened to tear the whole thing to the ground. He said the upkeep was costly, and he was rumored to be having plans drawn up for a new building. Neighbors and the press questioned, but Abrams refused to answer. No one really knew what would rise from the ashes.

Night after night, Griffin pulled up his barstool next to mine and bent over his glass like a guy staring into a hole dug out just for him. One night, after he'd had an infinite amount of booze, he started babbling, "I had it coming." When I probed, he said only "Valasco." Then he waved it away as if I wouldn't understand. But I knew what he meant. Griffin didn't think that I'd seen that damn piece of paper he'd stolen off the arch, back when we were kids. The one I'd practically made him steal. But I'd seen it. He'd left it under a stack of baseball cards in a corner of his bedroom bureau for months. *I cannot have a baby. I will never have a child. Please receive my anguish.* I remembered. I wanted to explain to him that Keira's miscarriage and the fire at Fidelis had nothing to do with anything written on any wall. The rules of cause and effect didn't extend outside the natural world. That was nonsensical.

But certainly, I take some responsibility in this. I may have had information, but I didn't have the whole story. I should have considered Keira's feelings and respected her discretion. If I hadn't interfered, Griffin would never have driven into Fidelis. He likely would have been at home with Keira that day instead of out in his truck. Or, at the very least, he'd have been going at a Sunday driver's pace, as was his usual way. The phone call I made to Griffin telling him of Keira's secret was more a cause of these unfortunate events than anything he had innocently done as a child.

I wanted to set things right. Griffin was the one person I could count on. It had been that way since we were kids. He didn't let many people in, but once you were a friend of Griffin's, you were always a friend of Griffin's. Sure, we'd had a few disagreements over the years. They were things we could work out over a handshake and a milkshake; when we got older, a beer. But this was different. When he looked at me now, his eyes were narrow with a distant resentment congruent with his own self-reproach. It wasn't that he blamed me for what happened between him and Keira. No, he took all the fault himself, saying he hadn't been paying attention and that he should have given more to Keira while he had the chance. But the sight of me seemed to be a constant reminder of the painful truth I'd forced on him, and the glower in his eye ate away at me like acid on the brain. I wanted him to see me as his old friend who had his back. A guy with noble pursuits who had become a private investigator for the purpose of helping people, not hurting people. The only solution was for me to find something consequential to do for him, something that could turn everything right side up again. I was looking for an opportunity.

I paid for our last round at the Ale House, and we headed back out into the street. It was well past six, and we were late to meet Teddy and our buddy P.J.

"I hope Teddy saves us some of those hot wings," I said. "I'm tellin' ya. Hot enough to bring a corpse back to life."

Griffin stopped in the middle of the sidewalk. "I think I'll go to his funeral," he said.

"What?"

"I should go to Wilder's funeral. For Gracie."

I had to catch up. "You're gonna go for Gracie?"

"To see if she's okay."

It made sense to me that Griffin wanted to help Gracie Wilder in a lonely hour. He knew what it was like to lose a parent. He'd been losing his mom for years. But be wary of the naked man offering you his shirt. I didn't think he had any solace to provide.

"She's out of your league, man," I said.

"It's a funeral, Coop. Maybe I can help her somehow."

And then it occurred to me. I might be able to help her too. If Griffin wouldn't let me try to put the pieces of Fidelis back together, maybe I could still show him that I wasn't in the business of wrecking lives.

I could help a grieving young woman find an email from her father. A little pro bono work would be good for me, and it was sure to be a smash-and-grab job. Griffin could take me out for a beer after and say, "You did good," and I could say, "It was nothing," and then maybe I wouldn't have to regret the phone call I'd made that changed Griffin's life forever.

9

GRACIE

There was a chill in the apartment, though the heating vents were humming optimistically. Ana was out and would not be home from her gig at the jazz club for hours. It would be dawn before I'd be able to tell her the news of my father.

I sat across from Mark at the little dinette table in my living room, twirling spaghetti on my fork, but not managing to eat any of it.

"Can I get you anything else?" he asked.

"No, I'm fine. Thanks." I watched Mark pour himself a glass of Cabernet. I didn't drink alcohol, but I did wonder in that moment if the bottle might contain a disappearing act of sorts. If the idea hadn't scared me so much, I might have pulled another glass from the cupboard and had a go. "It's very good," I said of the dinner he'd tossed together from what he could scrounge up in my kitchen. But he could tell I was lying. I'd not had a bite.

"Babe, would you mind not shaking your foot under the table?"

"Sorry." I retired my fork to my plate, rendering it useless. "What if I never find the nurse who helped my father? Or his laptop? Which may have the email sitting in an outbox, never sent. The laptop that is being shipped to his office where it will be scrubbed by the bloody company for security reasons." I was mentally spinning, but not exactly hysterical. I resumed shaking my foot under the table and pulled at my eyebrows. They would again be bald in places and require more brow pencil. "Do you think Daryl Cooper could help me?"

Mark's head shot up from his dinner. "Cooper? Oh no, Gracie. You don't need to go about this like detective work. Besides, that would just make things uncomfortable for me at the office. Give it a day or two. You'll find what you're looking for."

"I'm sure you're right," I said, though I was far from sure. "I'm grasping at straws." I took a long sip of water and felt the cool liquid ease all the way down into my empty stomach.

"It's been a tough day," he acknowledged.

Yes, it had indeed been a tough day. I was supposed to resurrect my career. Reconnect with my father. Celebrate over dinner. Gorge myself on chocolate croissants. What had happened instead was cataclysmic.

"You'll get the answers you need," he said. "A man like David Wilder would have firmly documented every aspect of your inheritance."

I paused, mid eyebrow-pluck.

My inheritance was the furthest thing from my mind. But Mark did not understand. How could he? He did not know the recently-orphaned-daughter part of me that had sought her father's affection and lost the chance to hear his great hopes for her the night before he died. He did not know my stories, because I had not taken the risk of sharing them.

Maybe Ana had been right. Maybe I didn't know how to do intimacy.

I could have sat across from Mark and explained that I knew what my father's will would reflect. He'd been an open book about it. He would leave his Chicago flat to Aunt Flora. His business would be maintained by the board; his charitable funds would be continuous. For me there was a trust, which I would receive in installments after age thirty in the hope that money wouldn't "ruin" me. His remaining assets would be left in individualized parcels to artistic foundations and companies he wished to support. He'd spelled it all out several times in his all-business tone of voice, "Just in case." But I did not share any of these details with Mark. Outside of the sparkly box containing the blackbird and a key, my father's will was of little interest to me, a subject of which I would waste no breath. I only said, "I just want him back."

After dinner, Mark offered to spend the night, though he had an early morning and would need to be up at five. I told him that I thought I might prefer a bit of quiet. He understood. "You need time to grieve. You let me know what I can do. I'll be right over if there's anything I can do," he assured me. He was pulling his coat on by the door when he said, "And Gracie, I'm sorry the showcase today wasn't what you'd hoped. I'm glad you have another opportunity to impress Olivia Garza."

I felt a tug of disgrace and leaned into him, wrapping my arms around his lean frame. But he was going for the door, and my grip only triggered further desperation.

It triggered the thought of *her*:

> Madame Bisset was saying goodbye. "*Je t'aime*. I love you." I was clutching my arms around her neck and wailing, but she was going, and my heart was breaking, and I had no one to blame but myself.

Mark returned me to the moment with a kiss. "I'll call you later," he said. I blinked up at him and managed to nod in agreement.

But once he'd gone, I didn't know what to do with myself. There would be no sleeping for hours, no TV, no books, no long chats with friends. I could not focus on anything but my own confusion, too big for these walls to contain.

I pocketed the small bronze key from my father and went for a walk. There was only a streak of light left in the sky as I wound my way through the neighborhood, passing rows of brownstones, restaurants, and shops. Every now and again I'd try the bronze key in the lock of a bookstore, an art gallery, or a bakery after closing. It was a strange game that subtly amused me, but of course, my key opened nothing.

I hailed a taxi for my father's penthouse and tried the key in the various-shaped locks of closets and drawers. Unsurprisingly, my key opened nothing. I found only empty spaces he had left behind. Empty rooms. Empty halls. An empty seat at the kitchen table. Though he had often been gone from these spaces, he had occupied room in this world. In my world. He had been reachable, at least in principle, until now.

When I got home, I didn't bother with switching on the lights. I just sank into the couch by the window, turning the blackbird over in my hands and new fears over in my mind. Would I be able to find the brass music box that had been my mother's? Would I have to meet the woman who had driven her car into my father? Would I ever be able to hear Vivaldi or the sound of coffee brewing without thinking of him? And would those thoughts always lead me down the road to heartache and shame?

I watched leaves drift past my window in the darkness, a dance of shadows, and thought of my father's heartache over losing my mother, how he'd fought to conceal it. Now his pain must have finally gone to rest. His emotional shield, too. I nearly smiled, wondering if my father might somehow be more reachable now than he'd been before. If I asked the emptiness of my living room for a gap in time, could I reach up and find him newly available to carry me around on his shoulders? If I simply peeled back a fold in the sky, could I ask him to tell me everything—to tell me what I was to do now?

I got to my feet and climbed onto the windowsill. Balancing on my toes, I flattened my hands and my forehead against the cold glass. The glow of city lights became a gentle haze under the fog of my breath on the windowpane. The city skyline went on forever, fading into the ink-black sky. It all seemed so vast, but maybe there was a way I could signal to him that I was here in the middle of it all, and he could know my regret.

I sucked in a deep breath and screamed as loud as I could. I yelled until my ears were ringing and my vision was blurred, until I was sure I'd either receive a response from the other side or from my authoritative neighbor in 3D, Mrs. Perry. But that night, neither Mrs. Perry nor the universe seemed to hear me. I squeezed my eyes shut and met a darkness spotted with flickers of light like fireflies in a jar.

And then, one of those glowing spots solidified into the spark of a question, small at first, then vivid. How, in those few hours before his death, could my father have obtained this treasure from Old Montreal and arranged to have it set into a box for me? He couldn't have. He must have gotten it at an earlier date. Which meant he had been back to the shop in Montreal at some point and held on to it. But why? To save as a parting gift should he tragically die? It didn't add up. While I watched my breath collect in patterns on the window and evaporate, one thing became very clear. My father hadn't merely given me a sentimental gift. Despite my emotional fatigue, this was the clearest thought I'd had since receiving the news from Mr. Brockwell and Aunt Flora.

I needed to figure out what it was my father had wanted me to understand. "There is much to explain," he'd said in his voicemail. I didn't know just what I believed about this world or the one beyond. Maybe life was nothing more than a game of chance—a human folly to which one can connect the dots that lead toward any finality, as Daryl Cooper had suggested. But what if you could trace the line further? What if the blackbird was my father's voice calling into the glass window from the other side?

10

ÉLOÏSE

"I need to tell you all the stories so they don't die with me," my mother said one afternoon while I was fixing a salad in the kitchen. I lifted my head in surprise and saw that her face was a map to her fear. "Do you remember the legend of Sedna the sea goddess?" she asked.

"It's ingrained in me," I told her. I had heard it nearly every year of my life—by then, at least twenty-five times.

"And the story of Lumaaq?"

I thought I knew most of the details of this one too.

She pulled one of the wooden chairs out from where it had been tucked into my small kitchen table and sank into it, gesturing for me to do the same. I wiped my damp hands on a dish towel and complied.

"I need you to understand the meaning behind each symbol in the shop so they can live on without me." I knew what my mother was telling me. The totality of her livelihood had been stitched into her blankets and her art. She'd woven the past into the future to give to others. She wanted me to care about this work as much as she did. If her illness progressed, she might even want me to take up this work as my own.

"Every culture has asked the same questions, Éloïse," my mother explained. "Who are we, and what is the purpose of this life? Modern culture has adopted an ideology that is false." She leaned closer to me, and I could see the pain of many lives behind her eyes. "It tells us that we are separate from the rest of the world. That the faces we pass each day in the street are separate too. It tells us that we must conquer one another to grow. This is what we have been taught. But this is not who we are."

I smiled at my mother, but I was beset with a sense of dread.

"Separate means we don't feel the pain of our brothers and sisters or the pain of the sea and our land. We become lonely. We wrap our grief in indifference or hate. We don't hear the stories of those even closest to us." My mother lowered her head into her large, reliable hands. After a moment she regarded me lovingly. "Éloïse, I have no power left outside of you. You are the best thing I have ever created. I must rely on you now, and our ancestors will rely on you too."

I tried to slow the drumming of my heart. I did not know how to carry this for my mother. "I do not have a strong voice, like you," I told her.

She lay her warm, crinkled palms over the tops of my smooth hands. "Your voice will grow stronger," she said. "It will help other voices to grow stronger too. Change does not come from a single voice. It will come when all the storytellers gently pull children into their laps and share tales of loss and resilience, of sharing food and respecting others, of redemption, love, connection, luminosity." She rested back into her chair, and I knew then—the way a daughter of a storyteller knows—that the ending must be close.

"I will think about it," was all I could promise her then, but she and I both knew that I would come through.

I had my own ambitions. I feel guilty saying it even now. I had helped with the shop since graduating from college. My mother was ill and needed me. I thought I might be free of it when she passed, but instead, I took it all on. In the last weeks of her life, I wrote down everything my mother wanted me to remember. I let her teach me new ways of quilting, echo stitching designs into thick fabric. When I felt my work was done, my mother would tell me to go back in. "Make it more beautiful than it asked to be," she'd say. I did the work. I wrote the stories. I honored my mother. And when she exhaled her very last breath, I wrapped her in her favorite quilt and sobbed a story I had never dared to utter.

Uninspired but dutiful, I took to running the little shop in Old Montreal that had been in my family for forty years. It was called The Heirloom.

My mother's stories and her store had been my inheritance, and surprisingly, they slowly nurtured my own gifts. Soon I understood the difference between the skills she had passed on to me and the abilities that were naturally mine. I could see the pain written in the lines on someone's face, and I felt compelled to lean in. I made my mother's shop my own by marrying her artistic symbols to the stories I collected from the new life that soon graced the timeworn doorway. People came to try on healing stone rings or to buy a wind chime made of sea glass. As they shopped, I listened to them tell me about their lives. One winter I brought a tea table and two chairs into the store to keep for customers, and on some occasions I would say, "Sit if you like," and we would piece together fragments of stories there among the textiles and books, shifting our own personal mythologies.

I had been charged with caring for others in a unique way, and the idea of it soon quieted other hungers in me. My mother's stories subtly leaked out into my conversations and into my art. Our two lives merged, long after her death, on a path of love.

But never had anyone come and requested something that had been distinctly my mother's until David Wilder wandered into my shop. It was a crisp day in June. I'd opened at ten o'clock, counted the cash in the register, and laid out a new quilt I'd sewn from patches of fabric with raspberry-colored medallions and emerald embroidered vines. My first customer was a woman in her midthirties, near my age, with a jacket heavier than the weather required. When I greeted her, she explained that she was just in to look around. She paced the room and quickly settled where I was among the quilts.

"They're each unique and handmade," I offered.

She ran her hand over a large blue-and-green one I'd toiled over for months. "My grandmother had a quilt on her bed throughout my childhood. The colors were the same as this one," she explained. She told me that her grandmother had died, and they'd had to give away many of her things. I was commenting on how it can be difficult to know what to hold on to, when the bell on the old door rang and a man stepped in.

"Let me know if I can help," I said to him before bringing my attention back to the young woman. She asked me to spread the quilt out so she could have a better look.

David, as I would come to know him, moved around the shop slowly while I laid the quilt along the wooden countertop. The woman's fingertips grazed the fabric and landed on a special patch of material. "Is this a mermaid?" she asked, pointing to a figure stitched in deep indigo, bold and prominent against the paler cotton underneath.

"That's Sedna, the goddess of the sea," I explained. "As a young woman she was deceived and tormented and thrown into the water, where she became a sea creature and now controls all sea life."

"And people still believe in Sedna?" she asked suspiciously.

I smiled gently. "As long as young girls are mistreated, Sedna is still among us. A reminder that we'd all drown if we didn't sprout fins."

The woman's face softened. "I like this story," she said, holding back a sea of her own. She was not the only one who had become interested. David stood just steps away, studying the quilt with sober concentration.

"Would you like to see a quilt?" I asked him.

"No. No, thank you. I'm here for the birds. You used to carry birds." For clarification he added, "The ones with crystal wings?"

Instantly I remembered my mother's handmade fabric birds. I'd sold the last of them many years before and had focused my merchandise on the more useful items. "I'm sorry, we don't sell the birds anymore."

He sighed. "I wanted to buy one for my daughter. I'm in town on business, and I hoped I might be able to buy the blackbird for her at last." The young woman and I were attentive. David looked to the door, but something made him stay. "She's lost," he said. "I miss her."

"*Elle te manque*," I said, because this is what we say in French. Word for word, it means "she is missing from you."

"Yes," he said. "She's long since passed age nine—she's nearly fifteen— but I thought the gift might be a heartening gesture."

We'd had many patrons over many years, tourists and locals who would come to buy something soft or shiny or indigenous and go home happy. But only some connected with the stories my mother told. Fewer still returned for more. As David spoke of his daughter, it collected for me. The story my mother had written out by the fire, hoping the nine-year-old girl would return to the shop to see the blackbird. My mother had said that this was a story the child needed.

"I can make you the bird," I told David. "I am not as skilled with a needle and thread as my mother was, but if you give me four or five days, I can have it ready for you."

"Thank you," he said with a smile that lifted his whole face.

I sold the young woman the quilt with Sedna's story, and then I set to work ordering silk fabric and Swarovski crystals for the blackbird.

Each of those four days that it took to make it, David came to visit the shop. He'd check on my progress and fill empty moments with the textures and tangibility that the shop provided. The quieter the day, the more David spoke. He told me about Gracie. I listened to his story, often understanding even the parts that he left out.

Gracie had been given the opportunity to chase her dreams, but as my mother would have put it: she felt separate. Her life had sprung from wounds. She had lost her mother, and along the way, she had lost herself. She was a child with holes where things could slip through her. I expected that the story my mother had given her had slipped through her too. I could tell that David valued his daughter's potential, but I wondered if David valued his daughter's pain.

For the first time since my mother died, I paced through the story of the blackbird in my mind and stitched it into the little silk bird. Objects do not have power until we give them power, or meaning until we give them meaning, and this small work of art was charged with an energy of love and healing. I willed for it to take flight and help Gracie find her way out of the dark. I thought she would receive it on her fifteenth birthday.

But human hands can be unsteady, not always as brave as the rest of us. A simple gesture from a father who longed to see his daughter happy would become difficult to give.

Still, the blackbird would find its way. The story would come back into Gracie's life, a gift my mother had set in motion all those years ago.

I liked thinking of my mother at peace. She would be glad that the quilts were still beautifully displayed in the shop window. She would enjoy the way I kept fresh flowers in her old pottery vase at the end of the sales counter. She might grumble about the line of handblown glassware I'd introduced in the spring, but she'd be terribly proud of the way I stitched together that blackbird. I had made it more beautiful than it had asked to be.

11

GRIFFIN

David Wilder's funeral service would be at a church in Uptown. Since I'd recently totaled my truck and the train didn't exactly support a funeral procession, I was going to have to gas up the Falcon.

Pop spent his retirement restoring a royal blue 1962 Ford Falcon convertible that I think he drove twice. About three months after he finished the restoration, Teddy and I had the unpleasant experience of having to tell the poor guy that it was probably safest if he didn't drive anymore. In all things, Pop had become apprehensive and unpredictable. He'd almost totaled my brother's Honda while trying to park at the grocery store. He hit the gas instead of the brake and luckily only killed a few grocery carts. His life was a familiar game, he'd just forgotten some of the plays. Teddy and I thought it was the stress of Mom more than anything. "Just a part of old age," Pop said, but seeing him hand me those keys felt pretty close to fatality. "She's yours now, Beau," he told me. But I didn't have the heart to take her out of the garage more than to circle her around the block once a month and keep her alive. It just wasn't my car.

Now that I had also been accused of being less than competent behind the wheel, I felt like a hypocrite. But I was determined to make the funeral of David Wilder, so I would put on my black suit and borrow Pop's car.

The rails of my garage creaked when I lifted the door. The space was small and the Falcon so long that the door nearly grazed her round taillights. Her paint still gleamed, and her white-rimmed tires showed no sign of experience. She was all dressed up with nowhere to go. It felt surprisingly right backing her out into daylight that October day.

I pulled in front of Fidelis for a minute on my way through town. The sight of its boarded windows made my breath fall heavy in my chest. There would be no funeral here; no ceremony; no closure. They say that more than fifty percent of car accidents happen within five miles of home, but it's not like I hit a tree. A tree would have been nice. Instead, I jumped the curb that gave Abrams a reason to throw in the towel on history. I was Fortune's fool.

—

The church was decorated with hundreds of white carnations for the funeral. They filled the entrance and were draped over the end of each pew. There was a large poster-size photo of Mr. Wilder propped on an easel in the front of the church alongside a cremation urn. The seats were two-thirds full of men and women in dark clothing when the organ began to play, and Gracie Wilder walked down the aisle with a woman moving stiffly beside her.

When it was time for the eulogy, Gracie walked up to the pulpit without anything to read. She adjusted the microphone and stood silently for what felt like several minutes. The whole church waited in anticipation.

Finally, she began. "My father used to let me polish his shoes," she said, and I found myself exhaling with relief for her. "Though he could have stopped for a shoeshine at the airport on his way from city to city, he preferred to do the job himself. And on some occasions, about the time I was eight or nine, he'd let me help." There was a warmth to her voice, as if she were talking with a close friend. But her eyes did not stay fixed on anyone. They swept over the room. "He showed me how much polish to use and how to buff them. And when I was done, I'd stomp around the house in those big shiny shoes until he'd march me off to bed. There was something powerful about walking around in those shoes." She paused and everyone sat in wait, urging her on with sympathetic expressions.

"When I sat down a couple of days ago to think of what I might say today, I first thought of the shoes, but then I got stuck. I spoke to a few family members and asked them what they thought of my dad. Someone said *honest*; someone said *hardworking*. Another person said *tall*! That was Cousin Millie over there," she pointed, and the crowd murmured a laugh. "The thing is, I'm not sure I really knew my dad. Not in the way that I would have liked. I knew pieces of him. I suppose that's true for most of us. Maybe my mother was the one who knew him best. I don't think anyone can adequately find words to encapsulate another person—I certainly don't know how to do this for David Wilder—but I can tell you that people like my father are not ten a penny. He was something of a contradiction of terms, wasn't he? He enjoyed English tea *and* Italian coffee. He read Charlotte Brontë novels, but his subscription to the *Economist* was always on top of the heap of reading material in every home we ever lived in. He loved foreign-language films, but also enjoyed physical comedy and Mr. Bean movies." She smiled at the thought. "While some carry on about their experiences, my father rather kept to himself, didn't he? He could close a deal with no wasted words and tell of a momentous trip across the Atlantic in a short, handwritten note scrolled out in perfect penmanship. He believed in perseverance and prided himself on hard work. He did not play much; that is certain. But when he did allow for a break, he sought nature, teaching me to love it too. The simple shade of a tree or the song of a bird." She seemed to push down a tidal wave of sadness. "I always thought I'd have more moments like that with him. We do that, right? We always think there's going to be more." She struggled not to cry. "But the fact of the matter is that every show comes to an end. The music stops, the curtain closes, and it's done. Even if you wish there were another act."

The mood in the church was somber. Some people shifted in their seats, uncomfortably. But me, I was entranced. She was warm, soulful, honest.

Her melancholy voice finished with this: "I have big shoes to fill now. If I slipped into a pair of his oxfords today, I'm not sure I'd walk any more gracefully than I did as a child. But I'd like to try. I think that's what he would want. He would ask us not to cry or fuss. He'd tell us to get on with doing great things." She gave herself a moment, then bravely smiled. "So, we must try. Thank you for being a part of his life, and many of you, a part of mine." She lowered her head and stepped away from the pulpit.

I had an urge to clap, stand in reverence, or at the very least, go put a hand on her shoulder. Clearly, no one else had the same compulsion. The congregation stayed still as Gracie returned to her seat, her heeled shoes tapping across the floor tiles.

When the organ had shared its last depressing sounds, I followed the crowd out of the church. I awkwardly stood by a tree, watching Gracie receive hugs from friends and a guy I presumed was her boyfriend. Before I could approach to offer my condolences, she was ushered into a black car. So, I followed to the cemetery.

We were assembled in a weathered chapel waiting for the reverend to give a final blessing when I glanced over my shoulder and spotted Gracie backing toward the door. No one else seemed to detect her graceful exit. I suppose that's why I followed her. I figured someone should, and I'd been wanting to talk to her all day.

When I stepped out of the dim chapel onto the expanse of lawn, the sun streaming through the tree branches blurred my vision. I had to squint to make out shapes, and then there she was, holding her cell phone up to the sky.

I walked toward her. "Gracie," I said, and she whirled around. But then all I could think to offer her was a token, "I'm so sorry for your loss." She blinked as if to signal that she'd registered my presence. I apologized for startling her, then looked to where she still held her phone skyward and asked, "What are we doing out here?"

She followed my gaze and lowered her phone. "I'm trying to get a signal. To order a car. Do you have a signal?" Unlike her composed demeanor while giving the eulogy, she was frenzied.

"Well, I have a car. Do you need a ride?" She nodded quickly. I asked her if she wanted to go back into the chapel first, but she went a little pale and headed for the parking lot. Once we were in the car and I'd turned the key in the ignition, I saw that her face was completely drained of color. "Here," I said, reaching for the lever under her seat. I inched it backward, creating more space in front of her. "Maybe if you lower your head."

She bent forward without hesitation and took in air like thick milkshake from a straw—painstaking and audible. Unsure of what to do, I put a hand on her back. Her body trembled like she might break into tears, but with the air she sucked in, she seemed to slowly suck that back too, pushing it down. When I lifted my hand, she sat up and wiped her cheeks with the palms of her hands. "Sorry," she said.

"It's okay," I assured her. I let the car run idle, giving us both a minute, and then I drove away from the cemetery. "Where am I taking you?" I asked after about a quarter of a mile. "Can I get you home?"

But she didn't seem to hear me. "I love this song," she said somberly. "Don't you love this song?" Only then did I notice that "Across the Universe" by the Beatles was leaking through the speakers of the Falcon. I might have said something coherent about it, and then she asked, "Did you know my father well?"

"I didn't," I admitted, "but he was always really good to me. Honest. Fair."

"I don't think he was very close to very many people. I bet half the

people there today barely knew him. Even Mark only met him once."
She clarified, "Mark is the guy I'm seeing."

"Was he at the cemetery?"

"He had to leave from the church. He had an appointment in court."
She was gazing out the window.

"He's a lawyer?" I asked, knowing he was.

"Yes, an associate at Stetson and Lawrey."

"I have a buddy who does some work for them. Daryl Cooper," I
told her.

Her eyes flickered in my direction. "I've met Daryl. I like him."

We were passing through Lake View when Gracie slid out of her
black suit jacket and pulled a green sweater from her bag. I tried to focus
on the road and made weak attempts at conversation. "When I saw you
last week you were on your way to a performance. How'd that go?"

She pulled the sweater on over her blouse. "Oh . . . not that great,
actually. But I have one more shot to prove myself." She seemed more
comfortable now. Maybe it was the sweater. Maybe it was the distance
from the cemetery. "Griffin, if you were no longer able to do what it is
you do, what would you do instead?"

"Well, I don't know," I said, trying to digest the question.

"Me either," she sighed. We sat at a traffic light with the turn signal
tick-tick-ticking. After a minute she asked, "Well, are you going to tell
me how it is you drive the coolest car I've ever seen?"

"It's not mine," I replied impulsively.

"You're a thief," she teased. "Have you ever put the top down?"

"Never."

"Why not?"

"Like I said, it's not mine."

Moments later, she moved to the edge of her seat. "I'd love to get out
here, please."

I pulled over. "Here?" We were looking at a row of average shops
and eateries.

"Yes, this would be perfect. Thank you."

She stepped out into the bright, cool air and shut the car door. The sun was low and large. She seemed to shoulder its weight as she leaned over the open window. "Thank you, Griffin. I really appreciate the ride," she said.

"Absolutely." I watched her walk up the street. She peered in some shop windows and then opened the door of a twenty-four-hour diner and disappeared behind the glare of the glass.

I must have sat in the car for five minutes before I finally shut off the engine and went to find her. She was sitting in a booth gazing out the window. Despite her solemn expression, she was the brightest thing in the place, beautiful with her windswept hair and emerald sweater. She didn't see me until I slid into the seat across from her, and even then, she didn't say anything. Just tilted her head with interest.

A waiter appeared. "What can I get ya?" he asked.

"A slice of strawberry pie," Gracie said.

"Sorry. Just sold my last piece. How about apple?" He was ready to close the deal, but Gracie didn't comply.

"Just water then."

The waiter shifted his attention to me. "Nothing. Thanks," I said. Then he was gone. I looked to Gracie. "I know we don't really know each other, but I couldn't leave you on the side of the road on a day like today."

She glanced around the diner and then back to me. "Strawberry pie was his favorite. I wanted to have it at the reception, but Aunt Flora said chocolate cake was a more popular choice. I'm sure it doesn't matter since he's not here." She forced a smile. "I guess I just wanted to toast him with his favorite dessert."

"I understand," I said, an idea emerging. "And I think I know a place where we can find some pie."

She shook her head. "All the bakeries will be closed by now."

"Not this one." I got up and pointed myself toward the door, and to my astonishment, she followed me.

Senior care facilities are generously stocked with sweets. The nurses at Oakview were always trying to feed me cobblers and cake. Not exactly my thing, but this was not an ordinary day. When Gracie and I arrived, the dinner hour was in full swing. We strolled into the dining hall, and immediately Pop glanced up from his meat loaf. "Lara," he said, standing and pressing a hand gently onto Mom's left shoulder. "Look who's here."

"How is she today?" I asked.

"Fine," he declared with a single bob of the head. "Who's the girl?"

"Pop, meet Gracie Wilder. Gracie, this is my dad, Owen."

Gracie introduced herself with an extended hand, which Pop took and shook eagerly. He gave me a sideways glance with questions written all over it, but luckily, he asked none of them.

Pop pointed to me. "It's Beaumont," he announced to Mom, but she didn't look away from her meat loaf.

Gracie raised her brows with interest. "Beaumont," she echoed in my direction.

I waved off the sound of my ridiculous formal name and took a seat at the table. Gracie followed suit while Pop went to fetch drinks. I explained to Mom that we'd come for dessert, but she only shook her head in a usual sign of frustration.

"I don't have much of a sweet tooth either," Gracie told her softly. "Though I do like to bake."

"In her day, my mom could bake like nobody's business," I said. The mention of it triggered memories I could practically taste and smell.

"It's one of those things that stays with you, right?" Gracie said, still directing the conversation toward my mother's distant gaze. "For me, it's chocolate chip cookies."

I told Gracie about how Mom did Christmas when I was a kid. We would spend days rolling dough, melting chocolate, and sprinkling sugar. Then Teddy and I would fill dozens of cookie tins for teachers, neighbors, and of course, ourselves. We'd count to make sure we both got the same amount and steal a few from the other tins when Mom wasn't looking. The thought of it made me smile.

"You have an amazing mother," Gracie confirmed. Then she leaned over to the frail woman beside her. "Don't you agree, Lara?"

Mom searched Gracie's face. "Shouldn't we be leaving?"

"We're just having dinner," I said, hoping to bring her back from wherever she was. I whispered to Gracie, "One day she's getting on a plane, the next, she's going to the beach."

"I don't like planes," she said. "Sometimes I wish it were as easy as it was when I was a kid. When I could imagine my way anywhere I wanted to go in a cardboard box."

I gulped back emotion at the idea of my mother imagining her way through an empty box.

"Lara," Gracie said, "if you could go anywhere in the world right now, where would you want to go?"

Mom seemed to consider that. "Home," she said after a moment. "I'd want to go home." My jaw grew slack. Was she remembering our house on Park Avenue? Then her gaze fell on me, and the paper-thin skin of her forehead lifted with vague recognition. "You crashed your car."

I stammered in shock. "It was . . . just an accident. Everything's fine."

She glanced away.

"Mom?" I took both of her hands in mine. "Mom?" But she receded, pulling her hands away and my heart with it.

—

As I'd expected, Oakview had strawberry pie. I was able to secure four large pieces from the kitchen. Pop and Gracie got along like a house on fire—with burning enthusiasm—and we all raised forkfuls in a toast to David Wilder. Even Mom had a bite, before Gracie and I said good night and headed back out to the Falcon.

"You did a good thing for me today," she said when we were halfway across the parking lot. The sky was dark and the air damp. She folded her arms across her chest.

"You want my jacket?" I asked.

"No, but thank you, Beaumont," she said, grinning.

"It's just Griffin. If you have to, then Beau."

"Okay. It's a strong name, though. *Beaumont.*" She said it again as if she were tasting something unusual. "I mean, it beats Adolf. Or Gary."

I laughed. "I grew up with a Gary."

"Likable guy?"

"Kind of annoying, actually."

"Well, *you're* a very likable guy," she said, before sliding into the car.

Once we'd pulled out of the parking lot, Gracie said, "You must miss her." She vacillated. "Sorry, I—"

"No, you're right. I do miss her." It was nice to talk about my mom. People rarely asked about her anymore.

"This is going to sound strange," she began, "but ever since my dad died, I've had this impulse to talk to him. Like, out loud. I keep thinking that maybe he can hear me. And I was thinking about that tonight when you were sitting with Lara. Wondering if there's some part of her that can hear you, really *know* you, even when her mind won't let her. Does that sound crazy?"

"It sounds hopeful."

"She mentioned the accident."

I shook my head. "I can't figure it out. Why she'd remember that of all things. But she's in there somewhere. She flits in and out. If you blink, you miss her. I've seen her MRI scans and the damage on her brain. The neurologists can't explain exactly how things occasionally come through, but they can promise that it will happen less and less. I go over there several times a week hoping that maybe I'll find her, get more than a few seconds. It's dumb, I know, but it's just a part of what I do."

"It's not dumb," she said quickly. "Griffin, my dad was in my life for twenty-six years, healthy as a horse, but I'm not sure I could really find him either. And we weren't fighting against a mind-altering disease. We were fighting against something we constructed ourselves and didn't know how to undo. Knowing what I do now, if I could, I'd just go and sit too. Just sit with him, because sometimes maybe that's all there is to do." She paused. "If you could talk to her, really talk, for like two minutes, what would you say?" It was a question that only someone who had lost someone would know how to ask.

"I guess I'd just want her to know that I am still here. And that I'll remember everything I can for the both of us. What about you? What would you say to your dad?"

She fixed her gaze on the city lights flickering by the window. "That I'm sorry I caused him additional pain," she said, though I couldn't be sure she was still talking to me.

When I pulled up in front of her apartment building, Gracie sat smoothing her skirt for a moment. "I hit a rough patch there earlier at the cemetery," she said.

"It's understandable."

Her expression was apologetic. "Thank you. It was a nice ending to a tough day."

"I'm glad I was there."

She opened the car door. "Maybe I'll see you again sometime?"

"You bet," I said, not knowing how to prolong the moment or how to tell her that she'd turned my day around too.

I waited as she walked to the door. Then, I let go and drove away.

12

GRACIE

The night of my father's funeral, I was exhausted but unable to sleep. I stared at the ceiling for an hour, wrestling between sadness and regret with no clear winner, before finally forfeiting at ten thirty.

I rolled back the floral rug in the living room and sat in front of the turntable by the window. I lowered the needle onto a vinyl record, inviting Van Morrison into the room in a folky-jazz concert of sound. Then I got to my feet and danced myself across the floor. When my mind grew tired, I let my body decide where it would take me. *Arabesque, back rollover, split.* When my technique faded, I still kept moving until my muscles were weary, until the day was finally done.

When sleep came, it took me for fourteen hours. Ana came in at nine in the morning to check on me, then again at noon to try to get me to eat. Both times I rolled over and went back to sleep. When I finally pulled my body from the stale cocoon of blankets, she drew me a bath and fixed me a sandwich. I sat at the table reflexively chewing turkey, Swiss, and tomato while she untangled my wet curls with a brush and a little hair product.

"I've never had a friend brush my hair before," I told her. "It's nice."

"Never? Not even at a sleepover or before a performance?"

"I was not a very popular child."

"I'd have guessed you hung out with the cool kids."

I snorted. "You know I've never had a barometer for *cool*."

"Maybe it would help if you didn't say things like *barometer for cool*."

I swatted at her lethargically.

"Seriously though, what was your thing? Like at recess in grade school, were you gossiping in the bathroom or playing kickball with the jocks or smoking something behind the building?"

"I was sneaking in chapters of *Anne of Green Gables* in the library."

"For real?" She seemed disappointed, but the memories lifted my spirits.

"For the school talent show, I even altered one of my mother's old lace cocktail dresses and made a gown to wear while reciting 'The Highwayman.' I wanted to be every bit as dramatic as Anne Shirley."

"You're in a category all your own, G," she said, tidying one last unruly wave with the hairbrush.

"Maybe I was born at the wrong time, like one hundred years too late." I gave that a second's thought. "But then I would have missed women's suffrage, so—"

Ana shifted my chair to face her, halting my chatter. "We need to get you out of this apartment. Let's go for coffee. Wander down to the lake."

This was a thoughtful suggestion, but it would have prompted a conventional afternoon in the city, a normal occasion. And nothing at all felt normal. In the past week, not a single upturned stone had produced an answer to the questions that had emerged from my father's death. Outside of his very clinical medical record, the hospital had been unable to provide me with an account of his time in the emergency room; Mr. Brockwell could not explain the purpose of the bronze key; and no one understood the significance of the silk blackbird, let alone when or why my father came to obtain it. The only new development was that Aunt Flora had yielded to my request the day of the funeral and put aside half of my father's ashes to be buried at the base of an English oak tree in Surrey so they could mingle with my mother's in the rich clay soil. When she'd called the night before to inquire about my absence at the reception, she said she was booking a plane ticket and asked if I wanted her to book two. I thought, *yes*. With the right planning and a sedative, I could take a flight out the week after next—once my performance for Olivia Garza was complete and the dust of October had reasonably settled. But Aunt Flora argued that the ceremony would need to take place immediately—before the first frost. Apparently, ashes do not consort with solid ground and David Wilder is not meant to sit on a mantel until spring. So, I would not be able to join my father for his last trip across the pond, and today would be far from ordinary. It would be another distance, another void, another finality.

I told Ana I'd rather not stroll down to the lake. I would be poor company. It was best if I tried to distract myself with thoughts of choreography. I would just whip up an epic solo. That would do the trick. A cinch, really.

God help me.

The Garza Dance Company was at the Harris Theater all week rehearsing their upcoming show, *The Shape of Poetry*. I thought I might find a way in and glimpse something that would inspire my own piece. The notion was gutsy and certainly desperate, but it was the only place outside my sad little flat that I could think to go.

I took the elevator down to the lobby and gave a wave to Joel, our building concierge. He stood up from behind the desk when he saw me. "Gracie, I have something for you. A man came by last night and dropped this off." From behind the counter, Joel lifted the dark wool jacket I'd worn to the funeral. I must have left it in Griffin's car. I thanked Joel and told him I'd pick it up on my way back home. But I would not. I would never slip that jacket on again. If only heartache was a jacket that could be slipped off too.

I took a cab to the intersection of Michigan and Randolph and cut briskly through Wrigley Square. I spotted a family taking pictures in front of the Millennium Monument and paused in step for just a moment to point my attention in the direction of their cameras. I loved tourists. How they tilted their heads upward and always seemed to be searching for beauty. Madame Bisset had once called me *ma petite touriste*, "my little tourist." She gave me a film camera for Christmas our first winter in Montreal, and it was like I'd been handed a new way to see the world. I would peer through the small, square eyepiece and focus in on the interesting details of my life—my purple rain boots in a glittering puddle or a honeybee at a picnic. I saved these moments in the small black film canisters and stowed them in a shoebox that had once held a pair of my mother's heels. It was a collection of memories preserved, undeveloped, untouched. Years later, my American au pair discovered the canisters and suggested that we develop the photos to make albums. Like regular people. But I told her to throw them all out; I didn't want to paste the past into books. I regretted it now, of course. I would have liked to revisit some of those moments, to reach back and remember.

I felt genuinely happy for the family taking pictures in front of the monument. Their memories would persist; they'd be digital and forever retrievable.

When I reached the tall glass facade of the Harris Theater, I spotted a woman in blue jeans playing a guitar near the entrance. I remembered seeing her there before, playing music for those who passed by. "Spare change for a song?" she asked me.

I checked my bag. "I have five dollars," I said, handing her the bill and a smile before carrying on.

"Wait, your song!"

I spun back around.

"If you don't mind, it's more enjoyable to play for someone who'll listen."

"Yes," I reasoned. "Absolutely." I put my bag down on the sidewalk and gave her my attention.

"Okay," she said. "A five-dollar song."

She plucked some pretty notes on her guitar and hummed out a rhythm to herself: *dum-dat-dat-dum-dat-dat*. Then, as if a turntable needle had simply found the right groove, her guitar sprang to life, and she played a melody in high vibration.

> *My mama held me when I was small. She sang don't worry baby; I'll catch you if you fall. Oh, but I'm such a long way from home. Nobody here no more. To get me back on my feet, when trouble's at my door. And oh, this weary heart, has it forgot how to play? The notes to the song, that can find the way . . .*

All the hairs on my arms stood on end as she belted out the words and hammered out the rhythm. Despite the melancholy verse, the music itself felt light. And as commuters paused in stride to listen, only smiles could be seen among the crowd. Momentum built, and the singer bellowed:

> *Well, I'm not done singin' yet. I'm not a broken string. I may be down on my luck, but I ain't givin' in. Here I am, baby. Still alive in these shoes that have walked these old streets, to the tune of the blues.*

Her voice triumphed into another octave, lifting in intensity and volume as she strummed and hollered out the end. When her guitar fell silent, the city was still grinding forward, but I felt as though time had been standing still. I clapped, and she bowed her head with casual gratitude. The others who had gathered to listen echoed my applause and slowly dispersed. I extended a hand. "Gracie Wilder."

"Myla Jane," she said, taking my hand.

"You're wonderful, Myla. That *sound*."

"I was a gospel singer before I started playin' the blues." She grinned. "Put them together, it's like peanut butter and jelly."

"You draw a crowd."

"I sing the truth. People like that." Then she leaned in. "And I play behind the beat. It's a magic trick. If you sit back into the music then you don't sing the song, the song sings you. So clean it wasn't even written."

I was captivated. "You were singing about your own life?"

"That's right."

"Well, it seemed to deliver me from mine. For a couple of minutes anyway." I gathered my bag to be on my way.

"Where you off to this morning?"

"To figure out how to make a dream a reality. I have a lot of work to do."

She shook her head. "Hard work is only hard work. You go home and tell someone how hard you work, how bone-tired, but that's not how you build a dream."

"Do you have a dream, Myla?"

"I got dreams. I got 'em right here." She gently patted her chest. "And they're gonna happen. I've put it all out here on the street. I got my whole heart on this street too. You got to put it all out there."

I didn't find my way inside the Harris Theater that day. I didn't get further than Myla Jane before I realized: I wasn't ready.

It was the very first thing I said to Dr. Peck when she kindly squeezed me in for an appointment the next morning. When she opened the door to her office, she said, "Gracie, you look well," and I said, "I'm not ready."

I wondered if I did look well. Dr. Peck was wearing a blue knit pant-suit that put my pink hoodie with the glittering words *Move It* to shame. I tucked a few misbehaving curls behind my ears and sank into a chair.

"What aren't you ready for?" Dr. Peck asked.

"To prove to Olivia Garza that I'm good enough. I thought I'd done everything right. I mastered the choreography. But she said that I didn't unlock the anguish of the piece. Dr. Peck, I need your help. I want to be able to show *all* of me on that stage. I have to put all of myself out there if I'm going to give the performance of a lifetime, and I'm not sure I know how to do that." Dr. Peck wore a face of deep concentration. I was feeling impatient. "Shall we dive in?" I tried.

"Gracie," she began, "I believe you need to give yourself permission to grieve. I believe that is how you might get closer to putting all of yourself out on stage. If you don't mind me asking, when was the last time you let yourself have a good cry?"

It occurred to me that I might say *2004*, but I didn't want to sound snarky. "It's been a while," I told Dr. Peck.

She was sympathetic. "I understand the desire to outthink what you feel. Outdance what you feel. But eventually emotion catches up with us. A simple moment can trigger a flood of grief or a rush of anxiety without warning."

I knew exactly what she meant. Days before, I'd passed a house with a yellow door and felt sick to my stomach, sick with an ache for my home in Montreal with the yellow door.

"Why do you think it became difficult for you to cry?" Dr. Peck asked.

I sat with the question for a moment before a memory sparked. "My father's pockets always jingled when I was a kid."

She cocked her head with curiosity.

"He had small, mysterious objects in there—coins and things—and I remember hearing him fiddle with whatever was in there when I was crying. I think crying made him uncomfortable. He'd say, 'Don't fuss, Gracie dear,' and eventually I'd calm down."

She crinkled her brow. "Do you think that over time your troubling feelings became as uncomfortable for you as they were for your father? And now some of those feelings are . . . mysterious?"

I sighed and smiled. "As mysterious as the rattling of a deep pocket."

Dr. Peck gave us both a moment to take that in, then patted her legs with conviction. "I think that together we can identify some of those feelings, Gracie. We can use our sessions to thoughtfully explore what's coming up."

She really was terrific, and I told her so. Then I added, "The trouble is, my audition is just around the corner."

"This *will* take time," she confirmed. "But . . . when we're not in session, try getting out and changing the scenery. As things come up, and I imagine they will, try staying with what you're feeling instead of pushing it away. It might be uncomfortable at first, but this could really inspire change. Maybe even inspire your audition."

"That sounds like a good plan," I said.

"How is your energy? Have you been able to sleep?"

"Sometimes my questions keep me up at night, but then I sleep well into the morning."

Dr. Peck picked up a notepad and jotted something down. "What kinds of questions?"

"Well, I'd like to know why my father ran out into the street that night. The witness who called 911 said he *ran* into the street. But my father didn't run. He walked briskly at best."

"Perhaps he was trying to hail a cab."

"Not at that hour. He would have finished dinner, returned his calls, and been headed up to bed on schedule. As he'd always done. So, I'd like to know why he was running into the street. And that's only the tip of the iceberg."

She set the notepad down. "What else, Gracie?"

"Well, I'm desperate to know how he got the blackbird and why."

"Who do you suppose knows the answer to that question?"

"The woman who sold it to him, I suppose." It seemed like a perfunctory response. And yet, once those words had left my mouth, my hands started to tingle. I squeezed them a few times hoping the blood would return to my fingertips. I could picture the young woman who had spoken to me about the birds all those years ago. And the older woman who had written me the little book. "I remember that shop so well," I told Dr. Peck. "It was a long-established boutique. I bet it's hardly changed at all. Why is it I can remember things like that with such clarity, and yet parts of those years seem to be completely erased? I lived in Montreal for almost six years, but I only have a handful of memories from that time. I can't even remember the story of the blackbird, even though I read it over and over as a kid. Once Madame Bisset was gone, I put the book away, and now I can't remember any of it. It's gone too."

"Post-traumatic stress can impact our memories," she explained. "Or sometimes after a great loss, it hurts so much to remember how happy we were that we want to forget."

"Well, now I want to remember," I said, realizing. My eyes brimmed with tears as images flickered in my mind like a flip-book in time—the night my father took me to the ballet; the shop in Old Montreal; the bird with crystal wings. "What if I'm looking in the wrong direction for answers?" I asked unexpectedly. "I've been calling New York, but maybe the answers are in Montreal." A little voice inside me seemed to whisper *yes*. "I could go there and find the shopkeeper. She may remember my father, know when he was there, or why."

Dr. Peck had never appeared so surprised. "These are possibilities. But we should consider that she might not remember him or know anything at all about these things."

"But certainly *I* would remember something."

"You might have misunderstood what I meant by a change of scenery," she tried.

I noticed that I was standing. I'm not sure when that happened. "Maybe Mark would be willing to drive with me."

"Drive?"

"Well, I don't fly well, and I'd hate to add to the anxiety of it all." I lifted my bag off the floor.

Dr. Peck stared at me, mouth agape. "Gracie, I'd like to talk this through some more. Talk through what you're feeling."

"Thanks a million, Dr. Peck. But I feel . . . well, I feel that I've got to go."

———

When I arrived at Stetson and Lawrey, Mark was sifting through paper-work at his desk. "Gracie," he called out, coming over to shut his office door before wrapping his arms around my waist. "You okay?"

I came right out with it. "What do you think about loading up your car and taking a road trip to Montreal?"

I could tell that he thought I was joking.

"I know it's far, but the drive would be beautiful this time of year. I could show you where I lived as a child. We could stay in a cute bed-and-breakfast or something."

Mark's wide, white smile narrowed into a thin crescent shape. "Gracie, I can't drive to Montreal. It would take days. I have to work." He led me to the leather love seat adjacent to his desk to sit. "Look," he went on, "I know you've just been through a lot, but you have an audition to prepare for."

"I *will* prepare, but I'd like to do it from my old neighborhood in Montreal. Maybe it's what I need to inspire an authentic perfor-mance." I felt so confident he would see it the way I did, but that was an unfair expectation.

"I'm sorry, Gracie. If this is something you need to do, I guess I understand. But I can't take a vacation right now."

Cooper stepped into the room with a quick knock. "Here's the report," he said, tossing a file folder on Mark's desk. Cooper nodded a greeting in my direction. "Gracie."

"Good to see you," I said as he breezed back into the hall.

"Wait, Cooper," Mark called out to the closing door.

"Go ahead," I told him, realizing my interruption.

"I want to talk about this, but—"

"It's okay. We can talk later."

Mark left to track down Cooper, but he must not have held his atten-tion for long. By the time I reached the street below and walked half a block, I heard Cooper call out, "Gracie! Gracie Wilder!"

I turned into the blustery morning and saw Cooper jogging to catch up with me. The air smelled pressurized with rain. The clouds were awaiting their curtain call.

"How are you hangin' in there?" he asked when he reached me.

"All right, I guess." The empathetic expression on his face made me feel as though we were old friends. We both put our backs to the wind and managed our way up the block.

"I've been thinking about our conversation. Did you ever find that email?"

"Sadly, no. And no one at the Waldorf Astoria or New York Presbyterian Hospital has been able to tell me much." I wrapped my coat more tightly around my waist to try to keep the wind from cutting through me. "Everyone in my life seems to think it's silly of me to try to go down the technological rabbit hole."

"You said your father's laptop was being sent to his Chicago office?"

"Yes, but I can't sit around hoping they'll change their minds and give me access."

"Gracie, let me help with this."

"I appreciate it. But I don't want to complicate things. I'm thinking of taking a trip in a more sentimental direction. Maybe I can still learn something about what my father wanted to tell me and dust off some memories. Do you ever find yourself pulled in an entirely different direction when on a case?"

"Absolutely," he said. "Often the answer is hiding in a subtle corner and not in the direction of all the excitement." This was heartening. "I'm headed to the pub across the street to meet some friends. Can I buy you a beer? Or a tea?" he asked.

The threat of a downpour had become definite. Icy drops of water were beginning to slap the pavement. I saw the pub door standing open across the street and I could not refuse its warmth. "Tea would be great."

We jogged through the intersection as the clouds parted. I was nearly soaked through by the time we reached the door.

There was a long bar at the front of the restaurant, and in the back, round tables were filled with the lunch crowd. Cooper didn't want to wait on table service, so he headed to the bar to order. I hung back, surveying the room. It reminded me of a modest English eatery with its brass lights, baskets of fish and chips, and people in work clothes milling about. There were three men in the middle of the dining room, taking up space at the central round table, laughing and clinking glasses. One was thin and dressed in a collared shirt and jeans. The one beside him was built like a linebacker and dressed in a suit and tie. They were inclined in their seats and listening to a man with broad shoulders in a flannel shirt. He had thick, dark hair, and though I could only see his profile, I knew immediately that it was Beau Griffin.

He was mid-conversation and did not see me approach. "You're going to have to actually talk to her if you want to take her out," he told the thin young man. When he sensed that there was someone beside him, he glanced up. "Gracie." His chair made a loud squeak against the floor as he stood. "Guys, Gracie Wilder," he explained coolly. "Gracie, this is P.J. and my little brother, Teddy."

I gave a wave and then had a flash of self-consciousness. Not only was my hair hanging in damp clumps, but my slick jacket was dripping water onto the floor by Griffin's feet. "Sorry." I lowered my head and stepped back. "I'm a mess and have managed to get water all over your shoes." Griffin did not move away from my small deluge.

The bigger guy called P.J. looked to him. "She doesn't know?" he asked. Griffin shook his head. "She doesn't know."

"Know what?" I asked.

P.J. stood, took his hat off the back of his chair, and said casually, "That you're beautiful." He put his wool cap on his head and tipped it in my direction. "Good to meet you, Gracie." A burn of color tinged my cheeks.

Teddy followed suit. "Yeah, I actually need to take off," he said with a shy smile, "but nice to meet you, Gracie." And just like that, Griffin and I were left standing alone at the table.

"Want to sit down?" He pulled out the chair next to him.

I awkwardly sat. "Thank you again for the other night."

"Not at all," he said.

We were silent for a moment. "I'm going to be leaving town for a bit. To see my old neighborhood in Montreal." He leaned forward with interest. "I'm hoping I might be able to make sense of a few things. Maybe the universe will point me in the right direction. It's a new plan. All very seat of the pants. You're one of the first people I've told," I said, cheerfully.

"I'm glad to be high on the list."

"Yes, so far it's really just you, Mark, and the guy at 7-Eleven."

He raised an eyebrow in question.

"Awfully nice guy. Calls me sweetheart, but not in a creepy way, you know? In an old-school way. I was buying a bottle of water and a tin of mints, and he asked me where I was off to, and I said Canada."

Griffin was smiling from ear to ear. "So, when are you heading up there?"

"Possibly driving out as soon as tomorrow or the next day."

"You know they make these flying machines now that can get you there a little faster than a car."

"I don't fly if I don't have to. Seven hundred thousand pounds of steel should not be able to float through the air; it's nonsensical."

"Well, it's physics actually," he said wryly. "Isn't Montreal like a twelve-hour drive of rolling fields?"

"And Toronto," I added. "You think I'm nuts, don't you?"

"Only a little. I hope you have a good car."

"I don't have a car at all. I'll have to rent one."

"Griffin has a car," Cooper interrupted. He was standing beside the table with the drinks in hand. He set a mug in front of me and settled into the chair beside Griffin. Unlike the other guys, Cooper was very happy to be a part of the conversation. He also did not find it odd that Griffin and I were friendly. I decided Griffin must have mentioned me.

"You know, I don't really have a car," he said.

"Yes, he does," Cooper argued. "That beautiful old Ford that his father gave him. It's wasting away in the garage. And his social calendar isn't exactly full. Where are you going, anyway?"

"Canada," Griffin and I both said in unison.

Cooper cocked a grin. "Does this have to do with your investigative work?"

"Don't get any ideas, Coop," Griffin said. He leaned closer to me, and I could smell traces of his aftershave—a clean, woodsy, spicy scent like soap and palo santo. "Cooper might be able to tell you what happened, but it won't bring you answers."

Cooper appeared a little wounded but did not have a chance to defend himself before his cell phone rang. He glanced down and muttered, "What do you know. It's Mark. Is he going with you to Canada?"

I shook my head, strangely embarrassed.

"Excuse me. I've got to take this. They want to send me to New York for a corporate fraud case."

Griffin waved him on. "Sorry. My friends have no manners," he said just loudly enough for Cooper to hear as he walked away. Cooper shot him a playful frown.

"I like them," I said. "I seem to like all your people."

Griffin's relaxed posture made me feel at ease. There was something about how he leaned back in his chair with his arms on the armrests, his head tipped slightly forward, that blocked out everything else in the room. I saw only him.

"This is going to sound *completely* irrational . . ." I began.

"Which we've already determined is the only way to address an irrational problem," he said, and I remembered our conversation in my father's den: *You can't go about solving irrational problems with rational solutions.*

"Exactly. So, I know Cooper was kidding, but if you really are free this week, maybe you'd want to come with me to Montreal? I will rent a car, but I could use a driving partner. And you might need a vacation?"

The question was out of my mouth before I had the chance to consider its absurdity. It was one thing to have imagined it, but an altogether different thing to have blurted it out. I tried to swallow the suggestion back down—I'm sure I looked like I was sucking on a lemon. But there was no going back now.

He sat up straight, rested his forearms on the table, and seemed to select his words carefully. "I doubt Mark would be happy about you going on a road trip with a guy he's never met."

"Right. Of course. But then, I don't think he'll exactly approve of me going alone, either. I would explain that you are a perfect gentleman. You are a perfect gentleman, aren't you?"

"Absolutely," he said on cue. "The thing is, even though I have nothing going on this week, or next week, I'm just not sure it's a good idea."

I tried to laugh and breeze past the notion with all its awkwardness. "Of course. It was a ridiculous idea."

"It's just that I should stay close to home right now. Until I can figure a few things out . . ." his voice trailed off. I was sure I'd never see him again after my insane proposal. "But I really hope you find what you're looking for in Montreal, Gracie."

"Thank you, Griffin. Honestly, I don't really know what I'm looking for or if I'll find it. But I suppose that's the whole point of me leaving. I need to find my own direction for once in my life. I'm tired of following all the steps, trying to do what everyone expects me to do, and still coming up short. It doesn't seem to be working." Griffin was so focused on what I was saying that I felt a surge of confidence. I said exactly what I was thinking. "You may have a car that you rarely drive, but I had twenty-three rolls of film that I never developed. Can you believe that? And there's a ten-piece set of my mother's wedding china in my cupboard that I've never used, I suppose out of fear I might break something. Oh, and I have a beautiful set of letterpress notecards from Paris that sit in my desk drawer untouched. What special day am I saving them for? God, I've been so vigilant! So careful. Until recently, anyway. Last week I had the audacity to *ask* for a dream audition. And days later, I found myself fleeing the cemetery in your brilliant car. Apparently, I now take impetuous leaps when under stress. *Fight or flight* is now more *fling yourself over the edge*. It's like a disorder. But what if the alternative to leaping is going down with a sinking ship? Or realizing you *are* the sinking ship? Which is probably true in my case. I just don't want to wake up one day and realize I've lived my life being so careful that I've missed a chance at being happy." I was suddenly aware of how I'd been overemphasizing with dramatic hand gestures. My body was vibrating with conviction, my skin pink with honesty. I hadn't meant to prattle on, but there it was. I pulled myself from the chair. "*So* sorry about all this."

To my surprise, his expression told me that he understood. "Stay. Finish your tea," he said.

I wanted to spare us both. "I've said enough for one day, but thank you." He rose from his seat, a gentle tower beside me, and I gave him an apologetic smile. Now it was my turn to bolt. "Always good to see you, Griffin." I put my head down and pushed through the crowd.

I was steps from the door when I felt a warm hand on my arm. I pivoted back around and there he was, blocking everything else from view.

"Cooper was right. I do need to get that old Ford out of the garage once in a while," he said. He casually put his hands in his pockets and shrugged his broad shoulders. "It must be pretty cold up there this time of year. We'll have to bring a lot of sweaters."

It took me a moment to register what he was saying, and then I beamed. "I'll start packing."

13

COOPER

The reception area of Wilder Investment Group was as chic and shiny as the receptionist herself. Also as empty. "Good afternoon," she greeted me with a toss of her hair. "Who are you here to see?"

I ignored her question. "Wow, you have an incredible view. Do you ever just stare out at the water?"

She bought my bullshit and spun her chair toward the wall of windows. "I really should."

"They should redesign this whole space so that you aren't always backlit," I said while my eyes anxiously searched her desk. I was hoping for a name I could use to get past the lobby or some sign of where Mr. Wilder's office might be located. Then a message slip caught my eye. It read, *Geneva—Loren Conrad called for Mr. Wilder. She hadn't heard. Give her a ring.*

I had the name I needed.

"I'm Daryl," I said to the receptionist as she turned back around. "A friend of Geneva's. I was hoping to catch her before she left for lunch." I flashed my teeth hoping for a stroke of good luck.

"Well, you know she never takes a lunch."

I winked. "I was being ironic."

She laughed. "I'll just tell her you're here."

"You know, I'd like to surprise her. You think I could just head to her desk?"

I watched the receptionist peer down the long hall to her left, contemplating. "She could probably use a nice surprise."

"Enjoy that view," I insisted before heading in the direction of her gaze. I nonchalantly checked every desk, every door, until I spotted what I was looking for: *Geneva Wilks*, written on the nameplate of a desk in front of a large, elegant office.

"Geneva," I began as I approached the blonde with tortoiseshell glasses. She lifted her chin with impassive inquiry. "I'm Daryl Cooper, a friend of Gracie Wilder."

"How can I help you?"

"I'm actually hoping I can help you. I'm told that you may be in possession of Mr. Wilder's laptop."

"As I told Gracie, legally I can't let her find an email. She sent you?" Geneva seemed confused.

"Not exactly," I clarified. "She wanted to but felt she might be overstepping. I'm a private investigator, and I tend to rub people the wrong way. Which, let me tell you, does a number on my social life." I had yet to rouse a smile. "But I like Gracie, and I didn't want to see her give up on such an important search, so I've come down here thinking I might be able to be of some service. To help you help her by accessing that file."

Geneva stood up. "I'm going to have to ask you to leave."

"So soon?"

"A man has died, and you come here like a . . . grave robber, hoping to nab God knows what from his computer files."

"No," I calmly corrected, putting my hands in the air like this was a sloppy stick-up. "Just the letter, and I won't even need to touch the computer. I can talk you through how to reboot it in safe mode and reassign a password in less than five minutes. For Gracie."

"You need to leave, Mr. Cooper, or you will be physically removed from the property. Whatever you're looking for, it's not here. I don't even have the laptop yet."

That was disappointing. It must have still been on its way from New York.

Geneva's phone rang, and she quickly snapped it up. "David Wilder's office—Yes, thank you so much. It comes as quite a shock." Sadness flashed across Geneva's face. It was clear she had respected David Wilder very much. "Yes, of course. I appreciate that. Thank you." She put the phone back into its cradle and glared at me. Then she picked it back up. "I'm calling security."

"I'm on my way," I told her, but I didn't hurry down the hall. I leaned in, just enough to let her know I had nothing to be afraid of, and said, "I'm so sorry for your loss, Geneva. Mr. Wilder has left behind many troubled hearts. When the laptop comes and you see that you hold the power to put one of those troubled hearts at ease, call me." I placed my business card on her desk. I couldn't be sure that Geneva would take the bait, but it was worth a shot.

As I disappeared down the hall, I sent Mark Schaffer a text: *Go ahead and book me for that trip to NYC.* I figured while in town on business, maybe I could run a personal errand and see about a missing letter.

I waved to the receptionist while heading back through the lobby, but she barely acknowledged me. She was speaking to a middle-aged woman with a French accent and a chic updo not often seen in today's corporate attire. She had a travel bag and was asking about where she could find someone, though I didn't catch who. The French woman glanced in my direction, smiling briefly through bright red lipstick. I smiled back, thinking it wasn't every day that I saw a metropolitan woman carrying a vintage suitcase in a 1970s green. People fascinate me.

14

GRACIE

Mark was not keen on the idea of me driving to Montreal with Beau Griffin, but the mention of it did not tempt him to come in his place. I knew it was unreasonable to feel disappointed, and I hoped thirteen hundred miles of friendly banter with Griffin would be a nice alternative. I kept these thoughts to myself as I went about stacking pullovers into my suitcase. Mark watched from my bed.

"Do you really think you'll wear the V-neck?" he asked. "It could be in the thirties. I'd go with the turtlenecks." I surveyed my options and considered his point. "How long will you be gone?" he asked.

"Just one week. I'm so sorry I'll miss that black-tie event you wanted me to attend."

"Where will you stay?"

"I'm going to book something tonight."

"I'll do it," Mark announced, punching his finger to his phone. "I can figure out accommodations."

"You don't need to go to the trouble," I tried.

"It's the least I can do," he insisted. "Maybe we can even get your trip down by a day or two. Really make good use of your time. That way you can be back in the dance studio with plenty of time before your audition."

"I'll be able to practice up north too. I'll find a studio or even an open park. I'll prepare," I assured him.

"Just to keep things in perspective, your career rests on the outcome of this performance, and you're leaving for Canada with a guy you know almost nothing about to try to find an old gift shop."

Excellent. I was an idiot.

I may have been as unsure about this trip as I was about the turtle-necks, but I needed to see it through. I would try to follow my heart while following Mark's travel plans. I would try to create a brilliant piece for Olivia Garza while looking for pieces of my father. I would try not to disappoint anyone in the process. But I knew, when I zipped my suitcase closed, that I was leaving on impossible terms.

"You ready for bed?" Mark asked once I'd closed my closet door. He'd already booked two hotel reservations, carefully assigning separate accommodations for me and my traveling partner. This act of assistance seemed to calm him, and his syrupy tone indicated that he had read only the itinerary and not the emotional fatigue that had been stitched into lines under my eyes.

"I'm pretty worn out," I told him.

He extended one arm from where he was sprawled out on the duvet, and I surrendered, filling the space beside him. He ran his hand through my hair lovingly. It was possible that Mark was trying to be the kind of man who could hold on to things. People in my life had a habit of letting go before I was ready to be free of them, and so I didn't mind Mark's strong grip around my waist. But I didn't need his body the way he needed mine.

"Hi, gorgeous," he said running a hand down the front of me. I let my head fall back as he kissed my neck, unbuttoned my blouse, encouraged my lips apart with his own. I moved in step with his body, but my mind was far away, curiously searching the room for an explanation as to how the silk blackbird had taken flight at last and landed in my life.

Afterward I felt the familiar pulsing sensation of dull pleasure and shame. It wasn't that Mark made me feel uneasy; it was more the act itself or my body's part in it. It had been this way since my first time with Miles Winkler—how he'd huffed and heaved and hollered, and then dismounted me and asked, "How was *that*?" I couldn't believe I had to withstand such a self-indulgent, chaotic performance and additionally be expected to give a review. There had only been one other man in my bed between Miles and Mark—a boy named Conner whom I met at Juilliard. He was now married to James and had two adorable children. As much as I cared for Conner, we never fit right. I couldn't imagine anyone with whom I could feel completely intimate and at ease. I wasn't sure I even wanted to be unraveled in that way.

I awoke six hours later. Mark had already left for his workday. I vaguely recalled him kissing me goodbye and assuring me that he'd be checking in often. I lay in bed, the haze of sleep lifting, and when my mind was fresh and crisp, it occurred to me: the letter box.

I wrapped myself in my bathrobe, slid open the door to my closet, and pulled the chain on the bare lightbulb fixed to the ceiling. It cast a yellow light over the shelf above my clothing rack. I pulled over my desk chair and climbed onto the cushion so that I could see onto the shelf. There it was, right where I'd stashed it when I'd moved in: my pin-striped letter box. It was the closest thing to a time capsule that I owned. Dust sprinkled into the air when I lifted it down. I sat in front of it on the rug like one might an urn just withdrawn from a columbarium. This is where Madame Bisset had saved a few scraps of experience for me. Though I'd kept it, I hadn't looked at its contents in almost ten years. I did not make a habit of opening boxes to the past, but I hoped the story of the blackbird bound by string might be concealed somewhere inside.

When I removed the lid, I met an old friend. A stuffed lamb, now grayer than white, with floppy legs and a head that drooped forward. I brought her to my face and kissed her. "Hello, Lamb," I said, before lovingly tucking her into my lap.

The next treasure I found was *The Secret Garden*. My father had given the book to me when we moved from Zurich to Paris the year I turned eight. I gently picked it up and brushed off its jacket. Madame Bisset had read it with me so frequently that there were pages I once knew by heart. The spine creaked when I opened it, and I landed on a tactically dog-eared page that contained Madame Bisset's favorite passage: "I shall live forever and ever . . . I shall find out thousands and thousands of things. I shall find out about people and creatures and everything that grows . . . I shall never stop making magic."

I set the book down abruptly. It had been so long since I'd read those words or touched those pages. I'd nearly forgotten about the garden and the unloved little girl Mary and the boy Colin who had to overcome great things. Until that moment, I'd completely forgotten about the sleepless night I'd tiptoed past Madame Bisset's room in search of my father, and how he'd walked me back to my room. "What will you dream?" he'd asked once I was tucked back in bed, and I'd tried to come up with the most peaceful thought I could imagine. "A secret garden," I told him, "locked safely behind an iron gate. It's beautiful and green with nothing but happy creatures. And only you and I have the key." I watched my father's face bend toward mine. "Very well," he said. "We'll have an adventure in our secret garden. Now close your eyes and make daisy chains for the rabbits."

I'd forgotten. The guilt fell heavily into the pit of my stomach. How had I managed to push these beautiful details into the abyss with the awful bits that followed in the years to come?

———

The awful bits began the night Madame Bisset sat on the edge of my bed and said, "I'm sorry, Gracie. Nothing good happens after ten o'clock." I was fourteen, still new to our home in Rome, and sadly, Madame Bisset was my truest friend in the world. I wasn't a good match for my schoolmates who all spoke fluent English but chose to converse in Italian, and I hadn't exactly hit it off with the girls in my dance company either. They were unapologetically cooler than me; everything I said or did seemed naïve. But as a practiced follower of tourists, I was terrifically observant and learned to watch for patterns in my peers. I figured out when to laugh and when to look smug; when to step in and when to keep walking. I was nearing a rebirth of social status, no matter that it was soul suicide. And when a few of these girls, the leader of them called Jenna, asked me to meet them at a disco at ten o'clock on a Friday, I accepted the invitation before asking for permission. I was young, but not exactly too young for this scene in Rome. Maybe if I wore heels and lipstick, I would be able to blend in. Ignoring Madame Bisset and my own anxiety, I pretended to go to sleep, then snuck out onto the cobblestone streets and into the worst night of my life.

———

I wanted to put the lid back on the box, to lock the past away again. But something stopped me—a glimpse of a familiar scrapbook. I bravely lifted it out and flipped through pages of programs from dance recitals, school art projects, and a few photos that Madame Bisset had captured of my father and me. One photo was taken at Christmas dinner where we wore paper crowns. Another was of us sitting on the front porch of our holiday cottage just outside Montreal. The Blue Tilting House, I'd called it, as it was a blue Cape Cod that leaned slightly downhill. My whole body warmed at the sight of it. I remembered that day. We had spent it eating pancakes, skipping stones, and sitting in the shade of a willow tree. I hadn't known how magnificent it was while it was happening, but now this simple day glittered in my recollections like sacred waters returning to a dried-up riverbed.

When I turned to the last page of the album, there it was—the thin booklet with *The Blackbird* scrolled across the cover. I peeled back the

adhesive clear plastic and held it in eager hands. Then I read the story
the old shopkeeper had written out for me all those years ago. It called
up vivid imagery I'd long ago tucked away, and with it, hope.

> The Red-winged Blackbird was a special creature who was con-
> nected to both the sky and the earth. While some birds spent their
> days high above the trees, and others pecking at the ground, Black-
> bird knew the gateways between land and sky. Blackbird's song
> brought the heavens closer, the sun, the stars, and all things of
> light. When the creator saw that creatures on the ground were
> getting lost, Blackbird was sent to guide the way.
>
> Blackbird befriended Fox. Fox had eyes full of wonder, and
> together she and Blackbird went in search of great things. One
> dimly lit night at the mouth of the wooded valley, they spotted the
> Amarok—the wolf who ate those who wandered in the dark. Black-
> bird sang softly, "Let's go slowly into the valley. I will guide our way
> from above. The Amarok will not be able to consume us if we follow
> the light." But Fox was filled with fear. "Surely the Amarok will
> catch up with us," she cried. "We must outrun the Amarok if we are
> to survive." With that, Fox ran between the trees of the dark valley,
> over boulders and through creek beds, until she was sure she'd lost the
> Amarok. When Fox turned back to see if she was safe, she found that
> she was alone. "Blackbird?" Fox called out. But she could no longer
> hear Blackbird's song.
>
> There was trickery in the wood. The magpie who masquer-
> aded as Blackbird and the vulture who swooped and hunted. Fox
> managed to escape both of these, but still she was lost and unsure of
> what direction to go. A small arctic hare passed by. It whispered,
> "Where there is darkness, there is always something in hiding."
> Encouraged, Fox carried on.
>
> Soon Fox came across a strange tree. Only it was not a tree at
> all, it was a moose named Sauri with antlers reaching so tall they

might as well have been trees. Trees with many rings, many stories. Sauri had made a home in the thickest, darkest part of the valley, having become lost there some time ago. Sauri offered Fox a ride on his back in exchange for light. But Fox could only howl at Annin-gan, the moon, and beg him to illuminate their path. Fox's voice was weak, and Anningan only shined his moonlight long enough for Fox to see how weary she'd become.

Fox sat down on a rugged patch of earth to rest. She stayed still for a long time. Finally, she heard something stirring in the silence, saw something moving among the rocks. It was Blackbird awakening from sleep.

"Is it really you?" Fox asked, getting to her feet.

"I am here," Blackbird sang, and with that, Fox's strength was restored.

Blackbird plucked red feathers from the end of each wing and braided them into Fox's fur. Blackbird was now a part of Fox, and Fox would always have a guide. The creator was pleased. And so, it was done for all creatures—that they might always know the way through the dark by the spirit braided within.

PART TWO

Hope is the thing with
feathers that perches in the soul,
and sings the tune without the words,
and never stops at all.

—EMILY DICKINSON

Everything in the universe has a rhythm,
everything dances.

—MAYA ANGELOU

15

GRIFFIN

"What are the sleeping arrangements?" Cooper asked me as he downed a cup of coffee. My kitchen seemed colder than usual; I pulled on a hoodie and refilled my cup.

"She's handling all that," I told him. "Some Canadian hotels."

"Two rooms?" he asked.

"Obviously. I'm just going to take in the freezing cornfields and hopefully check out some Montreal architecture."

"I don't understand this trip." Cooper sounded amused. "But go ahead and get after it."

I was pretty sure it had been his idea. *Griffin has a car*, he'd said to Gracie in the pub. It was nice to have a reason to leave town, to not have to see Fidelis boarded up every single day. But I had the sinking suspicion that over the course of that week I'd end up letting Gracie down, exhausting Pop's car, or worse, missing a chance to save Fidelis. It would be poetic justice, but it might just finish me.

"For what it's worth, I don't think Mark is planning on popping the question any time soon," Cooper was saying.

"And you think this because . . ."

"Well, for one, I saw him Thursday night in a hotel lounge with his arm draped over a paralegal, and she's definitely not his sister."

"He's an asshole."

Cooper nodded affirmatively. "I know I'm a PI, but he's not exactly discreet with his extracurricular activities."

I had a low tolerance for assholes. "If I ever see that guy . . ."

"Slow down," Cooper interjected. "As far as Gracie knows, they're a good thing. And no one gets laid for being the bearer of more bad news." He had an eloquent way of bringing everything back down to the basics.

"I won't say anything. I'll just drive," I promised. "What do you have going on this week?"

"Stetson and Lawrey are sending me to New York for a couple of days, but not much else. Want me to check in on your folks?"

From outside, Teddy's voice drifted in through the screen door. "Bro!"

"Check with Teddy," I told Cooper with a nod of thanks. I grabbed my duffle bag and followed him out onto the front porch.

"I brought you some stuff for the drive," Teddy said, as animated as ever. He tossed a paper bag into the trunk of the Falcon. "Some snacks and my wool jacket."

The morning was becoming a real send-off. "You guys know that I'm only going to be gone for a week, right?"

Teddy walked around the car with his hands in his pockets, admiring Pop's handiwork. "I can't believe you're taking this thing on the road."

"You should take that girl from your office out for a drive when I get back," I told him.

"How's Project Angela coming along, man?" Cooper asked.

Teddy smiled and stared at the ground. "Well, I got up the nerve to walk over to her cubicle on Monday and say good morning. I didn't want to go empty-handed, so I stopped by the shop in the lobby first. They didn't have any flowers, so I thought . . . donuts."

"Donuts?" I asked. "Well, what did you say when you gave them to her?"

"Just, 'Hi, Angela, I brought you some donuts.'"

I could see Cooper stifling laughter. "And what did *she* say?" I asked.

"She said, 'Thank you, Ted. I love donuts.'"

"And that was it?"

He threw his hands up like I'd missed something huge. "It made her happy."

I loved Teddy and his subtle victories. "She'll be head over heels in no time," I told him.

Cooper was laughing. "Oh, buddy, you're the best," he said, slapping Teddy on the back.

I had just finished loading the car when a taxi pulled up and Gracie stepped out. She was wearing a caramel-colored sweater, jeans, white Converse low-tops, and oversized sunglasses. She had one rolling suitcase and a small bag slung over her shoulder. She looked travel-ready. I walked over to greet her, and for the first time, I gave her a modest hug.

"Do these two manage Griffin's Rent-a-Travel Companion?" she asked, smiling at Cooper and Teddy.

"No refunds or exchanges," Cooper called out.

"I'll bring him back in one piece," she promised.

God, I hoped so.

She pulled some papers from her bag and handed them to me. "Mark believes in a good travel itinerary, so he put this together last night. Everything's here: maps, hotel info, numbers."

"Great," I said, biting back my disdain for the guy and jamming the papers onto the dashboard.

"So, Cooper," Gracie said, "I hear that you met Geneva over at my dad's office and ruffled a few feathers."

"About that—" Cooper started.

"It's okay," she said. "But it's not worth your time. The email from my dad is lost in cyberspace."

I was piecing it together. "Cooper, you can't leave anything alone."

"No, it's fine. Really," Gracie tried.

But when she and Teddy went to put her bags in the trunk, I pulled Cooper aside. "Stop meddling," I said under my breath.

"Man, I'm trying to do a good thing here," he said defensively.

I was so damn tired of Cooper intervening. I squeezed his shoulder so he would look me hard in the eye. "Stop picking things apart. Keira. Fidelis. What Gracie's lost. There's no getting around any of it. Shit just happens. Leave it alone. Stop fumbling around messing with other people's lives."

He managed a nod before Gracie called out, "You want to drive the first leg?"

I released Cooper from my grip and turned back to her. "Yes, ma'am."

"Shall we put the top down?"

It might have been only sixty degrees, but her smile was like sunshine. I gave in and unhooked the Falcon's canvas top.

You would have thought that Cooper and Teddy were sending me off to battle, the way they stood watching me back down the driveway. As I drove through the city, I kept both hands on the wheel and tried not to be distracted by how the wind played with Gracie's hair.

———

I had traveled those roads out of Chicago into Michigan many summers with Mom, Pop, and Teddy. Long before Pop bought the Falcon, he had a silver station wagon, which accumulated several thousand miles on I-94. Pop would have us up before the dew was dry. "You wait too long, and the fish won't bite," he'd say. We'd rumble down the highway, and when the morning fog finally lifted, we'd see arches of kelly-green maple trees framing our drive away from the city.

Today, though, the fog came in the form of Gracie Wilder. I had so many questions but tried to fight them off as if they were bugs hitting the windshield. I waited until we'd lost reception on the local radio stations then turned to her and asked, "So what exactly will we do in Montreal?"

"Well . . ." She pulled something from her bag. "My father left me this," she said, holding up an ornamental bird and carefully hanging it from the rearview mirror. "I was once enamored with it as a child. I made a fuss about it but only just received it after my father died. And I don't know why. So, I want to go back to where I first saw it. I'm hoping it might also help me understand what this belongs to." She lifted the gold chain that was tucked into her sweater and showed me a key hanging from the end. "It would be nice to have the letter he wrote likely explaining everything, but I'm hoping this trip will help me put some of the pieces together . . ." Her thoughts seemed to drift into the long stratus clouds that streaked the sky.

"So, we just need to find the shop where your father bought the bird?" I asked.

"It sounds crazy," she said, as though she'd just heard her own idea for the first time.

It did sound strange, but also sort of charming. "When you've lived your whole life on the straight and narrow and haven't gotten very far, crazy starts to sound pretty damn good," I told her.

She threw her head back and raised her arms, letting the wind that rushed over the open convertible slip through her hands. "We're taking chances," she said to me or the wind—I couldn't be sure. "We're in charge now."

Whatever air she was breathing, I wanted some.

"What's the craziest thing you've ever done?" she asked, returning her hands to her lap.

"Maybe this," I said, and she laughed, but then I gave it some real thought. "I once cliff dived at Jackson Falls. I ran in the Chicago Marathon the morning after throwing a bachelor party. And . . . I got married."

That got a reaction. "You're married?"

"No. We split six months ago and were divorced shortly after."

"Same time as the . . ."

"Yep. It all happened in one perfect storm."

"You've had a tough time of it," she said. "Tell me, what was she like?"

I went a little stiff. "It's kind of an exhausting topic." Gracie didn't say anything, but for some reason I went on. "She was my high school sweetheart . . . beautiful, fun, hilarious, spontaneous."

"She sounds like an adventurer," Gracie said.

"How do you mean?"

"I have this theory that people are either planners or adventurers," she explained, self-consciously. "Planners are reliable and can create something step by step. Adventurers prefer flexibility to set plans; they crave connection and excitement."

"Your theory seems a little black and white."

"Certainly, there are variations and exceptions. But don't you think people seem to naturally fall on one side or the other?"

I wasn't sure about Gracie's theory. But I was sure that over the last few years, while I'd been building my business and looking after my folks, I'd not showed up for Keira in the way she needed.

Gracie tried to read my expression. "No sad face."

"This is just my face," I assured her.

She squeezed my arm in a small but electrifying way. "A planner and an adventurer can be well suited together. The planner might learn to take risks, and the adventurer might discover the rush of commitment."

"I suppose I'm a planner type," I said. "Though nothing at all has gone according to my plans."

"Maybe there's something better in store for you," she suggested.

"I don't believe it's all charted out, if that's what you mean."

"No, but do you believe in meaningful coincidences?"

I thought of the paper I'd stolen from the arch of Fidelis and wondered again if it had somehow set into motion the trouble in my life. "I haven't ruled it out," I told Gracie.

"I think we get signs or invitations to help us find our way forward," she said. "But how we go about responding, well, that's entirely up to us. I like the idea of being a co-creator of my life instead of just a pawn in a game. Don't you?"

Her optimism, despite everything, was remarkable. "So, you believe in God?"

"Yes, I still do. I wasn't raised very religious, but when you lose your mother as a baby, it helps to believe in something bigger than the loss in your life. I guess you could say theater has been my church. A place to come together and be inspired. To listen to music or watch sorrow and joy danced across the stage. It's a reminder that we're all connected. One human race." She paused a moment, as if deep in thought, and then announced, "Griffin, I think I need to revamp my theory. What if we're all adventurers in our own right, but we miss the connections? We aren't a captive audience—we don't always notice what's right in front of us. Some of us plan three steps ahead to try to control what comes next. Some of us don't look before we leap. We miss the signs." She lowered her voice. "I think I do that. I avoid certain things, and in the process, maybe I miss some of the good stuff."

I knew she was no ordinary girl, but I was blown away by this road trip dialogue. "So you're an adventurer?" I asked.

"Of the worst sort," she decided. "An adventurer who once loved to explore, but took to following *other* people's plans. I used to love dancing because it felt like what it means to be free. I think I lost some of that to the conditioning and choreography." She moved closer to me, her face serious. "Someone told me recently that you have to give your whole self to a dream. You know, risk everything and put it all out there. Do you agree with that? That a dream should be more of a free fall than a plan?"

"You'd have to really know what you want."

"I think that's what makes it a dream. The passion."

"So what's yours exactly?" I asked.

"To dance and become a great choreographer one day. Bring real joy to the theater. I have one more chance to perform for Olivia Garza, one of the best in the biz, and really impress her. Really make something of myself."

"Oh, you'll make something of yourself," I told her.

"You think so?"

I met her gaze and nodded, then reminded myself to watch the road.

"What about you? What do you want to find out there?" she asked, letting her arm fall over the open window.

"I don't know." It pained me to say it.

"Well, we'll figure it out."

"We?"

She seemed to think about that for a moment. "Yes."

I grinned. "Well all right. We're in this together now. No matter what it is or what comes our way."

"We're taking a leap. Throwing caution to the wind."

"With a carefully planned itinerary."

"Shit," she said, realizing. She grabbed the papers from the deep corner of the dashboard and gave them one last look. Then she flung them into the air. The pages spread out like paper doves. I twisted in my seat and saw them fly.

"You just . . . well, littered."

"I'm sorry," she winced, "but I have to admit, that felt *amazing*."

———

We got a sandwich in Kalamazoo and then Gracie took a turn driving. Despite her new aversion to a schedule, she was completely in control behind the wheel. We listened to any music we could find on the dial of the Falcon's tube radio and sang along to classic '90s tunes when conversation was at a lull. Sunglasses on, Falcon top down, sweaters and sunlight keeping us warm, we sped down the highway. I couldn't remember when I'd felt so good. The hours flew by, and before long we approached the border and crossed the massive Ambassador Bridge over the Detroit River into Canada.

"What's your favorite movie?" Gracie asked me when we pulled into a gas station.

"I don't know. For a long time, it was the original *Superman*. What about you?"

"*Casablanca*. Or *Butch Cassidy and the Sundance Kid*," she said, sliding out of the car. "I never grow tired of the banter between Newman and Redford."

I got out of the Falcon and swiped my credit card in the gas pump. Gracie pulled some change out of her bag and dropped the coins into an old vending machine standing nearby. "Favorite book?" she called out.

"*The History of the Decline and Fall of the Roman Empire*."

"Ah, light reading." She handed me a Coke. "Okay, favorite song?"

"Too hard." I pulled a window washer from a dirty bucket of water and began swiping it across the windshield.

"You're not a bad singer," she said after a long sip from her Diet Coke.

I shrugged immodestly. "I was Tony in my high school's production of *West Side Story*."

"Stop it. I would have pegged you as a football player or some kind of jock."

"Hockey."

"Yes, hockey seems more up your street. So let me get this straight. You played center on ice by day and center stage by night? I bet the girls *loved* you."

I put the window washer back in the bucket. "Really just the one. And that didn't work out."

"Oh, I'm sure you broke some hearts," she insisted.

I liked the way she crinkled her nose when she was being playful.

"Will you sing me something from *West Side Story*?" she asked.

"No way," I said, retuning the gas pump to its cradle and cracking open my can of Coke.

"Please? Sing me 'Something's Coming.'"

"I'll sing if you dance, but it's not going to be that song."

She laughed but then realized I was serious. "You want me to dance *here*?"

I moved the garbage can over to make more space in front of the car. "Griffin. I'll look ridiculous."

I glanced around at the balding gas station attendant and otherwise empty parking lot. "And all these people here will tell everyone you know."

She put her drink down on the pavement. "Okay. I'll do it."

I sat on the front of the car and tapped out a gentle rhythm on the hood while she stood poised in front of me, waiting to get a feel for the tempo and trying not to laugh. Then, in my best Scouse accent, reminiscent of the Beatles, I gave a rendition of "Across the Universe."

I could tell she liked my choice of song. As I sang about words flowing out and slipping away, she danced as though we weren't in the middle of a desolate chapter in the middle of nowhere. Her eyes sparkled as she jumped into the air and reached for the sky like liquid in the sunlight. She seemed to rise above gravity or heartache or anything that could pull her back down to earth. I felt genuinely happy watching her, but as I sang lyrics of limitless love shining like a million suns, I didn't trust that the feeling would last. Just like the song says, nothin' was going to change my world.

We drove through the rest of the afternoon in a long, smooth gust of wind, the blackbird swinging from the rearview mirror.

16

GRACIE

My father didn't trust everyone who crossed his path. He evaluated before stepping into any relationship, personal or business. I was not allowed to sleep over at a friend's house unless the family had been fully vetted with research and formal introductions, all of which were very infrequent processes. As a result, I did not stay up late making brownies with girlfriends and watching Leonardo DiCaprio movies. Instead, my sleepovers were with Grandmama Marie on holiday breaks from school. These evening rituals consisted of Seven Up for me, bourbon for Grandmama, and an old classic film from her impeccably organized library shelves. I think she had the very first VHS tape player that was on the market back in the 1970s, and it was still clicking and cranking and playing movies years later when I was curled up on her goose-down, floral couch. We had our favorites—*The Philadelphia Story*, *Roman Holiday*, *It Happened One Night*. Grandmama would jingle the ice in her glass and occasionally double over with a howl of laughter. I would giggle from under the blanket that had been lovingly tucked around me, delighted in equal parts by the movies and by Grandmama. I could still quote the lines from any one of those films, even do an uncanny impression of Katharine

Hepburn or Claudette Colbert. Those characters were as much a part of me as any living family member.

As Beau Griffin and I took to the road that led into Canada, I could hear Claudette Colbert speaking up inside of me in her prim, level voice. It had been years since I'd watched *It Happened One Night*, but I could still hear her urging Clark Gable to get her to New York. *"I've got to get to New York without being stopped. It's terribly important to me."* I felt like a silly woman in an old movie dragging an innocent man, and his gorgeous royal blue 1962 Ford Falcon convertible, into the autumn foliage and then likely right over a cliff.

Griffin was a great travel partner and the idea of leaving town on a whim had been exhilarating, perhaps for us both. But once we crossed the Ambassador Bridge into Canada, I felt the size of my decision. Maybe this would become a real screwball comedy: me, the curious orphan, venturing into my own demise; and poor Griffin, unknowingly steering us toward disaster. Good Lord.

Dr. Peck had suggested that I take time to address my childhood memories, to explore my feelings and sit with what was coming up. I'd not been patient enough to do that work. Instead of dipping one toe at a time into the stormy seas of history, it seemed I'd packed a small bag and swan dived into the great ocean of the past in one swift jump, hoping it would be more comfortable this way.

I had flung Mark's itinerary into the air in an impulsive show of faith. Still, I felt familiar feelings of self-doubt, which I properly stuffed down with a smile the way one swallows acid reflux after indulging in a rich meal. I did not share my misgivings with Griffin; I just watched the road with its cascading maples turned vibrant red and wild. I enjoyed his thoughtful conversation and my sixty-mile-an-hour transport of emotional rebellion.

⁓

"Will I need to speak French in Montreal?" Griffin asked me from across the rickety tabletop. We were sitting in a booth along the front window of a roadside diner. He was having a bacon burger, whereas I'd made the bold decision to try the eggplant burger—a greasy and surprising beef alternative. Griffin eyed it suspiciously.

"No, most people speak English. But do you know a little French?"

He chewed back a bite. "*Un peu.*"

"Terrific. *Où avez-vous fait les études?*"

"Not that much."

"I just asked you where you went to school." I was selecting a tea bag from a small selection lined up in a tin box. I pulled out an English Breakfast, unwrapped it, and dunked it into a mug of hot water.

"Don't you think it would be more useful for me to know how to ask where the bathroom is? Or the pub?"

I pointed to the sugar packets sitting closest to Griffin's pint glass and he handed me a couple. "I'm asking you because I'm interested."

He put down his burger, wiped his mouth with his paper napkin, and told me about how he went into an apprentice program as a carpenter after high school. From there he went to work for his mentor crafts-man, John Myer, while chipping away at college at night. He'd started in the architecture program at the University of Illinois Chicago, but he couldn't handle the schedule while working full-time. Instead, he went with a management track and eventually started his own business. "I didn't study a whole lot of French," he explained, "but I did have a good thing going. For a while, anyway."

"You put yourself through school, mastered your craft, and started your own company. That's incredible. I can't imagine you giving it up." My comment was casual, but it triggered something abrupt in Griffin.

"I'm not giving it up. It's giving *me* up. Who's going to refer me now?"

I hadn't fully considered the impact his accident with Fidelis might have on his career. But in those brief seconds from across the Formica tabletop, his negativity around the subject seemed a little unreasonable. "Well, *I* will," I said.

"It took me a long time to build a network, to gain trust, and to convince people that I was the guy they wanted. I focused on the neighborhoods close to home so I could be . . . close to home. And there's not a soul who didn't hear about me destroying local history."

"Your accident is not a reflection of you or your work. Not a reflection of the homes you've built."

He shook his head. "You don't understand."

"Then help me understand. Can't you rebuild your business, restore your good name? Restoration is your specialty, right? Maybe if you could change the way you see this thing, other people will too."

"Is that how you get a handle on things? You change the way you look at something, and *poof*, it changes for you? Well, I don't have that kind of power or influence. That's not how it works for me, okay? I'm cursed." He waved off his frustration before leaning back against the booth.

I set my mug down, trying to process how we'd so quickly gotten off course. Then I saw something slip across Griffin's face that I recognized. Something akin to shame. I shuddered. I'd not meant to kick him when he was down. I'd meant to do quite the opposite, and it had gone horribly wrong. "I'm sorry," I began, inching forward in my seat, wanting to get closer to broad-shouldered Griffin, whom I'd practically shoved into the corner of the booth with my boorish perspective. It didn't matter that I believed what I'd said; I never should have said it. I had no business giving lectures on how to correct mistakes. My life was riddled with mistakes, and I wasn't sure I knew what to do about any of them. "I only meant to say that I thought you could improve your business. But that's just it, it's *your* business—not mine. And I know it can't be put back just as it was."

He slowly resumed his position of leaning on the table, of drinking his beer.

"Please believe me when I tell you that I have a handle on very little in my life. I'm in charge of virtually nothing. That was just a nice idea I had in the car earlier. Wishful thinking. If I had any real power, well, I'd be cozied up at home right now reading the letter my father wrote to me before he died."

His face softened. "You'll get a handle on things. You have more grit than you give yourself credit for."

"You think I have grit?"

"You're not afraid to face what's in front of you. To go after what you want."

"I'm constantly riddled with fear. I just do it anyway."

"See? Grit."

This was a revelation. I might have even sat a little taller.

"And maybe my business isn't *totally* finished," he added. "I may not be irredeemably screwed."

"If you are, then I am," I quipped. "We all are. That guy for sure," I said, pointing to a man picking his teeth at a nearby table.

He grinned.

"You aren't cursed," I assured him.

"That's debatable; my life has been brutally ironic."

Our waitress, Lucy, popped by to top up my mug with hot water and to ask Griffin if he wanted another beer. She was young and blonde with a too-tight top and a darling Canadian accent. Griffin agreed to another pint, and when Lucy was gone, I was still sitting there mystified by how the blaze of tension between us had cooled nearly as fast as it had ignited—a very short match. If I were to blink, I was afraid the whole scene would change yet again. But Griffin didn't hold a grudge. He simply handed me another sugar packet for my tea, a roadside diner's olive branch, and dug back into his burger.

"Thank you," I said.

His eyes met mine and lingered. "Of course." Then he added, "And I know that what you've just been through and what you're doing . . . well, it can't be easy."

I stared back at him, subtly scanning his fine face. I couldn't find a single flaw. His nose was perfectly proportioned to his chin, his eyebrows arched evenly, and as far as I could tell, his expression was one hundred percent genuine. I couldn't seem to find anything at all wrong with Beau Griffin. Sure, he'd lost his way, but he was a perfectly decent person. Someone I could be at ease around. And I was seldom at ease around anyone.

"Do you know what job your father might have wanted done?" he asked. "Why he might have called me? He was willing to hire me when no one else would, and I wonder what I missed."

"Well, it might have been the guest bath," I thought aloud. "He'd talked about having it redone. It could have been that." He nodded a little. "There will be other jobs," I said optimistically. "You must win people over with the initial handshake." He didn't seem so sure. "And you must be very popular with the ladies."

His forehead lifted in surprise. "Now, that's a different subject," he said with a mouth full of burger.

"Have you dated much since your divorce?"

He forcibly ingested his bite. "Not a whole lot."

"I would think you'd be a man about town."

"No, I'm picky. Particular," he rephrased.

"Would you ask out someone like our waitress?" I glanced in her direction. I was only curious.

"Well, I don't know. Maybe I'll get her number." He moved to the edge of the booth and lifted a hand to get her attention. "Excuse me, Lucy," he called out.

I nearly ducked, embarrassed. "Now, don't lose your scruples, Griffin."

He glanced around the booth as if searching for them. When Lucy reached our table, he only smiled and said, "Can we have another order of fries, please?"

"Sure thing." And she dashed off.

I threw a fry at him.

"I decided Lucy's not the one."

"I guess," I said with a laugh.

"Yeah, I'm only just getting back out there."

"Well, you'll find someone when you're ready. When you're not hitting on the wait staff, you're a very nice guy."

"Too damn nice. But yeah, thanks."

"You think you're too nice?"

"I mean, it's not the best idea to go around saying, 'sure, no problem,' every time someone wants something. But I guess I have a history of going with the flow, picking up the slack."

"Griffin, did you tell me 'sure, no problem, let's go to Montreal' because you're too damn nice?"

"No," he said without missing a beat. "I told you yes because you're too damn cute. That's different."

I threw another fry at him. "Well, I might have you beat in the too-nice department. I apologize when people bump into me. And I'd rather get a bad haircut than make the stylist uncomfortable by saying I want less fringe. Spare us all the embarrassment."

"You officially have me beat," he said with a lopsided grin.

Lucy returned to deliver the fries and Griffin's fresh beer. He offered to buy me one, but I declined.

"I don't drink," I explained.

"No taste for it? Too much of a taste for it? Or bad experience?"

People usually assumed that the choice was one made in health. The average dancer doesn't crack open a beer after a day of work. "Are those the only choices? The last one, I guess."

He was sitting against the booth with one hand on his glass. The posture of a guy who was two beers deep. I sat the way I always did— the kind of posture that says no beers in twenty-six years. "I can't drink tequila," he told me. "The taste of it reminds me of the worst hangover of my life. What's yours? Vodka?"

His question surprised me. "No. I don't know. It wasn't like that."

It must have been the shaky tone of my voice, or perhaps it was the way my face turned a warm shade of pink, but somehow Griffin sorted out that we weren't talking about the same kinds of experiences. "Sorry," he offered, leaning toward me while I faked interest in the dessert menu fixed into a plastic frame on the end of our table. "I can be an idiot about things sometimes."

Griffin had accidentally opened a door that I thought I'd clearly marked *Keep Out*, and I wasn't sure how to shut the damn thing. "It's fine," I said, hoping that would be the end of it. Done and dusted.

But Griffin wasn't really the door-shutting type. Worse, he seemed genuinely interested in acknowledging this thing that I wasn't eager to talk about. "I'm sorry you had a bad experience."

"It wasn't your doing," I said. "Anyway, it was a long time ago."

"Too long ago to find someone and kick their ass?"

Damn. His sincerity was threatening to melt my so-called grit like wax in the sun. I mustered a smile and waved to Lucy for the check.

When I tried to take out my wallet, he held up his hand. "I got this one."

I stood with an eagerness to move, to get out of this conversation, to smooth everything over and head for the door. "You know, Griffin," I said, slinging my bag over my shoulder, "my father was an excellent judge of character. He must have really trusted you. I'm guessing that's why he saw past what was written in the papers." I excused myself and went outside.

———

I was born soft, and then like an oyster, grew a shell of armor to protect my tender center. Yet that immutable center still made itself known, often when I least expected it. I stood in the parking lot with anxiety coursing through my blood. If the coming days were going to roll in like waves in a storm sent to break me open, well, I could only hope that somewhere along the way I'd figure out how to make a bloody pearl!

Griffin stepped outside. He was holding a small paper bag. "The remains of your eggplant burger, madame," he said, offering it to me. "In case you're still hungry."

"Thanks." I snatched it from his hands and wrapped my arms around it as if it were valuable. "I'll drive."

He dug into his pocket for his keys. "You're tough as nails, Gracie Wilder." Clearly, he couldn't see me at all. "You must be tired. I can drive."

Tired? Yes. Come to think of it, I was exhausted. My back ached, my shoulders were stiff, and my head felt heavy. The long day's drive had done a number on me. Certainly, it must have been that and not the length of years that had me feeling so burdened. If I just held my head a little taller, pushed on a little further, everything was sure to become a little easier. That was how it was done.

But Griffin wasn't hurrying anywhere. "Are you okay?" he asked, eyes level with mine.

I might have been if he hadn't asked. Damn his thoughtfulness. "Of course," I told him, but now I could barely breathe. Maybe there wasn't enough oxygen in Canada for both of us. I couldn't get into the car, either. My legs had gone fuzzy with the adrenaline of emotion. I couldn't find a single thought to grab on to that would seal away history. His caring gaze was bewildering. "It's a long story, Griffin . . ." It seemed the only explanation possible, and I hoped it would be enough to end it all right there.

He lifted a hand in a gesture that he wasn't there to pry and tried to offer me a friendly hug. But that put me over the edge. As if he'd triggered my security system, my body began to go into lockdown. I went stiff. I was unmoving. Everything came to a standstill—the whole universe maybe. The night sky with its streaks of moonlight and gleaming stars might have frozen. The sounds of cars, any evidence of life, had lifted into the distance. It was just Griffin and me and the exhausting weight of memories, standing on the pavement in the biting night air.

He stood in front of me, his concern obvious. "I'm sorry," he stammered.

"What exactly are you sorry for?"

The poor guy. It was an impossible question. *Everything and nothing* would have been the only thing he could have said that would have made any sense. I was now swelling with anxiety, ready to burst with rage while simultaneously wanting to fall apart with despair. "What can I do?" he asked. His face was so confused that it too seemed frozen— halted in an upward direction revealing new lines across his forehead.

I wanted him to stop talking. I wanted him to back away from me and let me have a proper panic attack in privacy this time. "Maybe you *are* too nice," I heaved the words out between breaths. "Why the hell are you even here?"

"You want me to leave?"

No. No. No. Don't leave. But he couldn't stay there either, looking at me like that. Like he'd just peeked behind the curtain and could see I was nothing more than a gooey human poured into a determined shell.

"Gracie, what happened?"

I lifted my chin to the wind, hoping the temperature was cold enough to freeze the tears balancing on my lower lids. "You don't want to hear about it."

"I do if you want to tell me."

I knew that there were horrible things in life with the power to crack us all wide open. But until Griffin was standing in front of me in the parking lot, lingering without agenda or expectation, unfazed by the cold wind cutting through his shirt, I had no idea that kindness could have equal or greater power. I didn't recognize this kind of benevolence, and the sight of it struck me hard. I felt my armor cracking under the strain.

"It's just that I make bad decisions, Griffin. I break things," I said. There was no keeping it from coming now. All the feeling, all the anger and sadness and shame, it wanted out. It dared me to say things I never dared say, to someone I barely knew, in a town I couldn't remember the name of. Unexpectedly, the not telling of it felt entirely more life-threatening than letting it seep through the cracks. I wanted to be free of this feeling for a while. I wanted to crawl into a stiff hotel bed and pull the covers over my head and disappear.

I would say it fast. I would focus on choosing the words—the way one might recite a poem they had to memorize as a school assignment—that way I wouldn't have to feel it all over again. I wouldn't look at Griffin. I'd focus on the horizon, a shadowy cluster of trees behind a row of buildings. Then it would be over. I could put it away, close the door, reseal the cracks.

I took a long sip of air, hugged my dinner bag to my chest, and said, "When I was fourteen, and an idiot, I snuck out one night to meet some friends." I hated the sound of my own voice; it was shaky. But Griffin stood as still as the sky. "We were all in secondary school, but I was the only one in the group under sixteen. The dance club scene was big with these girls, but I'd never been. I'd never experienced anything like it before; it was overwhelming. The energy. The deep bass of the music. Everything felt . . . alive. We met three seventeen-year-old boys, Luca, Gianni, and Enzo, who bought us each a soda. Then another and another." I tried to take a deep breath, but I was resigned to shallow gulps of air every few seconds. "Enzo seemed nice and danced with me. I'd never danced with a boy before. After an hour or so . . . I didn't feel well, and I wanted to go home. I was drunk but didn't yet understand. Enzo said he had a car and offered to drive me and the girls home. I wanted to leave on my own, but once I was outside, he kissed me. I'd never been kissed before. In the car, I could tell we weren't headed toward my neighborhood. The girls wanted to stop by a party. But it wasn't a party. It was Enzo's dad's empty flat above a convenience store, and there were lines of coke on the coffee table. I stumbled down the hall to use the bathroom. The walls were spinning around me, but I managed to find the landline in the hall. I called my au pair and told her that I'd found myself in a flat above a co-op market and she needed to come get me right away. But Madame Bisset didn't have a car and my father was at a dinner. She could hear the panic in my voice, and she said she'd find a way to get to me as quick as possible. She'd find my father. She'd find me."

I paused, my throat constricting. Maybe I couldn't do this. But then my eyes met Griffin's for just a moment, and his attentive gaze eased my urge to run. I was so tired of running. "Enzo found me in the hall and said the girls had gone home. I couldn't understand why they would leave me there. I cried to him that I wanted to go home, but he took me to his room. He grabbed me, kissing me so hard and rough that I could barely breathe. I tried to push him away, but he was so much bigger than me. He took off my clothes. He kept saying, 'You don't know what you do to me,' as if this were *my* doing." My words were coming out in rapid fire now. "His friends yelled from the other room, said that the party was in there, and for a moment I thought I might be free of him. But he pulled me down the hall toward their voices and their music. I was naked, and there were three of them, and I remember Enzo was laughing and saying, 'She's a dancer.' I was terrified and stumbling, but it was a show now. I was on display on the coffee table being told to dance. I remember staring at the ceiling so I couldn't see their eyes on me. I let my mind float around the room, thinking that maybe then I wouldn't feel their hands on me. I silently sobbed, holding out hope that my father's car would pull up. But when he was finally there, carrying me from that room, I wished that I had never called. Because he saw me there like that, too, and then he couldn't see anything else."

Winded, I inhaled and told Griffin the worst part. "My dad couldn't blame me for what had happened. I was fourteen, a stupid child. So, he blamed the only person he could. The one I betrayed: Madame Bisset."

I wiped away silent tears, hot and shameful. I would never be sure of which offense it was that had me pack up my childhood and stash it away. The silence that fell between my father and me, the loss of innocence, or the loss of *her*.

Humiliation is like violence in designer clothing, but there it was. I had exposed the secret kept under my skin like shrapnel. I waited for Griffin to push past the uncomfortable subject or try to cheer me up with platitudes. But he did not. He leaned against the Falcon so that we were shoulder to shoulder. I clutched my leftover dinner bag, my hair thrashing in the wind, and when I finally looked over at him, all I saw standing next to me in the dark was compassion. The sight of it let loose the tears that hung on my lower lids. He wrapped one arm around my shoulders, tilted his head so it was touching mine, and stayed like that until all those tears had fallen. I was offered the grace of a two-hundred-pound man's presence in the middle-of-nowhere Canada. A gift I never knew I'd been waiting for.

When he eventually turned to face me, I didn't see pity or awkwardness.

"I broke everything," I whispered.

He shook his head, a silent *no*, and gently swept away a few strands of hair that were sticking to my damp cheek.

"I broke rules. I wasn't allowed to go out after nine; wasn't allowed to travel beyond Via del Corso; wasn't allowed to drink. Because I broke these rules, the other rules—the ones meant to protect me—didn't apply."

"*They're* the ones who broke things, Gracie. Broke rules," Griffin said. "*They're* the ones to blame." He softened. "Not you."

"The doctor in the hospital told me that I had not been assaulted. And because I could not spell out exactly what had happened—not then, not yet—I had no power over what happened to me. When the details came back hours later, when the vodka and gin were out of my system, still I didn't tell anyone. Just as the girls I'd been with knew I wouldn't. My father put me in a new home, in a new school with new people. And when I thought I might go to pieces, he'd say, 'You are bold and brave and bright, Gracie.'" My voice quivered. "He wanted to see that I was all right. That we were all right. He just forgot to see . . . *me*."

I let my head fall back to meet a sky full of stars—some brilliant; some only pinpricks of light. He followed my gaze and rubbed his palms together for warmth, though I couldn't make out why. He seemed a heat source all his own.

"I'm not sure I've ever been brave enough or bold enough," I said. "More like a single pinprick of light in a massive night sky like this one. But my audition with Olivia Garza is next Thursday, and I hope *she* can see me."

He sighed and I watched the white vapor that flowed from his mouth disappear into the freezing air. "She'd have to be blind not to," he said. His face was filled with so much kindness that again I had to look away. "I know what it feels like to be a single light in a galaxy wondering if anyone will ever notice that you're there. But I'm not made of the stuff that you're made of. There are all kinds of people in this world. I've met most of them, and trust me, none of them are like you. *I* notice you. And this Garza person, she will too. If you let her." I wanted to acknowledge all he'd said, to thank him, but it seemed I had no words left. "Let's get you out of the cold," he said, sensing that if vulnerability couldn't kill a person, Canadian air possibly could. He reached for the paper bag still wrapped up in my arms. "I'll carry that."

I handed it to him. "Turns out I don't much like eggplant burgers."

He laughed. "No one does."

I couldn't help but smile. "I'll drive."

"Lead the way, Wilder," he said, and my heart quickly obliged.

———

I drove the Falcon through a town where Victorian architecture mingled with simple brick buildings. Griffin commented on the differing design styles and the eras from which they originated, while I watched the indignity that had been unearthed with my story lift into the darkness. I had thought that after telling it, I would feel small and want to plummet below the surface of the day like a sinking stone. Instead, I felt a dizzying lightness and a void of thought like waking from sleep. As the car's heater warmed us through, my whole body seemed to be tingling with circulation and resurgence. I focused on the road in front of me, changing course at random and eventually stopping in front of a large old home with a sign that read *Guesthouse.*

"Is this us?" Griffin asked.

"I think so."

"That's red slate on those turrets. Richardsonian Romanesque style. You just stumbled upon this?"

"Yes," I whispered, bewildered by the events of the day.

He was surveying the architecture. "Well, I'll be damned."

Remarkably, the guesthouse had rooms available. A middle-aged woman with cat-eye glasses and squeaky shoes led us through an entryway with large gleaming wooden moldings, up a staircase with an impressive banister, to two adjacent rooms on the third floor. I said good night to Griffin and went to get settled.

My room had pale wallpaper with simple navy-blue stripes to match the navy tiles around the fireplace. There was a settee by the window, milk glass light sconces to either side of the bed, and a vintage burgundy rug spread across the hardwood floor. I sat on the bed with a little bounce. The mattress was good. I unpacked some items and then phoned Mark. He answered at the first ring.

"I was wondering when I'd hear from you," he said. "I tried calling you. How's the road trip going?"

"It's going well. We got on a bit farther today than planned. We should be in Toronto by lunch tomorrow."

"But you were going to stay in London, Ontario. I had it all arranged."

"We decided to make tomorrow a lighter travel day," I explained.

"Did you find accommodations?"

"I'm in my room now."

"And your new friend is in his own room?"

"Of course, Mark."

"I just have no real reason to trust the guy. What did you talk about all day anyway? Power tools and beer?"

I knew his mocking was just masking concern, and that I had not put him in an easy situation, but I was in no mood. "Mark, he's easygoing, but that does not make him a simpleminded person."

"I was only joking. If I didn't know you better, I'd say you were beginning to like this guy. That hadn't occurred to me because, let's be honest, he's not exactly your type. Just keep your guard up, okay? I miss you."

I wondered if I even had a type, but I was tired, and so I just told him that I had best be off to bed. "I'll call you first thing," I promised.

After I hung up, I sat in the stillness of my room thinking about Mark's advice to keep my guard up. Yet in that singular day, I had come to trust Griffin faster than I had come to trust nearly anyone. I dated Mark for weeks before I even let him up to my flat, and I'd just gone and nearly let Griffin into my whole life. I couldn't make sense of why I'd done that. Certainly, it helped that my father had liked him, but it's not like I was having Mr. Brockwell over for tea on Sunday afternoons, just because my father liked him too. Had I simply been charmed by Griffin's candor, his cadence, and the whole adventure? Had I just forged a relationship at random out of a deep need for companionship? Was I a lunatic? I couldn't be sure I wasn't.

I thought it might be best to assure Griffin that there would be no more demands placed on him in parking lots, assure him that ours could be an uncomplicated friendship. I paced the burgundy rug for ten minutes and then wandered out into the hall to find him.

"How's your room?" I asked when he opened his door.

"Good," he said. "Blue." From the doorway it appeared that the room was indeed very blue. Griffin was wearing only a thin T-shirt and athletic shorts, something that could be classified as pajamas, and I could hear the TV playing in the background. I would make this quick.

"So. Thanks for earlier," I said, my hands gesturing vaguely to the past as if it were now floating above my head.

"Oh, yeah. No . . . of course."

A grandfather clock chimed somewhere in the house, punctuating the moment with long reverberating *bongs*. "I certainly didn't mean to dump all that on you tonight. I'm really sorry."

He looked at me deadpan. "You have nothing to be sorry for."

"Well, it was a lot. And, uh . . . I just want you to know I'm okay. That stuff doesn't really matter . . ."

"It matters," he said. The expression on his face was warm but direct. It seemed to say, *you* matter.

I stammered a thank you. Then, oozing with honesty, I added, "It would be right for me to say that I really don't know what I'm doing here."

He glanced over his shoulder. "It's a change of pace."

"I sort of jumped—heart first—hoping for answers."

"Yeah, but at least you jumped." He leaned against the doorframe in a casual posture that led me to think that maybe the only apprehension lingering here was my own. "I spend hours trying to figure out what to do, how to do it, how to get everything just right, before giving something a shot. And I still end up letting people down. So . . ."

"Not today," I told him, but he only shrugged unassumingly. Griffin was quickly becoming legendary for inciting me to say exactly what I was thinking the very moment I was thinking it. It was a sleight of hand, a trick of casual exchange. "There are far too many people in my life whom I feel like I need to perform for, rather than just being myself," I said. The grandfather clock had completed its recital, yet there was still a vibration in the hallway. "I'm glad you're here." It was the most levelheaded thing I'd said all night.

"We'll drive into Montreal tomorrow and see what the old city has to say about our spontaneous visit," he said.

I smiled with relief. "Well, I should get to bed. You should too."

He stood a little straighter. "Yes, ma'am."

"Good night."

"Good night, Gracie."

I walked back to my room and washed up in the bath. I pulled on soft pajamas and curled against the ruffled pillows on the bed. The only sounds I could hear were tree branches rattling together outside in a gentle staccato rhythm. I let the sounds soothe me—*rustle, tap, rustle, tap*—and imagined that the whole world must be nearly asleep, save for me, fastened like a pin to the bedspread. I let my mind drift until everything settled, and then the only lasting thought was of my father. What would he have thought of me embarking on this journey? Might he have said it was a waste of time, a pathless path? *Go home, Gracie. There's nothing worth all this fuss.* Or would he say, *Carry on, my dear. Carry on, and you'll find me.*

I wished I could wrap myself in his words and know what it was he wanted to say to me.

I wished I could tell him how very sorry I was, how I wished I could go back.

I wished I could have stood at his side in the hospital, smoothed his hair, and said, "I need you to stay."

17

COOPER

New York always has a fascinating story to tell. This one was no exception.

David Wilder had gone about his last evening on earth the way he had dozens of evenings before. He sat alone at the end of the bar in the Bull and Bear restaurant of New York's Waldorf Astoria, wearing one of his finer three-piece suits. He finished reading the *New York Times* and enjoyed a dinner of sea bass and brandy.

Jed, the middle-aged bartender regularly stationed under the glow of yellow lights, was careful not to over-assist. Sometime after Wilder set down his empty glass, his attention curiously shifted to *her*. She was a young twentysomething perched on a barstool with her body bent forward and her hair hanging in her face.

Jed saw Wilder lean over the curve of the bar with his credit card pressed between two fingers, trying to make eye contact. Wilder set his leather briefcase on the bar with an audible sigh—another signal of his departure. Jed hurried to make two martinis for Mr. and Mrs. Swanson, a young couple that often ran a high tab, while pouring another round of tequila for a ruddy-faced man, his tall unmannerly friend, and her. "She looked like she'd had a rough night," Jed recounted. "But I see drunk people all the time, so I didn't think much of it."

When he went to print a check for Wilder a few minutes later, he noticed the briefcase still on the bar, but Wilder was no longer sitting beside it. He had pushed through a throng of people and was approaching the young woman.

"Mr. Wilder was not the kind of man to put his nose where it didn't belong," Jed explained. "He rarely engaged anyone, let alone a woman. But after he'd spoken to this girl for one minute, he signaled to me with a pointed finger. I told him I had his check and slid it across the bar, but he put a hand on top of mine and whispered, 'This woman is in trouble.'"

Jed asked Wilder if he'd seen the "trouble," or if the girl had asked for help. Wilder gave a brisk shake of the head. "I can see it in her eyes. I can see it in the men she's with."

Now the ruddy-faced man and his tall friend wanted to know what was going on. Wilder spoke to them firmly and explained that their friend needed a taxi, that Jed was going to arrange it. But the men threw money on the bar and pulled the woman from her stool toward the door. Wilder continued to demand that Jed do something. When Jed did not, Wilder hurried out into the streets of Manhattan.

He must have seen the young woman across Park Avenue balanced between the two men from the bar as they tried to hail a cab—just as the doorman had seen them and the violinist who had been perched nearby squeaking out the notes to "Till There Was You." When Wilder reportedly reached the sidewalk, he yelled for them to stop, and when his voice was lost in the consuming sounds of car horns and street music, he waited for a break in the traffic and darted out into the street.

But Wilder failed to see the black Mercedes that had just rounded the corner, headed downtown. The police report indicates that it was this car—a woman eager to make her dinner reservation—that barreled into Wilder, unable to break speed before impact.

No one can attest to what went on for Wilder between his going unconscious and his coming-to approximately ten minutes later. I don't know if he heard the crunch of his ribs breaking or if he felt his body being thrown into the air. I don't know if he thought he might be dying or if time stood still then. I have no sense of whether he was in pain or if pain, like time, also might have been gone from him during this period. Some say that when we come that close to death, we are charged with warmth and light like electricity. Could that have been Wilder's experience? I don't know. But when Wilder found his way back to consciousness, he couldn't understand why a team of medics was buzzing around him like a swarm of bees. He could feel pain coursing through his body, and he wanted to know why. Though the memories and events of that evening floated around for him like specs of white in a snow globe, one thought rose through clearly. He spoke her name from the gurney. *Gracie.*

Jackie Marley only had thirty minutes left in her shift when Mr. Wilder was wheeled into the hospital. As paramedics and doctors deliberated on vitals in rapid fire, Jackie stood close, taking notes. She did not miss the shallow attempts Mr. Wilder made to speak. One of the other nurses described Jackie to be attentive, compassionate, and no-nonsense with her patients. Also quick with an IV and meticulous with her charts. Jackie promised Mr. Wilder that she would tend to his personal requests after a few diagnostic tests.

Mr. Wilder was admitted to New York Presbyterian Hospital on October 8 at 9:32 p.m. and was in the operating room by 10:59 p.m. During that time leading up to surgery, it was Jackie who monitored Mr. Wilder's oxygen, blood levels, heart rate, and IV drip. When Jed the bartender showed up in the ER to see if Mr. Wilder's accident in front of the Waldorf had been grave, it was Jackie who briefly explained his condition before taking the briefcase that Mr. Wilder had left on the bar and securing it with the rest of his personal items. It was Jackie who assisted Mr. Wilder in making three phone calls. And most important, it was Jackie who assisted Mr. Wilder in typing a letter to Gracie on the laptop that was kept in his briefcase.

"We don't usually allow for that sort of thing," Jackie's supervisor, Tammy Smith, explained. "But Jackie was here well past her shift, and we try to do all we can in those dire situations."

"Well, if I could just speak to Jackie, then I'm sure I'll have all the information I need for the family," I said.

Tammy shook her head. "I'm sorry, Mr. Cooper, but Jackie doesn't work here anymore."

I was confused. "Where is she now?"

"No saying, really."

Mr. Wilder had been admitted to the hospital the night of October 8, and Jackie Marley had quit her job of nine years on October 9. Why did Jackie quit?

Tammy couldn't say. "She never said anything to anyone about her plans. And I would have really appreciated a two-week notice."

I didn't have any trouble finding Jackie's home address or phone number. But I found her windows dark, and her phone sent me straight to voicemail.

This had begun as a simple quandary. A shot at restitution while doing business in New York. An easy moonlighting gig. But the further I went into the story of David Wilder's last day, the more I wanted to obtain his parting message. Griffin may have doubted my ability to do something truly good for someone, but I knew why I was there. It wasn't just for my own benefit anymore. It was for Gracie.

I'd wait for Jackie Marley to return my call. I'd follow up with Geneva about the laptop. I'd string the pieces together and find Mr. Wilder's final words. I nearly had it in the bag.

18

GRACIE

The second day on the road was cooler than the first. We left the Falcon's top up and ran the heat until the sun was high. I watched trees drift by my window. Like dancers in a spotlight, their tops were bright and illuminated, their undersides dark and in the shadows. Griffin asked me about my travels, and I told him about my various homes and schools. He said, "You must have friends all over the world." I agreed that I did, but not *everyday* friends. "I have friends who would show up at my door on my best day or my worst day," I explained, "but life happens in between. And I don't have a lot of people with me in between." He told me that Cooper was an everyday friend, and that everyday friends can be a lot sometimes. I thought to myself that Griffin must be a wonderful everyday friend.

When we stopped for gas in Toronto, I stayed in the car and watched Griffin walk into the store in long strides, a man with a wide step but in no hurry. He brought me tea in a wax cup and wedged it into the console, saying only "It's hot" before starting the engine. Later, when he saw me pull my cardigan tightly around my shoulders, he kicked up the heat in the car. And when I spent an embarrassing amount of time in a public loo, he wandered into a convenience store and came out with an

"I love Canada" baseball cap. He put it on my head and said, "To keep the sun out of your eyes."

We had found a dyad of rhythm together. He stepped to a slow and steady beat, creating space for me to find a lighter groove. If I hadn't been so busy overthinking my return to Montreal, I might have worried that we were becoming too simpatico. When we came upon a sign that read *Montreal, 200 km*, Griffin lifted his chin toward me and said, "Home stretch. By this time tomorrow, you might know something more about your dad's gift." My stomach fluttered with the thought.

I closed my eyes and dared myself to remember. I pictured the stone building where I had lived, where Madame Bisset and I had sat on the front steps on warm summer nights and licked pink lemonade popsicles, dripping half of the juice onto the speckled cement. I could imagine the black postbox that hung to the right of the yellow door and the great railing on the foyer staircase that I used to slide down when my father wasn't looking. I recalled that the pantry door in the kitchen swung both ways and my four-poster bed had been too tall to climb into without a little pink footstool. I thought about driving out of town with my father for the weekend in a swirl of suitcases and cigar smoke and reaching the gravel driveway of our country house before dark. I'd run between the rosebushes to the front porch of the old blue house, wanting to be the first to claim the hidden key from its place behind the garage lantern. I could imagine it all, more vividly with every mile, as if I was in fact driving into the past. I wondered who lived in those homes now. I wondered if there was still a pantry door that swung both ways in our old flat or if the Blue Tilting House might have since corrected its posture.

We ran into a heap of traffic as we entered the city, but Griffin's calm was undisturbed. We edged our way through downtown, high-rises to either side of the highway, and then finally made the exit for Old Montreal. I directed him toward the area where I had once lived, not far from the basilica.

Notre-Dame de Montreal was just as I'd remembered—two towers bookending three mighty arches—though I don't know why I would consider it having changed in the last decade when it hadn't in one hundred and seventy years. I watched the people in the square: a man feeding pigeons, a family taking pictures with the basilica as their back-drop, a woman strolling hand-in-hand with her toddler son. With each road we turned down, muted memories from my time there prickled with pigment, coming alive in a montage of color and movement.

"You want to eat something before we find a hotel?" Griffin asked, pulling the Falcon into a parking spot.

"Dinner sounds good." I gathered up my things, carefully pulling the blackbird off the mirror and tucking it into my bag before stepping out of the car.

Griffin stuffed his hands in his pockets as we started up the street. I rightly did the same, though it would have felt more natural to hook my arm through his or, at the very least, to have walked shoulder to shoulder.

The city's buildings were gray stone, but there was color everywhere. Color in the mums that lined windowsills in quaint flowerpots and win-dow boxes. Color in bright awnings, in smartly dressed people, and in the foliage that mingled between the buildings. There was high energy too, flowing like steam from a cup out of each eatery and shop that we passed as we started down Rue Saint-Paul. It put a bounce in our steps.

Griffin and I considered one restaurant and then another, browsing menus and enjoying the search for the right place to land. He would ask me about the French cuisine, and I'd share what little I knew about truffles and shallots. We'd nearly decide to go inside, only to be lured by the fragrances and music wafting from the restaurant next door. For a while, this went on like a wonderful sensory game. I met aromas from my childhood, wavering between identification and curiosity.

But while bent over the menu of an old brasserie, Griffin was stand-ing so close behind me that I could feel his breath on my cheek; I could feel a restless kinetic energy between us. "Do you think I'd like *lapin*?" he asked, trying to decipher the French *plats du jour*.

I turned toward him, hoping to disrupt the connection, but his face was hovering so close to mine. I stammered, "That depends on whether or not you want to eat . . . a rabbit."

The next thing I knew, we were kissing. It was soft and deep, and practically every muscle in my body wilted. When I gently pulled away, we seemed to realize only then what had happened. I believe my first word was *shit*.

"I'm sorry," he said.

"It's . . . okay." Shit, shit, shit.

He ran his hands through his hair. "I just messed this up, didn't I?"

"It's fine," I assured him, but an indelible line had been crossed. We stood there for a moment, staring at each other, trying to think of what to say or do. Finally, I stepped away toward the restaurant beside us. A sign above the door read *Fleur de Thym*. It was not a doorway that I knew, but the smells coming from inside felt like old friends. "Let's go in," I suggested, and Griffin followed my lead.

We couldn't have stumbled into a more romantic setting. The bistro's walls were stone, the floors wide wooden oak planks; there was a burning fireplace and a dozen small tables with white cloths and dripping candles. We were seated at a table in the corner and given tall menus with a variety of seafood items.

Griffin sat back in his chair and gazed at me like a person would if he was hoping you'd ask him to dance.

"Nice place," I said, my voice a bit pitchy.

After a moment, he leaned on the table the way he always seemed to when he had something important to say. "I think we should talk about the kiss."

"I *strongly* disagree."

"It was an unbelievably good kiss. I mean, didn't you think so?"

"I don't think we should linger on it," I said, righting my menu so that he had to peer over it to see me.

"I'm really sorry. But also, not completely sorry." He wasn't going to stop. "Gracie?"

I put my menu down. "What?"

"Why are you with Mark?"

I immediately felt defensive. "Excuse me?"

"Why *that* guy?"

"Griffin, I'm sorry if I gave you the wrong idea."

He shook his head. "You didn't. But I'm just wondering. Does he make you happy? Does he appreciate you?"

"Stop it," I snapped, under my breath.

"I'm sorry. I just think you deserve better."

"And you think you're the something better?"

He shrugged. "I'm not exactly my favorite person."

"I'm not going to justify what I have with Mark just because you kissed me."

"Well, you kissed me too."

"*Bonsoir*," a female voice said. A woman in a long black dress placed a basket of bread on the table. "A drink perhaps?"

"Just water for now, thank you," I said. "What's the soup today?"

"It's a lobster bisque," she began, her eyes intent on my face. "And the special is a sole fillet with olives, capers—" she interrupted herself. "I'm sorry, but you look so much like someone I know." She was so delighted by her observation that she didn't seem to detect the awkward exchange.

"How funny," I said, extending my hand. "I'm Gracie Wilder."

She shook my hand. "Yes. Amazing. Excuse me just a moment." And then she breezed off as though she'd suddenly been called away.

"That was strange," Griffin commented with a mouth full of bread.

We stared at each other, a little mystified. It was a gaze that melted some of the tension away. Griffin, mouth now free of bread, reached over and took one of my hands in both of his. "I should never have kissed you. I'm sorry."

"It's okay," I said, not wanting to admit to myself how amazing that kiss had been.

Griffin gave me back my hand and sighed. "I just can't decide if meeting you is the best thing that could have happened, or if it would have been better if our paths never crossed." I recoiled. He noticed and tried to explain. "What I mean is, I never knew someone like you existed. But now, well, now I have to live the rest of my life knowing that you're out there. Maybe I should have known what I was getting into, but how could I have guessed that you'd be so, well, you know . . . wonderful."

It was a raw and tender moment, and naturally I had no idea what to do with it. I was still in shock from all he'd said, when the woman returned to take our food order. Only this time another woman stood at her side—a gray-haired lady in a beige skirt suit. "Ms. Wilder?" the older woman asked with a French-Canadian accent.

I nodded.

"I'm Sarah. My husband and I have had this restaurant for many years. It's a pleasure to have you and your friend here. Are you in for a special occasion?" Her interest in us was demonstrable, and I thought to myself that certainly her restaurant had been around for many years because she treated the customers like esteemed guests.

"We just arrived in town tonight," I explained. "I lived here many years ago, so I suppose it's a sort of homecoming." It occurred to me that Sarah might be of assistance. "I'm actually hoping to find someone, the shopkeeper who may have made this," I said, pulling the blackbird from my bag and holding it up to the candlelight.

Sarah touched her fingers to her lips. Then, without asking a question, she simply instructed, "Come with me."

Griffin and I exchanged a puzzled look while the two women stood by expectantly. I slowly rose from my chair. Griffin followed suit, taking a few bread rolls from the basket. Sarah took her coat from the rack by the door and led us outside.

We paraded up the road, Sarah, Griffin, and me, with a couple of others who followed behind from the restaurant—the young waitress and a man I'd spotted working behind the bar. I couldn't be sure who was attending to Fleur de Thym in their absence, since there appeared to be only a few servers to begin with. But there we were, dashing up the street.

"Sarah, what's this?" an older gentleman called out from the doorway of a quaint café.

"*Mademoiselle Wilder est venue rencontrer Éloïse,*" she called back. And the man joined our march. A chill ran up my spine. Who were these people? Had they been expecting me?

Griffin took my hand in his and squeezed. I did not let go.

When we finally approached the block where I'd once seen that display of silk birds, I recognized the shop window before Sarah halted the procession. The sign above the door read *The Heirloom.* Yes, of course, that was it.

I glanced behind me and counted six people standing in my wake. I was bewildered.

"She'll just be closing," Sarah said.

"Do you want me to go in with you?" Griffin asked.

"You stay here," Sarah said, before I could answer.

I slowly twisted the doorknob and stepped inside.

The shop smelled like cinnamon. There were tea towels and pottery on the front table alongside a large display of quilts, and in the back, behind a wooden counter, a young girl sat talking cheerfully on the phone. I guessed that she was eleven or twelve years old. "Thank you, that will be fine," she was saying. "Will we see you tomorrow?"

I poked at the pottery while I waited for the girl to finish her call or for the shopkeeper to emerge from somewhere. I examined a small, shallow bowl with swirls of blues and greens and a mermaid painted in its center.

"She's a sea goddess," said the girl from behind the counter. I hadn't noticed that she'd hung up the phone. "A girl who sprouted fins to survive." She stood from her chair. "Are you shopping for a gift?"

"Actually, I'm trying to find someone," I said.

The girl skillfully braced silver crutches to her arms and pulled her legs forward and around the counter. When she was half the distance to me, she exclaimed, "Oh my goodness, Grace Marie?" My blood ran cold and my skin prickled with eerie recognition. "You know me?"

"Of course. From your picture."

I took a few steps closer. "How is it you have my picture?"

"You don't know who I am?"

I shook my head in dismay.

"I'm Celina. Éloïse is my mother, and this is her shop. But if you don't know us, how are you here?"

I pulled the bird from my bag and held it out to her.

Celina sighed and smiled. "He gave it to you at last."

I had to sit down. My legs would not hold me. I found a nearby bench lined with pumpkins and found a seat among them.

"I've been wanting to meet you for so long," Celina tried to explain.

"Why?" The word escaped me as only a whisper.

She stood before me, balancing on her crutches with her feet pointed slightly toward each other. "Well . . . because . . . we're sisters."

I huffed a laugh, ready to dispute this insanity—to tell the child that she was sorely mistaken. But I could not. I could only stare down the hazel-gray eyes shining at me like mirrors.

Celina went on talking about a man I scarcely knew, my father, but I sat motionless. Intellectually I could understand what she was saying to me, but the pain in my chest made speaking impossible.

When Éloïse walked in through the back, I recognized her immediately. She'd hardly aged a day. She had the same long dark hair, the same engaging look about her. She strode over to me, her hands open at her sides, and said, "Grace Marie, we're so glad you're here."

Had my father made a secret life without me? I could only say, "He never told me." Once, and then again. Twice.

Éloïse's face filled with empathy, which made me feel more confused. She said kind, consoling things that I quickly disregarded.

I pushed questions down with the emotion lodged in my throat. Dr. Peck would have cautioned against this, but she couldn't possibly have understood what it was like to return to the place that held the most beautiful part of my childhood, only to find that I had been replaced.

Minutes passed. Éloïse flipped the sign on the door to read *Closed*, turned off the light, and opened the door to the street. I followed as if in a trance.

"Are you okay?" Griffin asked when he saw me.

All I could do was lift my head in a brave attempt to fool him, but he was not fooled.

"Thank you, Sarah," I heard him say. He gave a wave to the older gentleman who'd been keeping Sarah company. They took the cue and said good night before dispersing, somewhat reluctantly.

Something inside me felt fractured, as if I had received a physical blow. Griffin, clearly sensing my discomfort, gently gripped each of my arms as if to hold me together. "We're going to go find a restaurant and a hotel," he said.

"We'd be happy to have you at our home for supper," Éloïse tried.

Griffin looked to me for an answer, and when I stared at him blankly, I could tell he was ready to handle that too, to politely refuse. But I put one hand on his chest in a soft, halting gesture. I needed a moment. Everything was happening so fast. Was I hungry? Did I want to go to the home of Éloïse? Did I want a sister? I'd come all this way. Could I leave with so few answers?

"Turns out . . ." I said, peering back at Griffin's knit brow, "I have a sister."

If he was surprised, he didn't show it. Steady as steady can be, he made the decision I could not make myself. "We'll come for an hour," he told Éloïse.

I exhaled as he took my hand and wove his fingers between mine. It was strange how well Griffin's hand fit with mine. We followed Éloïse and Celina up the road beneath the streetlamps.

Éloïse let us into a small brick house. The front door opened toward a quaint living room adorned with stacks of books and colorful paintings on the walls. She quickly assembled wood in a fireplace and lit a match. Griffin and I stood idly in the doorway until Éloïse motioned toward the couch. "Please, make yourselves comfortable. I'll warm some soup on the stove."

Griffin put a hand on my shoulder. "I'm going to get a couple of hotel rooms nailed down and be back for you in an hour. Okay?" I nodded. I knew I needed to do this part on my own.

But once he was gone, I had no idea what to do. I found a seat near Celina. She had lowered herself into a chair near the hearthrug. Her dog, a beagle she called Claude, loyally curled at her feet.

"I hope you like leftover lentil soup," she said.

I was holding the blackbird between my hands, and I found myself glancing at it every few seconds the way one might check a watch. Or an explosive.

Éloïse came back into the room with a tray of drinking glasses and a pitcher of water. "It will just be a few minutes before the soup is hot." She sat down next to me on the sofa, careful to leave a bit of space between us.

"It's so good to have you here, Grace Marie," she began.

"She prefers Gracie," Celina corrected. She was clearly an observant girl.

"You weren't at the funeral," I pointed out.

"No, we weren't," Éloïse said. "Celina and I were able to speak to him in the hospital before he passed, and we opted for a small memorial here. We lived separate lives but will miss him very much."

It was too big to understand. "But you never tried to find me."

"I'm sorry. David asked me to leave that to him. Even the last time we spoke. He said he was going to talk to you and write it all down. I wish he hadn't waited until the end, but this was his story to tell."

"He told me nothing. I know nothing. I was only given this," I said, shaking the damn bird in my hand like the stuffed thing that it was.

Éloïse audibly breathed and the room fell quiet, save for the crackling of firewood. It occurred to me that she might know nearly as little as I did. Then she smiled tenderly and said, "Celina and I are grateful that you followed the blackbird here."

I wanted to unleash nervous laughter. I had wandered there on a whim. "Dumb luck," was all I said.

"Providence," Éloïse argued.

"This is crazy. You know this is crazy, right?!" I was standing now, wearing tracks into the rug like an angry giant in a small room. I was laughing and crying and yelling all at once. "None of this makes sense!"

Of course, it did make sense. But I wasn't ready to hear that my father had been lonely. That he'd tried to do the right thing and fumbled. That he'd been human. No amount of humanity was going to save him from my pain and anger that night. I was ready to stuff the memory of him away with all the feelings swelling inside me.

Then I noticed the painting hanging on the wall over Celina's chair. It was a portrait of a woman done in oil that played with light and shadow in the same fashion as the one that hung in my father's home in Chicago. I stared at it a moment and found myself saying, between breaths, "He had a painting like that."

"Yes," was all Éloïse said, and I heard the meaning behind the small word. There was still so much to learn and try to understand.

"I need some air," I told them.

"Please, eat something," she implored. But she did not rise to stop me when I moved to the door.

"I'll come back. Tomorrow maybe," was all I could manage.

I heard Celina say, "Oh yes, tomorrow please, Gracie. Please come back." I quickly stepped outside and slammed the door to the little house behind me.

I tightened my coat around me, tucked my bag safely under one arm, and wandered back out into the streets of Montreal. I walked three blocks without a thought in my head. My mind was as numb as my body was from the cold. Then conversations began to emerge in an unwelcome racket. Bits and pieces of dialogue I'd had with my father flitted in and out of my consciousness like a glitch in my mental programming, a virus of uncertainty, a system search for understanding.

Had he tried to tell me? Had I not been able to hear him? Surely my father would have opened the door to this life outside my own, and I'd not been able to walk through. Surely that had to be the explanation. Hadn't he tried to tell me of business trips to Montreal, and hadn't I changed the direction of our discussion to other affairs, desperate to not think of the city that held my fondest memories, that preserved Madame Bisset in space and time? I couldn't be sure if I had done that, but I might have. Hadn't he once, many years before, entertained the idea of me going with him to visit the Blue Tilting House in the countryside, and I'd declined, unwilling to fly? To remember. Yes, I was certain I'd done that. I'd told him, *I don't want to go back.* And he'd told me that he understood.

But I had not been unwilling to know my father. I'd been most willing.

I walked back down the road where I'd discovered The Heirloom. Hoping to push past the shop quickly, I tried to keep my steps in time with the sounds of distant street noise. Like The Heirloom, most of the shops along the cobblestone street were closed. But one light still shown from inside a small establishment. It bore a large plaque that read *The LeClair Studio and Gallery*, and through the picture window I could see a middle-aged couple talking inside. They must have sensed me staring because they glanced up. I slowed my step. Had they been on the street earlier when I'd emerged from the shop with Éloïse and Celina? And then they were walking to the door and opening it toward me.

19

GRIFFIN

The air smelled earthy and ionized. I figured I had about an hour before a downpour. I tried to familiarize myself with my surroundings and headed in the direction of what I hoped was the Falcon. My thoughts were scattered but insistent, like animals foraging for food before the storm.

The kiss had been a mistake. The city itself held the extent of Gracie's attention; I'd been a stand-in, a way to fill the emptiness between Chicago and Montreal. Even if she had feelings for me, she would have denied them. I was not the reason she was there.

But then there was that moment in front of the shop when she looked at me with those deep, pleading eyes, and I knew I would do anything to protect her. This trip had been an excuse for me to get out of town, but I was beginning to think there might be another reason I needed to be there.

I walked for twenty minutes, convinced I must have passed the street where I'd parked, and then decided to find the hotel that had been on Gracie's itinerary. I remembered that it had the name Gray in it, and from the listings on my phone I deduced that it must have been Hotel

William Gray. I found the address and headed into the sleek lobby with its falling lights and floating stairs. I got confirmation from reception that they were still holding our rooms and texted Gracie with an update: *Hotel rooms at William Gray locked down. Car nearby. Will be there to get you in 30. How are you?*

All she wrote was *Thanks. I'll walk. See you in a bit.*

I hoped the rain would hold off.

I wasn't dressed for the restaurant at Hotel William Gray. I was in jeans and a navy sweatshirt I'd gotten from Keira last Christmas. The other guys at the long white marble bar had shirts with collars. But I pulled up one of the brass stools just the same and ordered an elaborate meat-and-cheese plate. I assembled some prosciutto and artisan cheese onto a crust of French bread, and I was just about to take a bite when I heard a male voice say, "Excuse me?" I froze, the toast held midair, and turned to see a man in a wool blazer staring me down.

"Beau Griffin?"

He was familiar, like I might have seen him somewhere before, but I couldn't place him. Not until he identified himself.

"Mark Schaffer."

Yep, I'd seen him before—at David Wilder's funeral.

"I googled you," he explained. "Almost didn't recognize you without the full beard."

My first thought was *What the hell are you doing here?* But despite my aggressive hunger, I found a softer approach. "What brings you to Montreal, Mark?"

He smirked. "That's funny."

But I wasn't meaning to be funny. "Were you planning to surprise Gracie? I don't recall seeing your name on the itinerary." Mark's jaw tightened. I gestured for him to take the stool beside me so I could return to my food, and he sat.

"She sounded uneasy when I spoke to her last night. I wanted to be able to help her through this part, so I booked a flight. I wish I could have just dropped everything days ago, but I have a huge caseload right now, and it doesn't allow me to just take off at a moment's notice, so . . ."

I bit back my tongue with a bite of prosciutto.

Mark slapped me on the shoulder in a brotherly gesture that we both knew didn't feel right. "Thanks for getting her here safely," he said. "Really. I'm grateful. But I'll be taking it from here. I rented a car and can drive her back home in a day or so."

I stifled laughter. Did he really think she'd be ready to leave after one day? Did he have any idea what was unfolding here? "Well, we'll see what she wants to do."

"What does that mean?"

"It means, it's up to Gracie. Her trip. Her town. Her choice."

Mark eyed me suspiciously. "You know, I'd be happy to pay you for your troubles."

"Oh, no. I'm good."

The more I remained calm, the more agitated Mark seemed to become. "Griffin, what is it exactly that you're hoping to get out of this trip? Are you just along for the ride or do you have plans?"

I wanted to say, *I am the ride, asshole.* But I took another bite and went with: "I've never been up this way before. Lots of history and architecture."

"Oh, you're a history buff. You know, I don't remember reading that about you. I *did* learn that you're the one that crashed into that old building. I'm not sure I would have been thrilled about you driving Gracie had I known, but it seems you've straightened out your wheels. Still, that was such a shame. Are they going to be able to fix that goddamned place?"

I stood, my stool screeching against the floor.

Mark was clearly surprised by my reaction and possibly thrilled that he'd been able to push one of my buttons. "Relax. Let me buy you a drink."

"I'm good."

"I won't take no for an answer. What's your drink?"

I didn't want to be within ten feet of this guy, but I wanted to finish eating. I sat back down. "Macallan," I said, pointing to a bottle on the top shelf. It was the least he could do.

"Two," Mark told the bartender, and then returning his attention to me, "We'll go easy tonight, so you'll be fresh for your day at the museums tomorrow." He was a smug son-of-a-bitch. "You don't actually think I believe that's why you came up here, do you?" he asked.

"Why *do* you think I'm here, Mark?"

"Gracie is not just any girl."

"No, she's not," I said, and watched him flinch. "I mean, strictly speaking, she's not a girl at all. She's a twenty-six-year-old woman."

Mark narrowed his eyes and slung back his Scotch. I drank mine too. It was smooth, no bite to it at all, but Mark's pinched face told me that his palate was not as sophisticated as his cashmere sweater and wool blazer. "She's in a delicate situation right now," he said. "It would be easy for a guy like you to take advantage."

"A guy like me?"

"Yeah," he said, looking me square in the eye. "A guy with nothing to do, who'd jump at the chance to drive a gorgeous girl anywhere she wanted to go in his dad's car. How does that thing drive, anyway?"

I wanted to punch him, but instead I just ordered another round on his tab. "Mark, did you really expect her to make this trip on her own? It would be a long way even under ordinary circumstances. But her dad just died. Aren't you even just a little bit worried that you're showing up with too little too late?"

He smirked, but once again I wasn't meaning to be funny. It had been a straight question. "I feel sorry for you, Griffin," he said. "I really do. You're in a lose-lose situation. But let me do you a favor. Tonight, let me help you find a girl."

"No thanks." I tipped back another glass.

Mark downed his whiskey and leered at a tall blonde and a redhead a few seats down. I couldn't figure out exactly what he was trying to prove, but I think it had something to do with potency. Sensibly, the two ladies turned their backs away from us and returned to their conversation. I tossed my napkin on my plate with some finality and went for my check.

"What? We're done?" Mark asked.

"I'm done. Gracie will be here soon, and you can figure out where you go from there."

"Where I go from there is back to my deluxe suite with my girl," he said.

He'd hit a nerve, but I kept my cool. I signed my bar tab, pocketed my credit card, and abandoned my barstool. "I'll check in with her later."

That was supposed to be the end of it. But to my surprise, Mark stood and positioned himself directly in my path. What he lacked in size he tried to make up for with volume and false bravado, courtesy of the Macallan. "I don't want you anywhere near her. You understand?" Hostility did not look good on Mark. He reeked of privilege and pettiness. He took a step closer to me, chest forward, cheeks reddened. He was so wrapped up in himself that he didn't notice that the bartender and several patrons had grown uncomfortable.

"I don't blame you," I said. "If I were you, I wouldn't want me around her either. I'd be afraid she'd realize she was with the wrong person."

Mark started laughing obnoxiously, the spectacle intensifying. "And you think *you're* the right person? You take down everything in your path."

I wasn't sure I was good enough for the likes of Gracie Wilder, but with Mark breathing flammable fumes into my nostrils, I sure as hell wanted to be. I lowered my voice. "Maybe you can tell me why you're really here, Mark. Are you here to help Gracie with her search in Montreal? Help her find some answers? Are you here to try and impress a couple of uncomfortable ladies at the bar, make sure I know who's boss? Or maybe you're hoping to find a nice paralegal you can screw, before dragging your girlfriend home with you. You see, I've heard a few things about you too, Mark."

That pushed him over the edge. He took a step back and came at me with his right fist. I dodged most of the hit, but he grazed my chin with a knuckle, knocking my head to the right. I sucked in some air and threw him down with an open hand to his chest, his feet going out from under him. He hit the floor with a thud. Within seconds, the bartender was beside me, and with the help of two other guys who'd been standing nearby, they dragged Mark outside. It was a scene—one that this beautiful establishment likely didn't see on the regular. Jaws dropped. A crowd formed. Strangers offered to buy me drinks. And the two ladies at the bar moved in with morbid curiosity.

Twenty minutes later, I was trying to cool my nerves with a slow, long sip of Scotch when I saw Gracie standing on the far side of the bar. Her hair was wet from rain and her face was knit tight with stress. I stood from my stool and walked over to her.

"You punched Mark?"

I opened my mouth to defend myself, but not much came out. You can take the guy out of the old neighborhood, but you can't take the old neighborhood out of the guy. I may not have thrown the punch, but I had fueled the fight.

"Why would you hit him?"

I shook my head in dismay.

"I want my things," she said. "I'd like to go to my room now."

"I'll go get the car."

"You can leave my bags at the front desk." She waited a few seconds. Her eyes were wide and practically begging me to tell her that this was all just one big misunderstanding. Lord knows I wanted to.

"Gracie—"

"I trusted you," she said, her voice despondent, before she walked back outside.

Through the window I could see Mark pacing in the rain. Gracie walked up to him and tenderly put a hand to his cheek. It was a sobering moment. I collapsed onto the barstool and accepted another drink from an outstretched hand.

———

An hour after I'd found the car, gotten the bags, checked into my room, and raided the mini bar, Cooper called. I wasn't sure I was in the mood to talk but answered anyway.

"You should have seen this game today. Hawks got pummeled," he said when I picked up.

"They weren't the only ones."

"Having a good time, are you?"

"Terrific."

"What's goin' on?"

I sighed. "Mark's here. I might have hit him, which I'm pretty sure was necessary. And now Gracie never wants to see me again."

"Fuuuuuck," Cooper agreed.

"Yeah, I can't catch a break."

"Figuratively speaking."

"And I can't let Gracie go with Mark."

"You don't have a choice, man."

"This is total bullshit."

"Well, you weren't supposed to fall for his girlfriend. And I'm guessing that's what you've gone and done?"

"How do I explain hitting a guy? Never mind. Don't answer that." I didn't want more dirt on Mark from Cooper.

"So, what're you gonna do?"

"I don't know."

"Just come home. It's flag football season, and we're the team to beat. Maybe you could even hit up that friend of your dad's with the commercial renovation business. Jump on a project or something."

He wanted me to throw in the towel. "You know, I don't just do demo. I still know how to build things."

He didn't hear me. "Sleep this one off and head home, brother. There's only one way this thing with Gracie ends. No need to torture yourself."

But how could Cooper really know how this would end? Sure, he spent his days tracing lines backward for clients, and maybe he could predict a thing or two. But Cooper didn't hold on to anything for long. His longest relationship since the fourth grade had been seven weeks. He rented his apartment, leased his car, didn't have a pet, and always had an exit plan. Even his work as a PI was independent and relatively noncommittal. He had more of a relationship with me or his Hawks cap than anything else. How could he be sure that this thing with Gracie was a lost cause, when he'd never taken the chance to care about something he could lose?

20

GRACIE

Mark was standing outside in the rain when I arrived at the hotel. I thought I might be hallucinating, until he came in for an eager embrace. "I couldn't bear the thought of you having to go through this time alone," he said. "So, I hopped on a flight this morning."

"It hasn't been easy to be back," I said as he put his arms around me. I didn't know where else to possibly begin.

"It can't be when you're traveling with a Neanderthal like that Griffin guy. I tried to talk to him, and he hit me. Can you believe that?" He put a hand to his chest, the wind still partially knocked out of him. "I mean, who throws a guy down on the ground in the middle of an upscale restaurant? Who the hell does he think he is, judging *my* behavior?"

My head was spinning. "He hit you?"

Mark carried on, but I couldn't make sense of the particulars. I could, however, sort out by the smell of him that it wasn't just Griffin, but also whiskey that had set him off-kilter. I knew where to find both responsible parties.

Yet once inside, Griffin had been unable to offer anything to reverse the beastly scene.

Mark checked us into a suite and hung his clothes in the closet. He said we would drive back to Chicago in a day or two. I wanted to tell him why I couldn't promise a departure date, but the whiskey fog that hung around his head compelled me to only say, "We'll sort it all out in the morning."

After Mark passed out, I sat beside him on the bed watching shadows splay across the ceiling and trying to piece together alarming details from the day: Griffin's kiss, Celina's plea to stay, Mark standing out in the rain, and Griffin standing at the bar. A chorus of questions echoed in my mind. I almost didn't hear the small voice asking, *What behavior?*

But then there it was, that question. Mark had asked, *Who does he think he is, judging* my *behavior?* What behavior was he referring to?

The hotel room was too damn quiet, and the question wouldn't leave me alone. After twenty minutes of pulling at my eyebrows, I pulled on my shoes and slipped out the hotel room door.

The restaurant was still full of life. I maneuvered between the crowded tables and pulled up a stool at the bar for an herbal tea. The bartender brought me a miniature jar of honey with the chamomile sachet. I was there only five minutes before I was approached by two young women. "Excuse me," one said. "Didn't we see you here with that guy who got in the fight?"

I thought I might be able to duck and run, but part of me was curious. "I wasn't here when it happened," I explained. "But yes. Apparently, he punched my boyfriend."

"Wait," the other woman said, "the tall guy is your boyfriend?"

Griffin had at least four inches and twenty pounds on Mark. "No," I clarified." The guy who was in the wool jacket—*he's* my boyfriend."

That's when the ladies started dishing about exactly who had hit whom. I sat and listened to a play-by-play of the big brawl in Hotel William Gray. The ogling guy in the jacket and the tempered hunk who made a move of self-defense. I wanted to argue their story. I wanted to scream *liars* and run from the building. But I did neither. I sat at the bar sipping my tea, wondering how the hell everything had come apart at the seams.

When I finally keyed back inside the hotel room, I was assaulted by the smell of alcohol and sweat, courtesy of the drunk bugger, passed out and snoring. I locked myself in the bathroom, pulled on my plaid pajamas and bumblebee socks, and sat down on the closed toilet hoping for a good cry. But tears would not come.

Then there it was again, that faint and familiar voice inside me. This time it was offensively chanting, *leave*.

I paced the hotel bathroom like a caged animal having vague recollections of her wild heart. Did I want to be with Mark?

I couldn't remember making a choice about our relationship. It more or less just happened. We met at a New Year's Eve party in a hotel ballroom downtown, and when the DJ played "Auld Lang Syne," he found me on the dance floor and kissed me. After a few dates, it seemed we were an item. He showered me with attention, and later, when he became preoccupied with work, I still felt grateful to have someone in my life who wanted me in theirs.

Now I wondered if he had really shown up for me when I'd needed him. He hadn't been at my performance. He had been relatively absent since my father died. Maybe he was the sort of person who only showed up when *he* needed you. Who called the shots. Who *threw* the shots. I rubbed my thumbs and index fingers against my skull to try to soothe the ache and wondered what Madame Bisset would have made of all this. She might have pursed her bright red lips together and said, "Well, Gracie dear, it seems to me you know *exactly* what you want."

I curled up on the love seat that sat in the corner of the hotel room, and eventually, I fell asleep.

When I woke, I felt a deep ache in my back, the result of my contorted position. Then I heard snoring. I sat up slowly and located Mark sleeping like a starfish under the plush covers of the giant hotel bed. He took up so much space, while I took up as little space as possible. I was tired of feeling small.

As a female dancer, I was used to having a male counterpart hoist me into the air. I would put my weight into someone stable in order to spring forward, ascend, and land. In my upcoming solo performance for Olivia Garza, I would have to produce a similar dramatic effect without the additional force. I would have to propel myself, land on my own two feet, and unmask emotion without the aid of a partner to tell the story. The idea of it filled me with a sense of dread. I rarely took to the stage by myself. I'd grown accustomed to having a partner to elevate me. And I suppose I'd allowed Mark to play a similar role in this last performance as Gracie Wilder. I'd believed I'd be more supported, more lifted, by having Mark at the center of my life. But my first morning in Montreal, I knew I needed to find my solo act.

With shaky hands, I felt around in the dark for my things, quietly stuffing shoes and toiletries into my bags. When all was sorted, I switched on the small lamp beside the bed.

"Mark," I said, softly. When that didn't rouse him, I bravely increased my volume. "Mark!"

He sat up, confused and irritated, then lay right back down.

"I'm leaving," I announced, my voice unsteady.

"Bring back some coffee."

"I'm not going back with you."

He was awake then. He sat up against the pillows. "It's Griffin?"

"No. I just need some time on my own."

"Time on your own?" He nearly laughed. "How are you going to get home all on your own?" His condescension stung like nettles. "What is it you're looking for, Gracie?"

So many thoughts were running through my mind, but I couldn't manage to say anything at all.

He sighed. "I'm here, aren't I? What do you want from me?"

"Nothing."

I backed toward the door slowly, my suitcase in hand, wondering if I could go through with it. He pulled himself from the bed. "You're upset. Let's cool down, and we'll work this thing out."

"I need to go," I said, my strength wobbling. "It's over between us."

"The hell it is!" he yelled, and then quickly tried to calm himself. "I dropped everything for you, babe. I came here to help you."

It was a trap. He knew just how to keep me tethered, how to find the weak spot and press. "I'm sorry," I said.

Mark reached for me. "Where are you going? Come on. You walk out that door, you'll barely make it past tomorrow, let alone into the Garza Dance Company."

I shrank back.

"No offense, Gracie, but you're kind of a hot mess. You need me. We need each other."

"I'm sorry," I said once more, before twisting the doorknob with my free hand and managing to slip out of the room with a swift tug of my suitcase.

I hurried down the hall, the sound of his voice yelling after me. "Gracie!"

I made it down to the lobby, then outside. I walked several blocks before finally finding a bus stop bench where I could catch my breath.

I frantically took out my phone and called Ana.

Her voice was groggy when she picked up. "It's early, G. You in jail or something?"

"I just walked out on Mark at the hotel."

I heard the rustle of bedsheets. "Say more."

"He flew in last night, and sometime early this morning I decided I didn't want him telling me how to live my life anymore."

"Amazing."

"I decided he was a self-righteous prig."

"Hell, yes!"

"So, I got up and I left."

"Good for you!"

"But now I'm wondering if I've blown it out of proportion."

"No. No. Don't overanalyze it. Get out of your head for once."

"Ana, I don't leave people. They leave me. I don't know how to do this." My teeth chattered, either from the cold or from the chill of indignity.

"Well, you're about to meet the part of you that knows exactly how to do this. And she's going to march your fine ass down the street without looking back!" She added, "But then go inside somewhere, 'cause you sound freezing."

I stood and began dragging my suitcase up the block. "The only place left to go is . . . my sister's."

"You don't have a sister."

"I do now. Found out yesterday."

"Holy. Shit."

"I know. I'll catch you up when I get my head around it," I said, trudging like a nomad into the morning.

"Call me later. When you're settled somewhere. You could get another hotel room. Just be safe."

I promised I'd call.

"I love you, G. I'm proud of you."

When I hung up, I headed in the only direction that was left: toward Éloïse and Celina.

———

I had learned more about my sister the night before at the LeClair Studio and Gallery. Mrs. LeClair had smoothed her graying hair away from her round face and opened the door for me. "*Bonsoir*, Grace Marie," she'd said. Her painted-in eyebrows were like two one-dimensional caterpillars that arched their backs as she greeted me. Mr. LeClair was a round man with twinkling eyes and hair slicked back by shiny gloss. He took a step toward me and softly opened his arms as if ready to receive a large gift. I should have balked at the reception, but I let him wrap his arms around me as though we had just been reunited. I let him pull me into the collar of his shirt, which smelled of brandy and peppermint.

These people had been my father's friends. They whirred like hummingbirds as they led me through the gallery. Three small rooms conjoined in a jagged circle like a series of soda boxes open on both ends. The main room sat in the center and held a variety of works, primarily oils of the contemporary variety. But I was more focused on Mrs. LeClair, how she swayed gently as she walked, and Mr. LeClair, glancing over his shoulder to check on me before finally stopping in the farthest little room, an office of sorts, and saying, "Now . . . come sit, come sit. We want to hear everything."

They were the crazy aunt and uncle types who likely argued over who was going to carve the meat, who wrote long holiday newsletters and wore matching pullovers. I instantly liked them, even though they were another unsung verse in my father's overture.

The LeClairs explained that they'd come to know my father by way of Celina. Celina, they said, fancied herself an artist at a young age and wandered into the studio asking for art lessons. Mrs. LeClair taught only adult fine art classes, but Celina was persistent and became her first young student. "She's a remarkable girl," Mrs. LeClair said of my sister, and then popped up from her seat at the table to fish some papers out of a nearby shelf. She carried them over the way one might balance a tray of cocktails and placed the stack in front of me with maternal delight. "Here are some of her recent pieces."

I'd been expecting the typical wiggly water lines, stick figures, and *m*-shaped birds. But what I saw couldn't have been made by a twelve-year-old. I figured Mrs. LeClair had grabbed the wrong stack. I held up a drawing of water falling off a roof and another of a muted cityscape at twilight.

"She has a gift," Mr. LeClair said, as though she had done nothing more than learn to whistle.

I could see the unique beauty in the paintings, as well as the similarities in their composition. My mind flipped through the collection, then to the portrait in Éloïse's living room, and finally to the woman framed in gold in my father's office. They had been Celina's too.

I stood from the table, unable to articulate deepening feelings of deception. There was something about my sister's painting hanging in the backdrop of my father's life, right in front of me, that made a secret seem more like a lie. "Does her work hang in your gallery?" I asked, glancing around, bewildered.

"Éloïse has wanted her to paint for the joy of it, not the profit. But David encouraged them to think about the future. The doors her art could open," Mrs. LeClair explained. "And he wanted to see a children's art program take shape here. Teachers and students and enrichment classes."

Mr. LeClair chimed in. "He left us a generous gift when he passed, and we will be expanding to include the Wilder School of Art, beginning with a special exhibit and reception featuring Celina's work. We feel it is a wonderful way to honor David and uplift Celina."

I stood there, of little consequence, and it must have been obvious to Mrs. LeClair because she added, "Gracie, we'd love for you to be a part of this. If you're willing."

Was I willing to be a part of all of this? This enchanting storyline where my father had supported young artists while I had waited anxiously, a world away, eager for his affection?

I was mulling it over as I rounded the corner for Éloïse's home that next morning. It was eight a.m. when I knocked on her door. She opened it wide.

"I can't stay in my hotel room," I told her, this thought being the most immediate.

"It's no problem," she said in a hushed voice, and I gathered that Celina was still asleep.

Éloïse showed me to the spare room. It had an antique bed and a small matching bureau. She took my coat and laid it on a wicker chair in a dapple of sunlight below the window.

"Griffin is not my boyfriend," I said. She did not reply, but her eyes shone like she could understand things that were impossible to understand. She had an earthy and pragmatic presence, probably having to do with how she stood all day in her cinnamon-scented shop wearing thick-soled clogs and talking with strangers. I sat on the edge of the bed and fiddled with the seam on the end of a pale yellow quilt. "I have questions," I said, hoping she might say something that would reassemble my understanding of my life.

She tried. "David came to buy you the blackbird, hoping to give it to you for your fifteenth birthday," she began. I tried to process that. *Fifteen.* Over a decade ago. "He was worried about you, and in many ways felt responsible for your unhappiness. But he and I had loneliness in common. We took comfort in each other for a short time, and the news that Celina was coming upset his plans of giving you the gift. It was charged with a new storyline. Things grew more complicated with Celina's difficult birth, and David put off the news too long to ever tell you without hurting you." She paused. "He never wanted to hurt you."

"He was afraid he'd make me feel even less significant than I already feel?" I was teetering on a vulnerable edge. "Did he not think I deserved to know?" I fell backward onto the bed, sure I would fracture into a thousand pieces of flesh and bones right there on the yellow quilt.

But Éloïse said gently, "Sit up, Gracie." And for some reason, I did.

She slid my coat toward the back of the chair under the window to make room for her to sit. "You know better than anyone that your dad gave a lot of thought to his decisions. He thought about you more than anyone. That does not excuse him from the pain he has caused you. He made mistakes—of that, I'm sure. But his intentions were good."

I was incredulous. An anger rose in me that I hardly recognized. It was stark and foreign, and yet I knew it was mine. All mine. "You think he had good reason to lie to me? You preferred it this way?"

"No," she corrected, her tone indicating her certitude but her face revealing tenderness. "I did not prefer it this way." She reached into the square pocket of her cardigan and pulled out a loop of oblong black and tan beads. Some were shiny, some dull, and they were fastened at the end with a thin leather lace. At a closer glance, I could see the beads were each shaped like fish. They rested in her open palm. "Each fish is for someone in my life," Éloïse explained. "Every day I pray for each person, one at a time." She pointed to a faded ivory fish whose eyes had been worn away. "This one is yours. I have kept you close to me for a long time."

I stayed silent as Éloïse put the beads away. She sighed audibly, not with frustration, but more likely fatigue. It seemed we had both grown tired of waiting for a pronouncement of the truth.

"David did want to protect you," she said. "But after a while the secret seemed to become the thing he was protecting. And I'm not sure he noticed. Once he tried to arrange a meeting for us. When that didn't work out, I pressed for him to try again but—"

"What meeting?" I asked. "Why didn't it work out?"

"I don't know," she said.

"It was me, wasn't it?"

She shook her head.

"I wasn't well? That's what he would have told you. He would have told you I was struggling with depression and anxiety."

She hesitated. "He explained that you were having a hard time."

"Did he tell you how I screwed everything up in Rome and we had to move to Chicago? Did he tell you what a mess I was? Is that why I didn't get to meet Celina before now?" Again, I wanted to tip backward onto the bed and shatter, but Éloïse's voice drew my spine tall.

"Gracie, you can be angry at your dad, at me, at Celina even. But not at yourself. Not for this."

I was coming undone. "He wanted me to stay focused, to keep moving forward. There were hard times, and he worried I'd get stuck. He didn't trust that I could handle it."

"More likely, he didn't trust *himself* to handle it."

"He didn't want to rock the boat, but what if that's what I needed? Twelve years and no one asked me what *I* wanted. No one said, 'Gracie, would you like to know your sister?'"

Éloïse lowered the volume of her voice, and again I was reminded that Celina was sleeping. "He wanted you to be happy. And while trying to secure happiness for another person may be a noble pursuit, I have never been convinced that it works. My happiest moments have been as spontaneous and scary as they are beautiful. Like the day Celina was born. Like you showing up yesterday. I'm not afraid of messy, Gracie. I'm deeply familiar with it. So, it may be late, but I'm asking you now. Would you like to know your sister? Would you like to know me? Because we would like that very much."

A little voice inside me whispered *yes*.

"I don't know if I want to know either of you," I said, attempting to be hurtful, but Éloïse only nodded with understanding.

She stood and moved toward the door. "I will be leaving shortly to go open the shop. You may stay as long as you like." The door closed with a click as she left the room.

I lay back on the bed and closed my eyes. The texture of darkness that rested against my eyelids resembled linen paper with many lines crossing in grid-like chaos. I could hear the radiator clanking and a small clock ticking discreetly on the corner of the bureau. The gentle sounds should have soothed me. But the throbbing of blood flowing into my head, aching behind my eyes, drowned everything out—eventually my thoughts, too.

I woke an hour later when Éloïse tiptoed into the room to place an extra blanket and a pair of sheepskin slippers on the wicker chair. I sat up, my thoughts slowly assembling themselves of their own volition. "I don't know what he thought of me." The words sounded as though they'd come from someone else. It took me a moment to realize they were mine.

"He thought you were exceptional," Éloïse said.

A tear leaked from the corner of my eye. Then another, and another, until a slow, silent stream coursed down both cheeks.

She sat down beside me and bent her shoulders toward mine. "Exceptional," she said again.

"I never apologized," I said. "And he's gone. Everyone is gone." All at once, I was sobbing. My chest heaved and a flood of tears poured down my constricted face. Unstoppable.

Éloïse wrapped her arms around me, and I did not stop her. "Gracie," she said, her tone resolved, "you were sexually assaulted. You have nothing to apologize for. You were a child." This acknowledgment was another unknown healing embrace.

The child inside me cried into the soft neck of Éloïse, the mother of my sister, the mother that was not mine. I had nearly always been a motherless child, but I would borrow this neck for a moment and imagine a story about a mother and her daughter that could hold my pain. That could forgive my father. That could forgive me.

I sobbed until my face was slick and swollen, until my breath was nothing more than a thin sputtering from my tightened chest. Then Éloïse looked into my bloodshot eyes and said with a heat that nearly dried my skin, "Do not abandon yourself. The past does not have any power over you. Do you understand? Only you have power over this. And you will be *victorious*."

———

When I walked into the kitchen that morning, Celina was eating a bowl of cereal at a small wooden table, and Claude was curled up in a patch of sun by the sink. "*Bonjour, ma sœur*," she said when she saw me, clearly thrilled to utter the word *sister*. "I'm so glad you came back."

She braced her crutches to her arms and got up to pull something from the cupboard. The kitchen cabinets were lacquered in smoky green and topped with thick butcher block countertops. Delicate white tiles lined the walls in a pearl sheen, and copper pots hung above a small vintage stove. Hand-painted terra-cotta plates decorated one wall with images of animals and wildlife, like artistic snapshots of nature. Celina poured tea into a mug the color of sunrise and handed it to me, then she took a seat at the table. I followed suit.

"Sugar?" she asked, after scooping some from a porcelain bowl onto her cereal.

"Yes. Thank you."

She pushed the sugar bowl toward me.

"You look like him," she said. "The lines across your forehead when you're surprised—he had those same ones. Mine are smaller." She lifted her brow to show me a gentle wave.

I managed to spill more sugar onto the table than into my cup. "I've never much liked those lines on me," I told her.

She studied my face a minute more. "You're not sure you want to be here, huh?"

"Sorry. I'm still working it all out."

"It's okay."

"Aren't you . . . aren't you mad at him?" I asked after a moment. "I would have liked to have known you when you were a baby."

"Well, Mom says I was a difficult baby, so maybe you were lucky to miss that part." Clearly Celina had been given a lot more time to process the news of not being an only child. She took a bite of cereal so large that there was nothing to be heard but crunching for a whole minute. "You're a dancer," she said, once she'd gotten it all down.

"Yes."

"I'm obviously not." She gestured to her legs. "But I'm artistic."

I realized then that she was searching for connections—similar lines on our foreheads and creativity in our veins. "You're a talented artist," I told her.

"Thank you. Do you like art?"

"I do," I said vaguely, and I watched her take another bite. "Are those your books?" I asked, pointing to a colorful stack on the counter.

"Yep," she said, once her mouth was again free. "My mom makes me read them all. She's my teacher right now. Middle school wasn't exactly a great fit."

"Were they . . . mean to you?"

"It's fine," she said. "I don't mind not going to school. At least not right now."

Celina took another large bite of cereal; I sipped my tea and shook my foot under the table. Claude interrupted the awkward silence by positioning himself between us and tilting his head at me with curiosity.

"He likes you," she decided. "He doesn't like everyone. We found him in the alley four years ago. We couldn't find his owners, and he refused to go to the neighbors' when they offered to take him. So now he's Claude, and I can't imagine life without him."

Claude rolled lovingly across Celina's feet in agreement.

"I always wanted a dog," I told her. "But I moved around too much to ever keep a pet."

"Dad said you lived in six countries by the time you were my age." She relayed this enthusiastically, but it felt like an inequitable truth.

I finally got the nerve to ask. "Did he come here a lot?"

"A few times a year, I guess. Like a special weekend here or there. He'd come for dinner, and we'd watch soccer or something. Sometimes we'd play chess."

I pushed fallen granules of sugar into a neat pile with one finger and allowed myself to imagine that. "He taught me to play too."

"Yeah. He told me that you were better than him at the game, that he thought you could visualize the board in your mind, and that the pieces were like dancers that you could organize. I'm not that good."

It had been a long time since I'd played chess and even longer since I'd played with my dad. I was quickly realizing that it was possible to be mad at him and miss him at the same time.

"We both liked the Museum of Fine Arts," she went on. "It's a lot of walking for me, so he'd push me in a wheelchair and pretend he was a tour guide. He'd use this funny voice."

Immediately I knew the one she meant. "Was it high pitched and nasal?"

"Yes! It sounded like this." She demonstrated in a falsetto tone: "Helloooo, madame. Would you like to see the modern collection?" Her face was pinched tight with an air of importance.

"Why yes," I replied, giving the intonation a shot. "Lovely day for an outing."

"That's it!" Celina let out a laugh infectious enough to make me smile.

"He used that voice sometimes when we were out shopping. Or doing anything that felt a little boring," I told her.

"Yes," she said. "It drove me crazy sometimes, but I also loved it."

"Exactly."

I stirred my tea. She chewed her cereal. Then she asked, "Would you like to see my room? I mean, it's not anything special, but I do have a hamster and some cool art stuff."

I was ready to politely agree, but there was something about all this that felt particularly uncanny. I stilled my shaking foot with a thought: "You know Celina, I was about your age when I moved away from here. Hanging out with you is weirdly like picking up where I left off."

"*Good* weird?"

I hesitated, but only because I was surprised with how clear the answer felt. "Yeah, good weird," I said.

Her face lit up. "You know what would be fun? Do you want to bake cookies?"

My reticence was slowly eroding. "We could give that a try."

"Chocolate chip?" Celina rose from her chair. "Let me see if we have the stuff."

She found the eggs and butter in the refrigerator and the flour and chocolate chips in the pantry. I made the discovery of a small bottle of vanilla extract in a high cabinet.

Together we measured out the ingredients. She packed flour into a ceramic cup. I whipped eggs in a mixing bowl. We rolled dough between our palms into perfectly round shapes and lined them up on greased cookie sheets. The ceremony gave way to a light conversation between two chocolate enthusiasts, and when the recipe was complete, we sat together at the little table sipping our tea and welcoming the aroma lifting through the room.

By the time the oven dinged and announced that the cookies were done, an even greater alchemy had begun.

21

COOPER

I was walking into Chicago City Hall when my phone pinged with a text message from Mark Schaffer. The average person gets sixty interruptions a day—one interruption every eight minutes, or about seven interruptions every hour. Lately, Mark Schaffer was responsible for about seventy percent of my interruptions. But he was out of town interrupting something else in Montreal, and I figured I could respond to his text when I felt like it.

The marble-arched entrance hall was no warmer than the weather outside, but I was dressed for a day of meetings and already sweating under the collar as I waited in a thick line. The headline that morning was partly to blame. I waited forty minutes, skimming the rest of the newspaper, before I got someone to see me.

Her name tag read Meg, but she looked more like a Margaret. Her hair was cut bluntly just above the puffed sleeves of her cable-knit sweater, and her oversized circular glasses made her eyes appear larger than I suspected they were.

"Good morning, Meg, I'm Daryl Cooper, here to see someone in the buildings department."

"Who is your appointment with?" she asked.

"I don't have an appointment this morning, but I won't take up much time. I just need to have a quick chat with someone about a building record."

"Are you a contractor?"

"No ma'am."

She tilted her head to one side as if waiting for me to say more. When I did not, she asked, "Are you inquiring about a public building, sir?"

"Well, one that means a lot to the public. Fidelis. The Abrams Building."

The vertical line above Meg's large glasses increased in depth with her perplexity.

I sighed and fished the morning paper out of my leather bag. Slapping it on the counter in front of her, I pointed to where the creased black-and-white print displayed the headline: One of Chicago's Oldest Buildings Faces New Uncertainties.

"Have you heard the news, Meg? It says here that Carl Abrams believes the land is worth more than the structure. That repairing it would be financial suicide. It says he sold it to a small real estate company."

She stared at me blankly.

"This interests me. It interests a lot of people. And I'd like to speak to someone who can tell me who the real estate group is and if they plan to tear down this historic building and replace it with an apartment complex. Or a parking garage."

Clearly, Meg was not hip to the controversy around the Fidelis fire, but she was not going to admit as much. She shuffled some papers around on her desk, jabbed a few keys on her keyboard, and came back with, "All I can tell you is that it's under review for a permit."

"Okay, but what kind of a permit?"

"I'm sorry?"

"Is it a new build permit? A renovation permit? Are they after restoration or demolition?"

Meg shook her head. "I'd have to put you in touch with someone in permits to say for sure."

"That would be great. Who can I talk to in permits?"

She studied her computer screen for one, two, maybe three minutes. Finally, "I can make you an appointment with Lewis Chan on November tenth at two o'clock."

"November tenth? That's not for weeks."

"It's a busy time of year, Mr. . . ."

"Cooper. Thanks, but I plan to get answers long before November." I put my card on her desk. "Call me if you can be of assistance."

I'd wasted an hour, but this was not a dead end. It was a detour. Information isn't something a person can possess. It's always out there. You just have to know where to look.

Permits take months. My buddies in the trades were often waiting on permits before they could bulldoze or lay pipe. And if there were plans for Fidelis, there were plenty of people who already knew about them. By six p.m. I'd likely be able to find one or two of those people at Richard's, a dive bar icon in the Fulton River District. Somewhere wafting through the cigarette smoke and Sinatra songs, I was sure to find an answer. I didn't actually think that I could stop Fidelis from being torn down. I'm not delusional. This was damage control. I wanted to get in front of it. Griffin would read that article and imagine the worst. If it was a renovation, I wanted to be able to tell him. And if it was going to be a demo, well, I wanted to find a way to soften the blow.

I read the text from Mark, something about the Simmons case, nothing urgent, and scanned through the rest of my emails and phone calls while I headed up South LaSalle Street. I still hadn't heard back from Jackie Marley, but there was a lot of day left. Something significant would come through. I would have put money on it.

22

GRIFFIN

I read the *Chicago Tribune* online every morning, so I saw the headline before Cooper texted me. Abrams had chosen money over history.

I found a pub and ordered an eye-opener. Whiskey, brown-sugar syrup, cold-brew coffee, and a stout beer. The bartender fixed the concoction fast and focused. It was early and there was only one other person in the place—an older guy who looked up briefly from his sudoku puzzle when my phone buzzed on the bar.

Cooper wrote: *I'm sure you heard. But I don't think the news is all bad.*

His subtext was obvious. He was trying to manage my reaction, dampen my rage, in typical brotherly fashion. I texted: *You think there's a chance the company he sold it to will restore it? Abrams says financial suicide.*

I watched the three little dots vacillate, and then read: *Abrams is an idiot.*

That much was true. I wrote: *He had hair stylists as tenants. He went about it all wrong.*

Cooper ended it with: *Go set things right with Gracie and just get on back here.*

The bartender put my drink in front of me. I hoped it would be a hearty elixir.

"Whatcha reading?" he asked. He had the energy of a guy at bat. He looked like he could have been a former ballplayer too, gone soft in places.

"The news."

"No wonder you look so beat. It's all bad news these days. Scary shit out there."

Scary, yes. And until now, Fidelis had been my safe haven. A place to go when things got scary. It had been that way ever since the eighth grade, the year things turned for the worse. I knew when Mom missed an after-school meeting with me and my math teacher that she was declining. I was afraid that if I went home, she would ask about my day as if nothing was out of the ordinary. I couldn't bear it, so I went to Fidelis instead. I sat in the atrium on the cold marble floor and stared at all those desperate pleas tucked into the wall. It gave me comfort knowing that the messages had come from people who'd walked in on a bad day, just like me. I didn't know if anything had improved for anyone, but just knowing that so many people bothered to name what they needed made me feel like I was going to be okay. I pulled my math notebook from my backpack and tore a blank triangular corner from a word problem page. With a number two pencil from my pencil box, I wrote: *Please bring my mother back. I need her. Thank you, Beau Griffin.* Then I stood and tried to decide where I should wedge the paper into the wall. I wondered if it mattered. I chose an uncrowded seam on the back left side. My hand trembled as I pressed the paper into the crevice. I rested my head against the cold stone and spoke the words aloud, hoping this might make my message stick. There were lots of days after that when I would go and sit with my back against the arch. The idea that Fidelis held all that pain for other people made me feel less ashamed of the pain that I carried inside myself. It was my place. It was a part of me. But when I went back to the wall after the accident, I didn't go for myself. I went for the people whose prayers were on that wall. We all needed Fidelis. I had wanted to make it right, and the idea of it being knocked down to the ground nearly knocked me over.

"You a Canadiens fan?" the bartender asked.

"Sure. Unless they're playing the Blackhawks," I said.

"In town for work?"

I shook my head.

"Play?"

"Not exactly."

"Well, if you're lost, I'm not sure this city can redirect you. I came here three years ago for a vacation and I'm still here."

"Must be a good gig."

"A good woman. Thinks I'm the answer to her prayers. Scares the shit out of me." He swiped the bar top with a wet rag. "How about you?"

"Newly single."

"I don't know how my girlfriend stands me, really. She's beautiful. Meanwhile, I have a roll of back fat that's like an awning for my pants. I think some hair is growing out of a mole back there too."

I was beginning to like this guy.

"Could be worse," he said. "I went to a reunion a few months ago, and I was the only guy who didn't have to unbutton his suit jacket *and* his pants when he sat down. But I'm not one of those dudes who's like, 'I'll have the double burger with kale garnish and a quinoa bun.' Fuck that. I'll eat what I want. I'll exercise too, but it really gets in the way of my drinking." He laughed. "And I won't give up the late-night social hour until I'm responsible for other humans. Babies are coming or Lisa's going. That much I know. The other day she thought I was checking out another woman's cleavage, but honest, I was looking at the baby carrier strapped to her chest and wondering if I could get one of those things over my back fat."

I stuck my hand out. "Name's Griffin."

He took my hand and shook it. "Dean. Nice to meet you. Another one?"

I nodded and he filled my glass.

Thirty minutes later I was back out on the cobblestones. The sign in the window of the local flower shop indicated that it wouldn't be open for another hour. It would have been nice to offer Gracie a small apologetic bouquet, even if it infuriated Mark. But waiting out in the cold was not the penance I had in mind for my morning.

There was a coffee shop nearby, and through the window I could see the barista cheerfully arranging pastries in the case. I went inside.

"Bonjour. What can I get you?" she asked.

"I don't suppose you have any donuts?"

"We have éclairs."

"I'll take four." It wasn't conventional, but it would do.

———

When I arrived at the home of Éloïse Fournier hoping to find Gracie, Celina was in the front room stretching on the floor with a middle-aged woman in a jogging suit—her physical therapist, I assumed. They pointed me to the back garden.

The garden was modest but still holding on to some of its leaves despite the change in weather. There was a small patio, and Gracie was pacing the length of it. She went still when I stepped out onto the brick. I took a breath but all that came out of me was, "Hi."

"Hi," she offered back.

"I wanted to see if you were okay."

She dropped onto the garden bench, and to my astonishment, made room for me beside her. I sat down and handed her the box from the coffee shop. "They're French donuts. A peace offering."

She studied the box in her lap, and I realized I didn't know what was supposed to happen next. Finally, she said, "The word on the street is that you didn't swing first."

This was encouraging. I thought about launching into a recap, but then reconsidered.

"What did you say?" she asked.

"How do you mean?"

"What did you say that made him so angry? It had to have been something pretty awful."

This was a tough one. "Uh, basically . . . what I said was that I didn't think he was . . . good enough for you. I'm sorry. He works with Cooper, and I may have heard a thing or two that rubbed me the wrong way. Anyway, things got a little intense, and . . ."

She dropped her head into her hands. "He's a shit, and I'm an idiot."

"No. Not the second part," I corrected.

"I always saw the good in him." She studied my face. "Have you ever done that with someone? Seen only the good parts?"

She didn't give me time to answer.

"I won't be going back with him."

I wanted to clarify, so I spoke slowly. "You left Mark?"

"Another sodding surprise courtesy of Montreal."

"We're really going to have to turn things around," I admitted. "What happened?"

"I'm not exactly sure, but in the end, I think it was something to do with control. He called me an hour ago, sure I'd change my mind and still leave with him. Can you believe that?" I absolutely could. "I don't suppose you'd still let me drive back with you?"

I didn't hesitate. "Of course."

"Are you sure?"

"What could go wrong?"

She laughed, but then her face grew serious. "Griffin, what you said in the restaurant, about not being sure if you're glad you met me or if you wished we'd never crossed paths—"

"It had been a long day. I'm sorry. I wasn't thinking," I said, hoping to conceal my feelings for her.

"It's just, I don't want to complicate your life. And it seems I have a knack for such things."

"You haven't," I told her, though she had *definitely* complicated my life. Mostly, I was happy about it.

"Friends?" she asked, the way one might call a truce.

"Wilder, we're in this together, remember? No matter what it is or what comes our way." She grinned. "Sure has been a surprising start to the trip, though."

"Right? I have a sister!"

I mimed a head explosion.

"I was ready to hate her, or at least resent her, but I can't. She's kind of wonderful. Éloïse too. It's a lot to process."

"I can imagine."

"I guess I will get to know them this week. And hopefully still prepare the greatest solo performance of my life."

"A light week."

She snorted a laugh. "I just hope I don't show up to the theater next Thursday and embarrass myself all over again. If that is to happen, then there will be very little point of me. I'll have lost my raison d'être."

"No way. I can think of ten plausible reasons off the top of my head why you must exist. You pulled me out of my miserable routine. That's got to count for something." I got up to seek a little shade from an olive tree. "I read in the paper that Abrams sold Fidelis," I said, maybe feeling the need to tell someone. Or specifically, to tell her.

"Griffin, I'm so sorry. Do you know what they plan for it?"

I stuffed my hands in my pockets and surveyed the brick under my feet. "No. I'm sure Cooper is trying to figure that out as we speak. I figure when I get home, I'll poke around and see what's up. I'm sure my pop will have a lot to say about it too."

"Your pop?"

"It meant a lot to them, my mom and pop. Anyway, I don't know what will happen but it doesn't look good."

"Well," she said after a moment, "a few things may be falling apart . . ."

"A few."

"But at least we have these!" She lifted the bakery box in her lap as if it were holy. "Now, are you going to explain how you know about my love of éclairs?"

"A lucky guess," I confessed.

"I'd sworn off junk food, Griffin, but I believe the last twenty-four hours call for an exception."

"Amen."

So, Gracie and I sat together in the garden, eating French donuts and watching the sun lift in the eastern sky.

———

That afternoon, I gave Gracie and Celina a lift over to the LeClair Studio and Gallery. "This Wilder daughter is actually going somewhere," Gracie said when we were in the car. "She's about to have her first local art showing." We were sitting at a traffic light. I twisted around to Celina in the back seat and gave her a high five.

"What is it you make?" she asked after seeing where my skin was rough and calloused.

"Woodwork. Cabinetry, mantels, that sort of thing," I said, accelerating as the light turned green.

"Do you use big saws and sanders and stuff like that?"

"Yep."

"You have the hands for it."

Years ago, my mother had told me that I'd inherited my grandfather's hands. "Good for playing the guitar, lifting children, and fixing things," she'd noted with affection in her voice. My grandfather had been famous for those things.

"You can park over there," Celina said, pointing to an empty space a short walk from the gallery. I backed the Falcon in and then jumped out to help her from the car.

Gracie, Celina, and Mrs. LeClair got right to work discussing where the paintings would hang on the walls in the main room of the gallery. My plan had been to visit Bonsecours Market that afternoon, but I found myself lingering with my hands in my pockets. "Let me know if I can help," I said to Mr. LeClair.

He was mumbling to himself from behind the desk. He pulled out a box of light bulbs with a proud, "Aha!" Then he was dragging a ladder out of a closet. I felt ridiculous just standing there.

"Where do you want it?" I asked, lifting the end of the ladder and helping him haul it toward the middle of the room. He pointed and I set it up.

"Thanks, son," he said. The tenor of his voice and the way he called me *son* reminded me of my old man. Back when he was still full of gusto.

I helped Mr. LeClair change half a dozen light bulbs, which could have been an awkward task to share with a man I'd never met, if it hadn't been for our shared love of hockey. It came up when I noticed a picture of a young guy in a hockey jersey sitting in a modest frame on the corner of the desk. When I asked, he explained that his son Alex had played in high school, and I told him about how I'd almost tasted a championship a few times.

When the light bulbs were all burning bright, I helped Mr. LeClair secure a loose floorboard. He held the plank while I drove the nails. When we'd finished that, we spackled a few holes in the wall, sanded them, and touched them up with paint. Mr. LeClair shook my hand and patted me on the back. "You're a good man," he said. And I felt oddly useful.

"So is Alex still playing hockey these days?" I asked.

Mr. LeClair offered a stiff smile. "He went into the service and died seven years ago." This left us both in a cloud of disbelief. I told him how sorry I was, but he only said, "We enjoyed him while he was here. And we'll enjoy you while you're here too, son." Never had I seen a sincerer look on a man's face. But I wasn't this man's son. This wasn't even a page in my own story. I'd only moved a ladder and hammered some nails.

When I was a kid, I thought I might one day build buildings; cities, even. If I was lucky, if I could find the right opportunity, I'd turn my drawings into walls and spires. Instead, I found a safe path in renovation. Now, watching young Celina with her eyes full of wonder, Gracie following her heart, and Mr. LeClair still open when he could have shut the world out, I could see that not everyone went searching for happiness, hoping to get lucky. Some people just created it. I'd been very busy. I'd made a lot of things. But I'd not made anything that could bring a man to say, *I'll enjoy you while you're here*. I'd not done anything so important.

———

Toward the end of the afternoon, Gracie found a painting of Celina's that reminded her of the old barn she used to play in as a kid. When she asked Celina about it, she confirmed that it was the very same one.

"He still has the Blue Tilting House? With the old barn out back?" Gracie asked, wide-eyed. They were huddled around the back table, standing over a pile of Celina's work.

"He loved it there," Celina explained. "Maybe we can go out and see it together."

Gracie lingered beside the painting. She sounded reticent when she said, "Yes, maybe we can."

I went to warm up the car while the girls finished their goodbyes. I sat scrolling through pictures in my phone of Keira before we split and Fidelis after the fire, torturing myself with clear visuals of the wreckage. It was something I did now and again, maybe out of disbelief or maybe for the purposes of punishment. This time when I reviewed the slide show of catastrophe, I was sure of one thing: I was tired of being a worthless set of hands and nobody's hero.

23

ÉLOÏSE

As a child, I had an elder teacher who taught me about the history of indigenous peoples, our ties to nature, and our traditional methods of healing. She instructed our class to study the four directions of the medicine wheel, the symbolism of sacred animals, and ceremonial plants. I was a devout student and stayed past dismissal one afternoon to seek approval on my project. She examined what I'd written on yellow and red paper and nodded her praise. Then she said, "You must learn a great deal about what is delivered from water. This is strong in you." I asked her how she could be sure. "It is in the emotion behind your eyes," she said, and I knew it was true.

I studied the interconnectivity between the physical, emotional, mental, and spiritual worlds, until I could see people through the lens of the elements, how earth, water, fire, and air fuel us from within and point us toward our own unique balance. If my mother, the storyteller, had been the one who taught me to listen, then it was my elder teacher who taught me to see.

In those days, my mother took her direction from fire. Her skin and her temperament were the temperature of August. My father had followed water—troubled waters that moved him away from those he loved.

David Wilder had so much rock. Steady in mind, stubborn in spirit, private in nature. The night he showed up at my doorstep to thank me for making the blackbird, I invited him in out of the damp air. He had a quality of someone who knew where he had been. He spoke about Gracie, her love of dance, her smile like her mother's. He asked me about my life in Montreal and thoughtfully listened. Later, after we'd talked for several hours, I invited him into my bed. And for a night, I was held.

I was sure I'd never see him again. Yet, two months later, I found myself looking up his number and giving him the news. "I don't expect anything from you," I explained. "But I thought telling you was the right thing to do."

When Celina was placed in my arms moments after birth, I saw a child with wind. I cradled her to my chest and marveled at her silken hair and her smooth complexion, both lighter than mine. Her perfectly round head, still dewy from her delivery into the light, fell back into my hand as she squawked like a baby eagle. I saw a little being that I could not identify as my own. She was a part of me I did not yet know. She was an ever-present dawn, a perfect spring day, imagination and vision swaddled in tender flesh. How had I been charged with the task of caring for her? I began a great adventure into the unknown.

She was born with a partially exposed spinal cord and a mild case of cerebral palsy, a nonprogressive paralysis caused by developmental defects in the brain. The doctors could not explain the exact effects, but they predicted she would struggle to walk. I called David to tell him of her diagnosis. Again, he appeared at my doorstep. We were never a family, but that day he held me while I cried, and a bond was cemented between us.

Caring for Celina began like a business for David. He researched treatments and challenged doctors while I took her to her appointments and raised her on my own. On her third birthday, David came for one of his occasional visits. When she greeted him at the door, his whole face lifted, and it was obvious that he loved her. Maybe he could see that she was the air of an eternal spring.

When Gracie walked into my shop that blustery day in October, no longer a little girl in a velour coat or a picture in a frame, but a grown woman, I was overwhelmed with the notion that she was made of the same matter that I felt inside myself. She was not mine, but she and I both belonged to mighty waters. Gracie moved with the ebb and flow of life and wanted to find understanding. I believed I knew how to support her.

The morning that she spoke of her pain, I tried to become a vessel that could hold it for her. And later that night, as she sat at the little table in my kitchen across from Celina, Griffin to one side and me to the other, I watched her lift her chin and bravely seek harmony. She listened to Celina tell stories about Claude as she fiddled with the key that hung from a gold chain around her neck—a key I feared would not unlock the passageway to her father that she greatly needed. When we had all had our fill, Gracie cleared her plate and followed Celina into the living room to play old records, and I let out a breath made of relief. Together, we had filled the space at the table. It was a small victory in a journey of love where the waters run deep.

Griffin appeared unsettled, and his attention remained on Gracie even when she'd left the room. I did not yet know Griffin, but all signs pointed to the physical world, as if he had been made with rock and silence, midnights and unlocked insight. Griffin filled a doorway or a glance like a great animal from the tundra. But it was clear he was not in his power. Most people are not and don't want to be. It's easier to play small than it is to create who it is we are meant to become. I knew this to be true because I had avoided my empowered self many times before.

Griffin was robust in stature, but it was as if some deeper part of him was actively bleeding. His liveliness faded in and out. As he stood there scraping his dinner plate above the open trash bin, he seemed to vibrate at a low frequency that did not match his presence. Maybe he'd once become so angry that he'd drawn a series of storms into his life to affirm his anger, and now he carried this as his job, his role, his affliction.

But Griffin had a luminescent face. His eyebrows lifted even when his shoulders slumped, as if he expected love to come walking into the room at any moment. I decided that I liked him, and I invited him to sit back down at the table while Gracie and Celina played music in the living room. I pulled out a bottle of wine and three stemmed glasses from the cupboard.

"She doesn't drink," he said, and I placed one of the glasses back, all the while wondering where this boy's pain was leading him and why my kitchen was on his path. Were we just another storm sent to uphold misperceptions, or was a Gracie-shaped door opening toward something as bright as the quizzical expression on his face? I poured the red wine, which spilled into Griffin's glass and then mine, reminding me again of all the wounds present at the table, not to be discounted but instead poured out.

"Thank you for dinner," he said when I handed him a glass.

"Celina says she'd like to bring Gracie to visit David's country house so she can use the barn as a rehearsal space. I need to work tomorrow, but Celina said you offered to go with the girls. I can't imagine that's what you'd want to do with your vacation time."

He rested his forearms on the table. His back curved like a spoon. "No, it's fine. I'm up for anything."

"I've never let Celina go to the country house with anyone other than me. She would need help. From what I hear from Caroline and Ames LeClair, you're the kind of man who might be able to lend a hand." I intended to get to know Griffin better before I made up my own mind.

"Happy to. As long as Gracie doesn't take me for a third wheel." He rested his jaw on a weary fist.

"You must be great friends to go on such a trip together."

The corners of his mouth bent with amusement. "We barely knew each other when we set out a couple of days ago."

"Does she know how you feel about her now?"

His eyes flickered with a rim of light like the borders of dark moons. "Is it that obvious?" He didn't wait for a response. "She's going through a lot right now."

"The heart pays no mind to timing, does it? Maybe for the better. Maybe just to piss us off." I winked, and he smiled faintly.

"Whatever feelings I have for her, I'm pretty sure they're not mutual, and we want different things. So, I'll just finish out the week, then go home and pull my shit together. Excuse the expression." He paused. "That's more than you asked."

"We're just talking." A friendly folk song floated in from the other room. "What do you mean when you say you want different things?" I asked.

"We're just different people on different paths."

"But then that's always true of any two people. And sometimes *different* can really work. Nobody has all the tools. We have to borrow from each other to move forward with life's projects."

"Well, I don't want to mess anything up."

"For Gracie?"

He shrugged.

I swirled the wine in my glass just to watch it move. "I've been asking myself if Gracie came here following the blackbird myth or if she came here following a deeper knowing in her heart. Now I ask you the same thing. Are you following a myth? One that says you are no good? Hoping you'll prove yourself wrong?"

"Is that what you think?"

"Everyone carries a myth. I'm only just getting to know you, but I see someone who is willing to help people he hardly knows. But maybe not himself. Because maybe you don't feel deserving?" I felt a little sorry then. Years of listening to stories and seeing what turns them upside down had made me rather outspoken.

"I have a habit of letting people down," he said. "Maybe it's better to be on my own."

I set my glass down, unsure if I should say anything more. But he looked so melancholy. "No one gets anywhere on their own," I told him. "That chair you're sitting in right now—there are at least ninety people involved in getting you there. Ultimately you make the choices that determine where you're going, and you can take responsibility for that. But you are not on your own. So, why not be with the people you care about?"

He bobbed his head in accord.

"Beau—I've learned your first name, it's a good name by the way, French even—you can't rule out a possibility until you've given it a chance. Take it from a woman whose life has never gone as expected. Don't give up on what you want before you try. I bet you'll surprise yourself."

"I take it you don't believe in self-preservation?" he asked wryly.

I laughed. "Ah, well there's that. But we're talking about life and love. And those things tend to hurt a little."

He bent his head over his glass like one might fold a bad hand in a poker game. "So, what then?"

"Follow your heart."

"And if it hurts like hell?"

"Then it hurts like hell. But you'll have tried, and that is never fruitless."

He sighed.

"We all go through shit, Beau. We're all blessed and broken like the bread at this table. The question isn't whether you'll get hurt again. The question is what the hell are you going to do about it? Feel defeated? Or find a new way?" I leaned over and refilled his glass.

"You know, I have a feeling that people go to therapy for years to be told what you just said in about five minutes over a bottle of Pinot Noir."

"I'll send you the bill," I teased. I got up and went to the sink. I let the water run until it was hot and then one by one, I began soaping the stack of dishes with a yellow sponge.

Griffin tapped his fingers on the armrests of his chair. "Éloïse, were you scared when you found out you were pregnant with Celina?"

The question surprised me. "Yes. Absolutely. But I've never done anything worth doing that didn't scare me. And it felt like the right kind of scary." I could revisit those first days in an instant. The swelling and tightening of my belly, the daily nausea. And later, fragile fingers gripping mine. The warmth of newborn Celina in tiny cotton pajamas against my chest, her legs tied up in a bow. Even in the wake of knowing how hard her life would be, that there would be surgeries and therapies and challenges to surmount, my fear had been cloaked in desire. "I suppose each person knows the good kind of scared and the bad kind of scared," I tried to clarify. "Celina was the good kind for me."

Griffin got up from his chair and joined me at the sink. He picked up a dish towel and began wiping the clean plates. "Were you in love with David?" He was asking the questions now.

"We were friends. Lovers, once."

"But you've been in love?"

I nodded.

"What happened?"

Deep down in my belly I felt emotions swirling up like old friends I'd gone through war with. I welcomed them. "His name was Oliver. He was a biologist with a passion for the life in the river. He moved to Quebec City fourteen years ago. After I turned down his marriage proposal. My mother was dying, and I could not follow him."

"Wow. And he couldn't stay here with you?"

I leaned deeper into the question and told Griffin the story.

―――

I met Oliver in the dead of winter. I had come down with a fever and was trying to get home from the shops, when I fell in front of his apartment building. He offered to get me home, but I could hardly see to point the way. I passed out the minute my head hit his couch and woke with a cold rag on my head, drenched in sweat. And there he was, this handsome man sitting across from me saying, "You had me worried."

By the time he walked me to the street the next morning, I was sure I was falling in love with him. It seemed sensible to blame the fever, but I knew I could not. I agreed to meet him the following afternoon.

I was approaching the area in front of Notre-Dame-de-Bon-Secours, what is commonly called the Sailors' Church, when I heard a voice coming from above. Oliver was in the parapet. He was leaning on the wall and calling out my name. Looking up at him, I could only think of a lighthouse shining in the middle of my life.

I climbed the stairs to meet him. "How is my patient?" he asked when I reached the top. And then he kissed me. It felt like Oliver was made of fire; his warmth was what made him so exceptional, so unlike any other man I'd known.

When he was offered an ideal research position at Laval University in Quebec City, he got down on one knee and asked me to go with him. But my mother was sick. Oliver offered to stay in Montreal with me, but I said no. I didn't want him to give up his passion and live to resent me for it.

I never saw him again.

—

Griffin was watching me, utterly perplexed. I took the dry stack of dishes and placed them on a shelf in the cupboard. "We think when we're young that something easier or better or timelier will come along," I said. "But don't do what I did." I shut the cupboard door firmly. "Don't throw what you want aside because you aren't sure if you're worth it."

We waited for the room to settle. "You regret it?" he boldly asked.

"Celina is my lighthouse now."

"You don't get lonely?"

I pushed the question away. "I do not regret the path I took. I only wish I took a few more chances."

"Sure would be easier if we could see fifty miles down the road."

I laughed. "Isn't that the damn truth?"

He returned to the table and to his glass of wine. "Have you ever tried to find him?"

"No," I said, staring out the kitchen window into the darkening sky. "But I'll admit, I never pass the Sailors' Church without looking up into the parapet, hoping I might see him. Sometimes I even climb the stairs to the top. Everything seems a bit clearer from up there." I wiped my hands on a dish towel and sat back down across from him. "Oliver is probably married with loads of kids. And I like the notion of him having that kind of happiness."

"That's good of you. I'd think it would be easier to picture him having grown bald, fat, and boring. Like you dodged a bullet."

"He did have a receding hairline."

"There we go," he said lightheartedly.

"But boring, he was not."

"How about overactive sweat glands? Or sleep apnea? Tons of snoring?"

I was laughing into my glass. "Oh, it's a horrible thing to lose a person."

Griffin's grin faded because there was nothing truer to say then.

Music drifted in from the living room, shifting our focus. "The records were his," I told him. "He loved music on vinyl. This is Puccini. 'Nessun Dorma' from *Turandot*."

"It's sad," he said of the melancholy voice filling the room.

"Sad, yes. But powerful, too. It's usually sung by a tenor, but here we hear it from a soprano. Gorgeous." It was the perfect sound for that night. Strong and wounded, like the rest of us. I sat back in my chair and took it in with my wine, and when the girls wandered back into the room, I could see quite clearly who was seated at my table.

24

GRIFFIN

Éloïse offered me the pullout couch. "So you don't have to scrounge for food in town," she said. Out of courtesy, I tried to argue. I didn't want to be in the way.

"It seems like I'm crashing a party," I said to Gracie.

"I'm crashing this party too," she pointed out. "I'll go with you to get your things from the hotel." Mostly I think she just needed a minute to clear her head, process the day. She wasted no time getting her coat.

"It's good of you to stay at the house," she said when we got in the car. "But I don't want you to feel obligated."

"I don't feel obligated," I said. I was happy about saving on the nightly fee, and I liked being near Gracie. "Just let me know if you need some space," I told her.

"I may have sworn off men, but *you* are welcome to stick around," she assured me.

"You've given up on men since this morning? You know, we're not *all* bad."

"Not all, certainly, but when I broaden the lens, it sure does seem to be quite a few." The Falcon took a long time to warm up, and she was shivering a little from the cold. "I had this idea for a big dance production this morning," she said. "It's the year 2045 or something, and women have sworn off men and banded together, become leaders and high priestesses. Sort of the reverse of how the Catholic church put celibate men in power in the twelfth century. Anyway, women are running the world, and there is peace throughout the land."

I was grinning. "I wouldn't let Mark get to you so much."

She sighed. "Yeah, it's probably a waste of energy."

"There are a lot of good guys out there. Attractive, too." I glanced over with a smile, but she didn't meet my gaze.

"I'm not sure I'm even all that attracted to men."

I figured she had to be joking. "What? Are you telling me you didn't feel something when we kissed?"

She covered her face with her hands. "Could we maybe go a day without talking about that?"

Damn, she was cute.

"What I mean is," she said, pulling her hands away, "it's not like it is in the movies when I'm with a guy. I don't get all . . . gaga."

"Gaga?"

"You know, head over heels, euphoric, smitten . . ."

"You're talking about chemistry."

"I guess so."

"Well, it just sounds like you've been with the wrong guys."

"It's more likely to do with me than everyone else. Part of me is just . . . broken."

I felt an ache in my chest; she'd been through so much. Still, she seemed far from broken. And I knew broken.

When we came to a red light, I said, "Look, I'm a guy, so take this with a grain of salt, but you know how in movies there are characters who are super-sexually charged, just looking to get laid? And then other characters who are charged by emotional connection, not just sex?"

She was nodding. Blushing, but nodding.

"Well, maybe you're more like the second one. And maybe to feel really . . . charged . . . or able to just let go, you need to feel really—"

"Safe," she said before I could finish.

"Yeah."

We sat there in silence for a moment, and then the light changed to green. I wanted to reach over and squeeze her hand, but the gap between our seats felt like a line that shouldn't be crossed.

When I saw a parking spot on the street near the hotel, I put the Falcon in reverse. "I'll just run in and grab my bags," I said, throwing my arm over the passenger seat and checking my blind spot. Gracie looked over at me then, and for a second it felt like we might be meeting at that invisible line. But someone honked for me to hurry, so I cut the wheel and backed the rest of the way in. Returning my arm to its neutral position, I threw the car into park.

"I'll go up with you," she said. "I'd rather not sit in the car."

———

The hotel lobby greeted us with a blast of heat and a flurry of activity. Gracie and I shrugged off our coats and carried them toward the elevator. When its steel doors slid open, we quickly entered its empty confinement. I jabbed the number three on the panel as six other people with large suitcases hurried into the elevator after us. We had to squeeze against the wall to make room for them, and because we'd been facing each other when the intruders forged in, Grace's face was practically pressed against me.

Instinctively I wanted to put my arms around her, shield her from the crowd, but I managed to keep my hands at my sides. As the other travelers fumbled with the elevator buttons and the doors finally closed, I could feel her hair brush my neck, her breasts graze my chest. The remaining space between us felt so ferociously energized that it also seemed to be bumping up against my defenses.

The doors opened on the second floor and two of our elevator companions wedged their way out. There was more room now, but Gracie didn't entirely back into it. Maybe only an inch or two. I felt a surge of dopamine rush through me, quickening my pulse. I had to remind myself that this was no time to demonstrate how I felt. Though I did let myself imagine it for a second—me obliterating the slip of space between us as I took her in my arms and kissed her the way I'd wanted to in the street that day. Like my life depended on it.

The elevator chimed with our arrival at the third floor. Seconds later the doors opened, and the four other passengers lumbered forward. I let myself lower my face toward Gracie's. She glanced up. Her skin was so smooth, her hair so soft. As strong as she was as a dancer, everything about her seemed soft. Her smile. Even her sweater was soft. As she turned toward the awaiting hallway, I wondered if she'd felt the molecules recklessly and wildly conjoining between us the way I had, or if for her that was soft too.

We noiselessly walked down the hall to my room. I swiped the plastic key card over the magnetic strip and pushed the door open, but we both hesitated. I hadn't thought this all the way through—its undertones. I mean, we were just grabbing my luggage, but we were also—correction, I was also—carbonated with sex hormones. And now I was walking into a beautiful hotel room with the one person I would want to be doing that with.

She stepped inside and idled near the door.

"I'll just be a minute," I said, grabbing a few loose items and stuffing them in my duffle bag.

"Are you sure you don't want to stay in this comfortable room, maybe meet someone at the bar with far less drama? I won't hold it against you. We could meet up in a couple of days."

"The room isn't all that comfortable," I said. "And I've already been to the bar. It was not without drama."

"Ha! You have a point there."

I finished packing up my things but couldn't help but notice how her eyes passed over the room.

"I just ran out of there this morning," she said while fidgeting with her necklace. "I took my things and ran. I never even told him about my sister. I'm really *not* good at intimacy. Ana tells me all the time. I don't let people in."

I stared at her, stupefied.

"I mean . . ." She seemed to backpedal. "Not usually. Funny, I seem to tell you every damn thing that comes to mind. Sorry, I don't know why I do that."

My words were as slow as my steps toward her. "I'm glad you feel safe with me, Gracie."

She seemed to take that in, its gravity, blinking up at me with awareness.

I wanted to dive into this moment like a pool of water and sink below the surface. I wanted to dive into her and everything about her. I didn't know if she felt the same, but I knew one thing for sure. We had chemistry.

I put an arm around her. "Let's go," I said. And we left Hotel William Gray.

25

GRACIE

When I woke, it took me a moment to remember where I was. The pale yellow comforter was my first clue, and the smell of pancakes was the second. Just the night before, Celina had requested that Éloïse make pancakes before she left for the shop. I sat up and caught a glimpse of myself in the bureau mirror. Long lines creased my right cheek from hitting the pillowcase way too hard, and my hair was monstrous. I tried patting it down, but it only sprung back larger. I gave up, slipped into Éloïse's sheepskin slippers, and shuffled toward the breakfast table.

Celina was abuzz with maple syrup and talk of our day trip to the Eastern Townships. "My mom said we can take the train out to the Willows so that Griffin doesn't have to drive," she chirped as I sat down with a plate of pancakes.

"The Willows?"

"It's what I call Dad's country house. In honor of the trees."

I had to admit that Celina had planned a lovely day for us. But I was feeling apprehensive about returning to that house. For me it held the last fragments of my childhood before everything changed. I might have objected to confronting it, had it not been for the key strung around my neck. I wanted to know if it was a match for the front door to the Blue Tilting House.

"Is Griffin up?" I asked.

"He left about an hour ago," Éloïse explained. "Said he was going for a run."

Less than ten minutes later, he was in the kitchen doorway, apologizing for his appearance: his face and arms dewy, his gray T-shirt clinging to his chest.

"Pancakes?" Celina offered him, holding up a plate.

"Thank you. I'm going to take a shower first. Gracie, you okay with the nine o'clock train?"

I self-consciously tucked my hair behind my ears and nodded. Everyone was acting as though this was normal behavior. As if sisters and pancakes and beautiful men who jog and make travel plans were regular things that just emerge like morning.

———

The Orford Express was a shiny silver-and-blue machine that hummed loudly as if warming up for a big performance. Celina took a seat by a window, and Griffin landed beside her with a thump. I took the seat that faced them, and we all watched out the window as people boarded the train.

Not long after we'd left the station, Celina said she was cold. Griffin put his coat across her lap as a blanket and made warm conversation about the countryside. I preoccupied myself with a view of giant pine trees under a gray sky and tried not to fidget in my seat.

"You okay?" Griffin asked after a while.

"I am," I told him, twitching my head back to the window.

"She has ants in her pants," Griffin said with a wink, and Celina laughed. He was so comfortable with her. I figured he must have other young people in his life, perhaps a cousin or a niece. "Are you warming up?" he asked her.

"A little." Her shoulders were drawn so tight that they concealed her strong, lean neck. She scooted closer to him in the seat.

"If I were a blanket, I'd wrap you up and make you warm," he said in a soft voice that I didn't recognize.

Celina smiled. "If I were chocolate, I'd make us some hot cocoa."

"Nice," Griffin said. "If I were a spaceship, I'd fetch you a bucket of sunshine."

"If I were a wishing well, I'd give you your wish."

Their exchange was so enchanting that part of me wanted to laugh in disbelief while the other part of me wanted to jump in and play the game.

"Well, if I were a garden, I'd grow you some flowers," Griffin said.

"Roses," Celina requested.

"Gardenias," I said, finally choosing to be a part of whatever this was. "White ones."

"Well, that's very specific. Okay, roses for Celina and white gardenias for you, Wilder," Griffin said, his eyes shining in my direction.

The taxi pulled up in front of the house, and the gravel crunched beneath my feet when I stepped out into the autumn air. Returning to this house felt like stepping into a river I'd once dipped into as a child. Old waters had run their course, and what filled the space now was a fresh unknown. I could not find the ring of rosebushes that had once bordered the circular drive like my own personal labyrinth. There were only withered sticks where blooms had once been. The house was still a pale blue Cape Cod with white shutters and a wrap-around porch. However, the porch beams seemed slimmer than I had remembered, and the house itself appeared less grand in size. Despite its ever-more-tilting disposition, it still had a cheerful white fence lacing the ground at its feet, and two dormer windows popped out of the roofline like bright eyes that had seen many things. Behind it, the bright red barn had faded to a wrinkled pink, but the willow trees on top of the hill were as tremendous as ever. Their leaves, an autumn yellow, glittered in the sunlight.

"I'll show you where the front door key is hidden," Celina exclaimed, leaning on her crutches and pulling her legs one at a time up the gravel drive with Griffin only steps behind.

I hurried to the front porch, imagining that my key would be a perfect fit for the front door. But when I tried the key in the lock, it would not budge.

"No dice?" Griffin asked when he reached the porch step.

"I guess it belongs to nothing." I tucked its mystery back against my chest.

Celina held up the spare she'd retrieved from the hood of a lantern on the garage. "Got it," she announced.

It had been fifteen years or more since I had stepped inside that house. I entered slowly, urging myself to be patient while I attempted to take in one solitary thing at a time. The familiarity of its pale wooden floors, its arched doorframes, and its vague scent of firewood surprised me. It was like stepping back in time. I stood frozen near the door, my bag still slung over my shoulder. Celina had to squeeze past me to get through the entryway.

"Great place," Griffin remarked, also wedging his way in behind me.

The house was cold and as silent as old books. I watched Celina switch on the thermostat in the hallway, and I had an unexpected hunger to be her size again, making a routine visit to the country and to the thermostat. To the simple pleasures that could fill an afternoon or a lifetime if you allowed it to be so. "It will take twenty minutes to warm up," she explained, and then she was going on about something in the kitchen. But I could not hear her. My eyes had met the frames that lined the hallway walls. I was far away in my mind when Celina brought Griffin back outside to see the barn.

It took me several minutes to understand what it was that I was seeing, and as the realization washed through me, I was immobilized. My father must have spared my old shoebox of film canisters from the trash bins when we cleaned out our lives and moved to Chicago. He'd developed pictures that I couldn't bear to see. He'd framed them and hung them on the walls of the country house that I couldn't bear to visit.

The images were oddly artistic, often pointing upward or even sideways. It had been so long since I'd seen a Christmas tree from its lowest bough or the light glowing inside a home at dusk from underneath the windowsill. I remembered the way the crystal in the dining room would catch the light; and how amazed I'd been watching the sun push through terrific storm clouds from my bedroom window. And all these moments were preserved behind clear glass.

I stood for a long time staring at a picture of my father laughing in front of the fireplace. I couldn't remember a time when I'd seen him that happy. He was smiling down into the lens of my camera with a glint in his eye that could only be affection. And there was one framed picture of me from when my father had borrowed the camera. I must have been thirteen years old—a fragile thing with a halo of frizz at the crown of my head and adolescent curls, courtesy of new hormones. I was sitting on the front porch, all legs and daydreams.

The house, the pictures, the overgrown fields outside, were vivid reminders of what had come and what had gone—my father and the child he'd once swung up into the trees and sat with on summer nights to catch fireflies. But there was something else drifting in through the open doorway—something powerful. It was a consciousness of what remained.

I was that child who had believed in love and harnessed beauty in photographs.

I was astonished at how full my heart felt as I drifted outside. My father had secured beauty in frames and secured love in time. In the hours that followed, I would come to find that I had been here all along and that he was *everywhere*. He was on the porch swing and in the rose garden, on the hillside and in the willows.

I walked toward the barn, trying to absorb all the details around me, not wanting to forget this time but instead frame this moment in my memory. The way the rose vines laced the eaves, the way the birds flew in *V* formation overhead, and then, the way Griffin stood on a ladder in the barn holding strands of Christmas lights.

The barn was designed to hold several stalls for horses, but for years it had only held dust and shafts of light, storage boxes and forgotten tools. Now also Griffin on a ladder in his element, full tilt. A thing of strange beauty.

"It sure will make it brighter for her," Celina said from where she was seated on an antique mounting block. I stood silently at the barn door. I could have made my presence known, but I was oddly content not to.

"This could be a great place for painting, too," Griffin called down to her. "How do you decide what you want to paint?"

"I guess I just see something, and then I paint it," she answered. "Sometimes I imagine it improved, and it changes halfway through. That's why my paintings aren't very realistic."

"That's what I like about them. You're not afraid to break the rules of scale or proportion."

"I guess I find a way to make what I see even better. Like when I drew this house, I made it lean even more to the side and I added a window in the attic and a balcony. Sometimes when I get here, I'm surprised when I don't see that window. Like I've remembered it wrong."

"I totally get that," Griffin said. He went about loosely wrapping strands of lights over the wooden beam. "There's this building back home that I've loved since I was a kid. I always thought it should be a community place where people could come to listen to music or hear great speakers, because when you stand in the center of the first floor and look up into the open space between the stairwells and balcony, you can see all the way to the roof. And if you say something, even softly, it reverberates. Like someone on the third floor might hear you. The sound in that place is incredible. And I used to imagine blasting out the staircases and the offices up above and being able to see every bit of every engaged column and all of the lancet window in the back. It was once a church, and one of the original pews is still in the atrium. It has this intricate detailing on the sides, and I always thought it would be cool to recreate some of those details and make comfortable seats for people to come and sit. And sometimes when I would walk in there, I'd half expect to see it the way I'd imagined it."

"Wow," Celina said. "You should tell someone your idea."

"Unfortunately, people don't believe the building is worth much. Not everyone has the vision to see things improve. Like you do." He climbed down the ladder and caught sight of me in the doorway. "There you are," he said. "Check this out." He took up the end of the cascading Christmas lights and plugged them into the outlet at the base of the wall. They glowed bright white. "Stage lights," he announced.

"They're . . . completely beautiful. And your idea for Fidelis," I said, still taking it in, "so beautiful too."

His face glowed like another strand of light.

"I think I should lie down," Celina said then, and Griffin and I both moved toward her. "It's just that my back is sore and lying flat helps."

She chose a bed of leaves behind the house. Griffin went inside in search of tea or coffee while I lay with Celina watching faint traces of clouds in the pale blue sky.

"I wish I had a hollow spine," she said after a while.

"Why on earth?"

"Because then I'd be able to fly like a bird."

I watched the sky for birds. "You sure I can't get you anything? A book maybe?"

"I'm fine," she assured me. "When I have to lie down like this I just paint. Not with brushes obviously, but in my mind."

"What do you paint?"

"Well, right now I'm going to paint willow trees."

"Can I paint too?" I asked, hesitantly.

She slanted her gaze in my direction and shrugged. "Okay. You can help me paint us sitting under the trees. I'll paint you wearing a yellow dress."

"Why yellow?"

"Because you seem yellowish," she said.

"And what color shall I paint on you?"

"How about green?"

"Like the fir trees."

"And the plume moss," she said. "I'm going to exaggerate the curls in your hair. Make them big and wild."

"Like a lion?"

"Like willow branches." Celina was quiet a moment before she went on. "We are on the hill together, and Dad is there too."

A chill ran up my arms. "He is?"

"Yeah." She smiled. "He's wearing a navy suit and getting ready to leave for work."

I could almost see him. "Does he look sad?" I asked.

"No," she said. "He's happy to see us together in his favorite place."

A tear trickled down my face as I tried painting my dad in my mind. "Celina, what side did he part his hair on?"

"The right, I think."

Yes. His face became vivid in my mind.

"Did he ever tell you that he loved you?" I dared to ask.

She considered that. "I don't think so, but I know that he did."

"You could just sense it?"

"Yeah. When it came to doctors and teachers, he always had advice on what I should do. But when I would ask him what I should paint, he'd say, 'well, now that's up to you.' He let me be me. Complicated, but creative me. That's how I know he loved me."

She made it sound so clear, so simple. I thought about my father's advice after I lost my position at Boden. I worried that he didn't care anymore which way I went. But perhaps I had heard him wrong. Perhaps he'd just wanted me to be me.

I watched Celina gaze at the sky, her imagination still fresh like a different season of my life. I could see her pain and her peace. I could see her crooked spine and her perfect heart. Her life was a fascinating paradox: a contrast between suffering and bliss. I was only just beginning to understand how to live in this space, in another dimension of possibility. Joy in a plume moss coat. Longing in a yellow dress with willow hair. Fresh paint from the hidden ground of love tracing patterns in the atmosphere.

She rolled her head toward mine and said, "I don't like that I'll never see him again. That's why I paint him every day in my mind, so I know then I will never forget." She blinked a few times. "I'm going to paint you too, Gracie."

I felt an avalanche of love for her. "You're not going to be without me."

She took my hand and squeezed.

By the time Celina and I got up from the field of bronze leaves, I could see something new within the embers of my father's life. The wind whipped around and revealed its presence like the green grass hiding below us: love. Celina was right, of that I was sure. My father had loved me. With quandary and determination, with carefully framed memories and high hopes for the future, he had loved me. Like a concealed gift with silk and crystal wings, love had been intended for me and was now making itself known.

—

That afternoon, I got to work on a dance for my audition. I tried to pace out steps in the barn, but my body hesitated in moving across the floor.

I was on the ground in a back rollover, all my weight on my arms, my legs isolated above me, when I heard, "Can't find your feet?" It was Griffin walking in with two mugs.

"What did you say?"

"You're upside down."

I righted myself and sat cross-legged. "Madame Bisset used to say that, *find your feet*, as a way of getting me back in the moment when I was stuck in my head." He handed me a mug that smelled like chamomile, and I thanked him.

"Did it work?"

"It calmed me down. Still does when I think to do it. She'd have me find a sound in my environment that I could dance to like music. It's weird, I know."

He shook his head. "No, you make *walking* look like dancing. And you're by far the best gas station dancer I've ever seen."

I grinned. "That's not the best example of what I do."

"Well, I also saw you dancing in your apartment once. Through the window the night I dropped off your jacket."

I straightened as if someone had just pulled a string attached to the top of my head. "You were standing down there skulking about?"

"No, I wasn't *skulking*. I was walking to your door. You should do that for your audition."

"Do what?"

"Whatever you were doing that night. I was captivated. Even a little choked up."

"Stop it."

"I'm serious."

"That was just me messing around. Sometimes I need to move

at the end of a long day. But this audition is about polish. It's about perfection."

He took a few steps toward the open barn door, then glanced back at me. "I don't know the first thing about dance, but I've seen you raw and real and it's . . . beautiful."

I was speechless. He *had* seen me very raw and very real, and he was still here.

"I'll just get out of your hair so you can do your thing."

"Thanks for the tea and . . . everything," I said as the sun obscured his outline in the doorway. "You're incredibly decent, Griffin."

But he didn't seem to hear me. "You know, I think this house is one hundred and fifty years old," he guessed, taking in the view. "Celina showed me the dumbwaiter. Totally awesome."

"Incredibly decent," I said again softly as he walked away.

Once he'd gone, the vaulted room felt even more quiet than it had before. I reached for my headphones but stopped myself. Instead, I closed my eyes and listened for outside sounds, but there was hardly one to find. The silence in the barn was like velvet—deliciously soft. The only faint rhythm I could detect was that of my own pulse, slow and steady, giving a texture to the silence that was all my own.

That delicate beat was enough to get me off the floor. I rose and began to move slowly. As my pulse quickened, so did I.

I performed several double tours; I left the ground and spun like a corkscrew. Doubling the energy, I flew through the room in a grand jeté, my legs parallel to the floor. Soon the rhythm inside me could not be contained.

Out in the garden, the dogwoods and tired stalks of primrose rustled alive like mature strings in a long-standing orchestra. I bounded up the hill toward the willow trees like a drum. By the time I reached the peak, the wind had become my soloist, singing of precious moments and lost time, of memories and forgiveness. I kicked up fallen leaves, my silhouette taking new shapes against the horizon. I leapt with utter abandon, unleashing my childlike self and sending her sailing through the sunlight. As the music made its crescendo, tears streamed down my face. I lifted, released, and inhabited my body in a way that felt entirely new and yet like home. I danced to heal my pain and the pain of my father, the weeping willows, and my family tree.

———

"Ana, I think I just found my audition piece," I said when she answered my call. I was pacing the barn in an air of sweat and excitement. "But it's weird."

"What do you mean, *weird*?"

"It's imaginative and quirky. Sad, but also uplifting. There's technique of course, but it's not the kind of thing I typically do."

"It sounds like *you*," she said. "You're really doing it."

I let out a puff of air. "I'm sure as hell giving it a shot."

"I'm proud of you. You going to be ready to come back?"

"I think so. How's Tess?"

"She's great. We may have found an apartment."

"I can't wait to see it," I told her.

"Thanks, babe. How's it going with Griffin?"

"Well, it's been terrific actually."

"Wait. Are you into him?"

"I might be," I said, biting my lip.

"This is big. You never get excited about anyone, G."

"After everything with Mark, I was ready to swear off men, but I just—I don't know. Bloody hell."

"This is *good*."

"I'm worried I'll just complicate a great friendship. I mean, how many great friendships do we really get? And how many times can a heart break and still survive? What if I'm almost maxed out? That would make this a huge risk."

"It's a risk worth taking, honey. Don't overthink this one. Promise?"

"I'll try."

———

We returned to the city after sundown. Celina stole Éloïse away to share the details of the day while Griffin set out to catch the hockey game with Mr. LeClair. I grabbed my coat and went for a walk.

I followed red ivy along stone buildings and down the hill toward the nightlife percolating on the street below. I watched families leave restaurants with arms wrapped around small children and couples enter bars hand in hand on streets too full of people for cars to pass through. I wandered alone but strangely found little comfort in it.

Mrs. LeClair opened the door and her arms when I arrived at the gallery. Immediately I could hear the guys cheering from the back room. "It's been quite a game," she said, bringing me into a hug as soft as her chest. "Only a few minutes left in the last period." She put her hands together in prayerful gratitude before taking my coat.

The gallery looked incredible. Nearly all of Celina's artwork was hung professionally on the white plaster walls of the main room.

"Has she seen it like this?" I asked.

"Éloïse thought it would be more fun as a surprise." There was a lot of joyous yelling coming from the back room. "Oh, those fools," Mrs. LeClair said with a hint of affection in her voice. "You better go see what the verdict is."

I walked back into the small office where the two guys were crouched over a TV in the corner.

"Hello," I said announcing my presence.

Griffin turned and smiled. "Hey there!"

"There's only a minute left in the game," Mr. LeClair said, not looking away from the TV.

"Then, I've made it for the best part!"

Griffin slid over on his chair and patted the small remaining section of plastic. I took the space beside him and watched the Montreal Canadiens hockey team fly down the ice while the Boston Bruins maneuvered for a turnover. I tried not to be distracted by Griffin's clean, woodsy scent, which seemed especially potent in the heat of the moment.

"He's got it. Fifteen seconds. Come on!" Mr. LeClair yelled.

Griffin ran his hands through his hair nervously. I wasn't sure if he was even breathing. Seconds ticked off the clock, and we all got to our feet.

Then the shot was made. Right into the net. We all howled with excitement. Griffin wrapped me in a bear hug and did not let go until Mr. LeClaire announced that it was time for the celebratory brandy.

"It's upstairs in my secret room," he said, "where I can smoke my cigars in peace."

"I can hear you," Mrs. LeClair called out from the next room.

Mr. LeClair led Griffin to the stairwell in the corridor. Griffin looked back over his shoulder at me, and my stomach fluttered. I quickly redirected my attention to Mrs. LeClair. She was hanging the last information card for Celina's collection.

"It's been so lovely having you both here," she said when the guys had disappeared into the large room above.

"It's been nice for us, too," I assured her.

"Maybe you'll come back and visit?"

"Maybe for Christmas," I thought out loud, not wanting to be alone during the holidays.

"Oh," she said, her eyes welling, "I'd like that very much."

I could see clearly then a tremendous commonality between me and Mrs. LeClair. We were both women seeking family in the wake of loss. I put my arms around her and squeezed.

The whole evening felt like a prolonged embrace, and when Griffin and I bundled into our coats and said good night to the LeClairs, I felt warm through and through, despite the drop in temperature.

"So, what happened in that barn today?" Griffin asked as we walked away from the gallery lights.

"I found my feet," I said, practically beaming.

"I guess," he said, mirroring my enthusiasm. "You seem different."

"It was hard to go back there today without him, but I still found a little bit of him, you know?"

He linked his arm through mine. We walked shoulder to shoulder like that for at least two blocks. It felt so warm and natural. I wanted to find a way to tell him how much he'd come to mean to me, how much I appreciated him. I threw my head back to inhale the crisp night air and found a sky full of stars. Even with all the city lights, hundreds of stars had found their place. And then I knew what it was I wanted to say.

"I notice you," I told him.

He slowed to a stop. "What?"

"I was going along one day, and then there you were. I notice you. And you're not like anyone else. You're . . . amazing, actually." I hoped I wasn't blushing. "And I just wanted you to know that."

"That you notice me."

"Uh-huh."

A heart-stopping smile crept across his face, but the thoughtful moment was interrupted by a small crowd swelling around us. A dozen people appeared to be queuing up to enter a restaurant where Motown music was seeping through the door. I was eyeing the distraction, when Griffin asked, "You want to go in, Wilder?"

I hesitated.

"Come on," he said. "Let's see what all the fuss is about."

Inside, neon lights were fixed to an exposed stone wall, and tables and chairs filled with people were scattered across the wooden floors. In the corner, a five-person band played Motown classics, trumpets and all, while a dozen people danced at the foot of the low stage. There was standing room only, so we threw our coats on a window ledge and lingered near the entrance. Griffin stood behind me, intoxicatingly close, occasionally using his back as a shield when someone new came through the door. I could have stood in the contentment of that spot for hours. But when the band struck up "Dancing in the Street," I broke away and unconsciously moved toward the swarm of people at the foot of the stage.

"Wilder?" Griffin called out.

"This is my jam!" I yelled back.

I may have been in control of very little in my life, but if there was one thing I knew how to dominate, it was a dance floor. As the golden-voiced singers crooned the classic lyrics, I found my groove and made friends in the crowd.

When the song ended, and the lead singer belted out another melody, Griffin wedged his way onto the dance floor. "I can't let you have all the fun," he said.

"Let's see what you got."

I half expected him to just step side to side. But as the band sang "Ain't Too Proud to Beg" powerfully enough to blow the roof right off the building, he looked me dead in the eye and brought on some serious swagger. "Holy shit. Why didn't you tell me you could dance?" He shrugged again and grinned.

Griffin and his understated confidence followed my lead on the dance floor, and by the time we stumbled back out onto the street, energized and laughing, my entire body was buzzing like the neon lights.

I wanted all of him. And it terrified me.

26

COOPER

I was eating a bagel in my makeshift office at Stetson and Lawrey. It was one of those everything types with garlic and salt, and after a few bites I felt poppy seeds lodged in the back of my throat. I went coughing down to the break room in search of coffee and ran into Mark's assistant, Lynn, squawking on her cell phone by the coffeepot. I had to wave her aside between coughs to fill my mug.

Lynn gave me an apologetic smile and went on talking into the phone. "No, Mark, she didn't pick up. I just left her a voicemail," she was saying. "No, I didn't give my name. I just said I was calling on behalf of Olivia Garza, like you asked me to. And that her appointment had been changed from Thursday to Friday at four o'clock, just like you said. Is this some kind of surprise?" She rolled her eyes as if she and I were in on the same conversation.

I had no idea what the hell she was talking about, but I gathered she knew how I felt about Mark.

I washed the poppy seeds down with weak coffee and tried to hide the fact that I was agitated. It wasn't just Lynn or the poppy seeds that were rubbing me the wrong way. I hadn't gotten a shred of solid information on building permits from the guys at the bar the other night—only one too many Sinatra songs. I still didn't know the fate of Fidelis. And it had been four days since I'd left Jackie Marley a voicemail, so I was trying not to give up hope of finding David Wilder's letter. Griffin would be home in a few days, and I wanted something to show him that I wasn't a fuck-up.

I went back to my desk and tried to focus on the new case I'd been assigned. A guy who had scored in the commodities market and started his own company was being charged with breach of contract. It was a nice distraction. But imagine my enthusiasm when Jackie Marley called at one o'clock.

"You're a hard woman to track down," I answered.

"Hello. I'm sorry, Mr. Cooper. I've been traveling."

"Daryl," I offered, and then I got right to the point. "Well, as I mentioned in my voicemails, I'm interested in the letter David Wilder sent to his daughter the night he died. Were you the one who typed it?"

"Yes, David dictated it to me before he went into surgery."

"So, you know what it said?"

"Yes. It left an impression. The next morning, I went to find my son who I hadn't spoken to in six years."

"That explains quitting your job. But Jackie, Gracie Wilder never got an email."

"She wasn't meant to get an email."

"What's that?"

"After his message was typed out, David decided that it would be a lot to hear in the form of an impersonal email. He said that he preferred handwriting his letters and that he wasn't sure if Gracie had ever received an email from him before. Other than to forward flight information or a dinner reservation."

"Go on," I encouraged impatiently.

"So, I suggested that it might be better if David emailed the letter to someone Gracie loved who could hand deliver it to her and be there for her when she read it. He said that the only person Gracie ever truly loved was also someone he'd removed from her life. He said it was his biggest regret. He had tracked her down years before but had never known how to reach out."

I was now pacing a hole into the carpet beside my desk. "Jackie, who did David send the letter to?"

"Michelle Bisset."

"Who the hell is Michelle Bisset?"

"I don't know. But she lives in Paris."

"As in, France?"

"Yes, but she must be in Chicago by now."

I grabbed a notepad and pen from my desk. "B-I-S-S-E-T?" I asked, scribbling a few notes.

"That's right."

"And if I don't find this woman in the next forty-eight hours, will you tell Gracie yourself what was in the letter?"

"I guess that would be the right thing to do."

"And I can reach you on this number?"

"Yeah," she sighed. "You know what he said?"

I was dying to know what he said.

"When he was asking me to help him get this letter written, he said, 'It's not too late.'"

"Too late for what?"

There was a new strength in her voice. "To change everything."

─────

Aer Lingus flight records indicated that a Michelle Bisset had landed in Chicago a week before. I called a dozen hotels in Chicago but couldn't seem to find a Bisset on the books. I tried calling one Michelle Bisset, a former nanny, age forty-five, from Sèvres outside of Paris, but it was an old number.

I went to Gracie Wilder's apartment building and casually smoked a cigarette by the entrance. When a woman and her poodle exited, I put out my smoke on the brick and stepped into the lobby.

I wasn't expecting an apartment concierge to greet me. He stood behind a counter-height desk. "Can I help you?"

"Joel," I said, reading his name tag, "I'm a relative of Gracie Wilder." He eyeballed me suspiciously. "Married in, obviously. Her cousin Nora's husband." I waited to see if he was buying it. I decided he was. "Anyway, as you know, Gracie is out of town, and she asked me to collect any messages that might have been left for her here. Since her dad died there have been a lot of people trying to get in touch. It's a little overwhelming."

"Well, a woman did come by," he began.

"Was it Aunt Laura? Or maybe Michelle? Michelle Bisset? It would be just like her to check in on Gracie."

Joel shuffled through some papers on the desk.

"Yes. Bisset." He held up a folded piece of paper. "She left a note."

"Terrific." I stepped closer. "I can relay that to Gracie right away." I put out an eager hand.

Joel hesitantly held the paper halfway between us.

"Any other messages?"

"I don't think so," he said, glancing down again.

I smoothly took the paper from his hand. "Thanks, Joel. Gracie will be really appreciative." I moved for the door.

"What did you say your name was?"

"Daryl. Nora's husband," I said as the door closed behind me. I walked a block before I opened the note.

Ma chérie, I am so sorry for your loss. I have come to town for a few days to see you and deliver something from your father. Please try reaching me at the Ivy as soon as you return. I have missed you. I keep you close in my heart. Love always, Madame Bisset

The Ivy. I hadn't thought of that one.

I called Bisset, but she wasn't in her room. No problem. I would wait, and when I found her, I would put her in touch with Gracie before she gave up and left town. I'd show Griffin that I didn't just fumble around and mess with other people's lives.

27

GRIFFIN

I left the house before anyone else was awake and went for a run. By seven o'clock, I'd slowed my pace and was cooling down in front of a row of houses with brightly colored front doors—light blue, red, hunter green. It was as if this particular group of neighbors had each agreed to a different color in the rainbow. I stopped in front of the blue door when my phone rang. It was Keira.

"Did I wake you?" she asked when I said hello.

"No. I'm up."

"How're you doing?" As if we talked all the time.

"Fine. You?"

"Good." Her voice rang higher than usual, the pitch of real effort. "I hope you don't mind. I went to see your parents yesterday."

I let myself imagine that and sighed. "I'm sure they loved seeing you. Pop always did like you best."

"He said things have been slow for you. That you're thinking of working for a friend of his in commercial design."

"Pop spoke out of turn there."

"Good," she said, supportively. There was a long pause before she went on. "Well, I've finally decided to go back to school and get my MBA. You'd be proud of me. I've gotten into some good programs."

We'd often talked about Keira getting her MBA. I couldn't remember why she hadn't done it sooner. "That's great. I always knew you had it in you." She paused again, longer this time. "You okay?" I asked.

"Yeah. Sorry. I just didn't sleep well."

"You still going to Joe's? You know their decaf is leaded," I said on impulse. It was so easy to fall back into old patterns. To think of her eating dinner at Joe's Café, ordering a cup of decaf, and then lying awake half the night.

"When will I ever learn?" Her laugh sounded strained. "Listen, Beau, I just wanted you to know, to hear it from me. I'm moving to San Francisco."

"California?" I asked, dumbly.

"Yeah. I've been offered a job at a start-up with a lot of room for growth, and I'm going to start classes at San Francisco State in January."

She was saying goodbye. "Wow," I said after a moment. "A whole new life."

"I guess."

The divorce papers had made it official that Keira and I were parting ways, yet she had stayed in the backdrop of my life. We lived in the same neighborhood, went to the same gym, frequented the same coffee shop and grocery store. If I couldn't remember the name of an eye doctor or if she needed a tool out of my garage, we could find each other. But now she would be gone, and the last seven years of my life as a married man would fade too, into a story that sounded like a nice idea once.

"I'm sorry, Keira," I said. "I'm sorry we weren't happy."

"We were happy for a while, Beau. We were young and in love long before we even knew who we were or what we needed."

"I think I'm still figuring all that out," I admitted.

"You weren't dealt an easy hand." There was a break in her voice that told me she was trying not to cry. I could hardly bear it. "We never discussed the ring," she said.

She meant her engagement ring. It was a vintage round-cut diamond that she had casually pointed to one afternoon when we were passing the display window of a jewelry store. It was gorgeous, with numerous facets that captured the light. I scraped together everything I had that summer and surprised her with a proposal.

"Keep it," I told her. "It was a gift."

"Thanks," she said in a small voice.

"Well . . . you take care now."

"You too," she said, before she hung up.

⁓

The productive start to my day nose-dived. I went to the pub where Dean worked the bar. It's not that my recreational drinking had escalated into an actual problem, it's just that I didn't know very many people in Montreal.

The door was still locked, but I could see Dean setting glasses out, and I startled him with a knock. "I'm not supposed to let anyone in before ten," he explained, opening the door. "Good thing I don't wear a watch."

I slapped him on the back with an assault of gratitude.

"What are you after so early?"

"A fresh start, I guess."

"I got something for that," Dean said. I sat down at the bar while he fixed me a concoction that was cousin to a Bloody Mary but had more whistles and bells.

"Rough morning?" he asked.

"My ex-wife is moving as far away as possible, and my old man thinks I'm all washed up." I forced a smile like a true cynic.

"This one's on the house," he said as he methodically assembled some garnish and set the highball glass in front of me with a thud. "For whatever it's worth, you don't look washed up."

"Thanks," I said, surveying the elaborate drink. If you could even call it that. It was more of a meal. I'd been expecting a stalk of celery, but the strip of bacon was a welcomed twist. "I don't know what happened," I told Dean. "I worked hard and kept my head down, but I think I forgot what I was working for. I lost sight of some things, and it took my life breaking apart to realize it."

"I know that story," he said. "Usually has a good ending. The kind where you decide to go after what you really want. Like a badass."

I considered that as I pulled the bacon from my glass and bit into it.

"I've learned a lot watching people," he went on. "Some of the folks who come in here treat me like I'm the water boy, but bartenders are like gods. We hear all your prayers. We deliver or make you wait for your cures. We know how the game is played, and it's not won by the timid. You have enough of that morning cocktail right there and you'll see I'm right. You'll remember what you came here for, and you'll go after it."

"Funny, I think I came here just hoping to forget. Leave everything behind."

Dean reached up to a top shelf and pulled down an unmarked bottle. He set it in front of me with an empty shot glass. "It's a hundred twenty proof and tends to make people forget a whole lot of things. But I'm not sure it's your drink." He was watching my face carefully, as if it was my turn in a game of cards. Or a test that he wanted me to pass.

I picked up the bottle and examined the brown liquid in the light. "You don't mind if I send a few people your way for this? There's not a whiskey in Ireland that could make my pop forget what a screwup I am, but I might send him to you just the same."

"Dads are the hardest," Dean agreed. "We remind them of their own shortcomings. There's no bourbon for that."

I set the bottle back down on the counter. "He named me after his brother. An honorable guy who died moving his family to America. He didn't come by ship during a famine or anything. No, he had the incredibly bad luck of having a heart attack in the departures terminal at

Dublin Airport at forty-nine years old. I was born that same year. That makes me Beaumont Cormac Griffin, the second. A ridiculous name that I have not been able to live up to."

"Man, you never had a chance."

I smiled and pushed the bottle back toward him. He returned my smile and the bottle to the high shelf.

I took one last swig of my Bloody Mary and lay some money on the bar. "You're a good man, Dean. And you make one hell of a morning cocktail. If you're ever in Chicago . . ."

He nodded. "Go be a badass, dude."

I was hit with a blast of cold air when I left the bar. I strolled through Bonsecours Market, then poked around the Pierre du Calvet Hotel. It was built in the early 1700s, making it one of the oldest historic homes in Montreal. I kicked a few stones in front of the chapel Notre-Dame-de-Bon-Secours and tipped my head back to take in the parapet of what Éloïse had called the Sailors' Church. Then I walked through its immense red door.

The chapel was impressive with its pipe organ and stained glass. I couldn't help but think of Fidelis, how it likely would be torn down by Christmas, and all because of me.

I followed a steep staircase down into the crypt and again was confronted with my captivation for particular history. There was evidence of fire. I read on a placard that fire had destroyed the original chapel in 1754. I half expected to see smoke filtering through the wooden palisade like ghosts.

When I finally made my way to the parapet on the roof, I was alone above the city. My only company were statues of angels said to be guiding the sailors safely into port. I watched people on the street below going about their lives, contributing something to a balance, like the city itself with its rich history and contemporary development. I could see where the Second Empire architectural style of City Hall sat alongside neoclassical architecture, both making the century-old courthouse seem infantile.

Their peaked roofs and spires sat like an array of hats alongside simple brick structures. I found one dilapidated stone building that stood out from the rest, because of the apartment that had been placed on top of it, clearly an afterthought. Its long horizontal seams sat on the edge of open air. It was quiet and dignified with incredible views of water. One might not detect its existence from the ground, where it blended in with brick and mortar, but those who looked up could find brilliance in its design.

In a way, that was what Gracie had done for me. She had seen something in me that no one else seemed to detect. It had been right there in her eyes, glittering up at me with sincerity from the start, making me want to see things differently too. She appreciated me despite my rough edges. Like Keira's diamond, maybe it's the jagged facets in a person that eventually reflect something worth noticing. Maybe the difference between being broken and being brilliant is simply being seen.

If that were true, then the only way to save Fidelis was to make sure people saw past the plywood to the bigger story underneath. Its bedrock soul had gone unnoticed for so long, covered up by commerce. The community didn't seem to remember that it was worth fighting for. They weren't in line to help rebuild it, like the Sailors' Church had been rebuilt, because they didn't know they needed it.

I called Cooper from the parapet. "Who's your friend at the *Tribune*?" I asked him when he picked up.

"Michael Kendrick. Why?"

"I need his number."

"What for?"

"There are fifteen thousand tons of steel in Fidelis. It was built to withstand far more than what it went through this year. But Abrams never respected it enough to get to know it. He's convinced the whole damn town that it's irrevocably damaged. And it's bullshit."

"You think you can fix it."

"I know I can fix it. It wouldn't be as hard as everyone thinks or as expensive. If I can get the community to see that it's not just a goddamned office building, they'll fight for it. Stand in the way of the bulldozers. You watch and see."

"You're a super-nerd, man. But I love you. I'll get the scoop on the real estate company."

"No. I'm going to the papers. I want to talk to the people." I crossed the parapet, no longer feeling shame with every step. I headed down the stairs toward the street with exhilaration in my veins.

"All right. Go get after it," Cooper was saying. "And then get back here, will ya?"

The next number I dialed was Michael Kendrick's. It was time to be a badass.

28

GRACIE

I dreamed I was waking. I rose from the bed in Éloïse's spare room, wandered down the hall toward the front door, and stepped outside into the morning light. The sun glinted against the brass postbox, where an envelope was protruding from the letter slot. I lifted it out and saw that it was a piece of my father's red-rimmed stationary. I carefully opened the note, eager to read what was inside. The message was scripted in large, bold letters: *Brava Gracie.*

When I woke, the first thing I saw were my fingernails. The day before, Celina had lacquered them in pale pink polish with flecks of gold glitter. I was examining them in the morning light when I remembered the dream and sat straight up.

I had risen from this very bed in this very house to retrieve a message from my father. *Brava*, his note had said. I wondered what I had done so well to receive it.

Sounds drifted in from the kitchen. I could hear Éloïse unloading the dishwasher and Celina making a case for chunky peanut butter instead of smooth. There was the scampering of Claude's paws and an uproar of laughter. Was this what a home was supposed to sound like?

Clinking plates, idle chatter, scampering feet, bursts of laughter. What a wondrous thing.

It seemed I had developed a talent for crying since embarking on this trip. I sat against the pillows blotting bittersweet tears with glittering fingers.

———

After lunch, Celina asked me to help her do something special with her hair for the art exhibit. We stood in front of the beveled mirror in the bathroom while I gently pulled the tangles out with a paddle brush. I gave her loose curls with a wide-barrel curling iron, then gathered the hair that framed her face and fastened it behind the crown of her head with a twist and two bobby pins. All the while, she chattered on, telling me of the time in first grade when Éloïse tried to cut her hair at the kitchen counter and lobbed off all her curls. "I'm already walking around with metal poles. I can't afford an asymmetrical bob," Celina said lightheartedly. "So, now Mom just sticks to what she's good at."

Éloïse was putting linens away in the hall and chimed in, "I can braid!"

Celina tilted her hand from side to side. "Sort of," she whispered to me.

I'd been folded into the fabric of their day with such ease that I thought I might be suddenly living someone else's life. It felt so ordinary and so remarkable all at once.

When Celina's hair was in place, I went through to the spare room to smooth out the folds in my blue silk dress. I'd brought it along in case an occasion might require something other than blue jeans or dance leggings, and I was pleased to have a reason to pull it from my bag and spread it across the pale yellow quilt.

I pinned my hair into a twist, brushed color onto my cheeks, penciled in my eyebrows, and glossed my lips. By the time I pulled the dress on and slipped into a pair of pale heels, I felt like a new person, relaxed and elegant.

I wandered out into the living room and found that Griffin had returned from his day in the city. He and Celina were flipping through a book he'd bought her about the architect Frank Gehry. He was saying, "See how he breaks the rules too? Exaggerates lines and angles—" but he stopped talking when he saw me and stood from the couch. "Wow," he said.

He was wearing a navy wool sports coat and a crisp white shirt that looked like they had been tailor-made just for him. "What do you think?" he asked, straightening his lapel with a little pride. "Picked it up this morning."

I had the impulse to gush and tell him that he was gorgeous, but then thought better of it. "You'll do," I said with a wink.

"Gracie, did you see what he got me?" Celina asked. She pointed to a small arrangement of pink roses.

"I got you something too," Griffin said, walking over to me. He pulled a freshly cut white gardenia from his breast pocket and tucked it into my pile of hair. A gesture that left me nearly speechless.

"Thank you," I managed to say.

"We should be on our way," Éloïse announced as she strode into the room. So, we pulled on our coats and piled into the Falcon. I rode in the front next to Griffin while Celina sat next to Éloïse in the back.

⌒

When we walked through the corridor into the gallery, Celina positively lit up. The main room was entirely filled with her work, and underneath the bronze logo for the LeClair Studio and Gallery hung a new plaque that read: *Wilder School of Fine Art for Young Artists.*

"He would have loved this," she said, squeezing my hand tight. I was sure she was right.

Éloïse helped the LeClairs set up refreshments while Celina eagerly led Griffin on a private art tour. I followed quietly behind, taking in one painting at a time. A rosebud standing high above blooms too heavy with beauty to hold upright in the sun. Hands—open, wrinkled, rosy—in the lap of an older woman, gray hair cascading. Faces weary and wonderful. Children at play. A boy with owl eyes. A girl with skin that shimmers. The Blue Tilting House with its newly appointed window in the attic and willows everywhere. Each painting exploded with life. Each invited me to borrow the perspective of Celina.

Guests arrived at five o'clock sharp, as Mr. and Mrs. LeClair had intended. To the newcomers, they handed out glossy cards with information about the new art program, and to old friends they handed out kisses, on one cheek and then the other.

Over the next few hours, dozens of people perused the artwork and congratulated Celina. I was introduced to nearly everyone in town as Celina's big sister, receiving hugs from charming strangers as well as condolences on my father's passing. I was overwhelmed but warmed by the reception. I found myself often skimming the room in search of Griffin, as if he were my anchor in new seas. I'd find him laughing with Mr. LeClair or chatting with guests, but his eyes always found mine.

I excused myself from Celina to use the loo and found Griffin near the door when I walked back into the gallery. "You're a popular guest tonight," he said. "You okay, or do you need a break?"

"I'm all right. But I might hang out on the fringe for a bit."

He led me toward a corner. "I've been wanting to get you alone all night. Do you still want to pack up tomorrow and hit the road?"

"I think so. I heard from Olivia Garza's office, and they've moved my audition from Thursday to Friday at four. So, I'll have an extra day at home to prepare."

"That's great. Why'd they move it?"

"They didn't say." I figured it had to do with their rehearsal schedule. I was so happy to have more time that I didn't give it another thought.

"I have a meeting that day too, at the *Tribune*," Griffin said. "A guy has agreed to meet with me and hear what I know about Fidelis. What it's meant to the community. Hopefully we can do a piece that will rile up some folks and stand in the way of a teardown."

"That's amazing! You can tell its story."

He seemed contented. "So many people want to believe the worst about things, but not you. You see the best."

"I just see what I see," I said innocently. The noise in the room amplified, but Griffin's eyes stayed on me, softening at the edges. "Please don't look at me like that," I pleaded.

"Like what? Like I'm falling in love with you?"

His words stole the air right out of my lungs.

"You're very lovable, Wilder, you must know that." I wanted to laugh, but instead it seemed I might cry. I blinked several times to combat another onslaught of tears. Griffin tilted his head to one side. "You know, I don't think I've ever seen your eyes so green."

That nearly knocked me over. I had to reach for the wall to steady myself.

"You okay?"

Honestly, I wasn't sure. "You might change your mind," I said.

"About what?"

"About me."

He smiled. "You're talking crazy. Do you need to eat? You want me to get you some punch or something?"

"People are always changing their minds. I can stand to lose a few people in my life. But I don't want to lose you. If we start dating, you might wake up one day and see that I'm messy, and difficult, and—"

He stepped closer and put a hand to my lower back. I could feel heat travel up my spine. "Let me be very clear," he said gently. "I want you in my life. I want you in my plans, in my arms . . . in my bed. Tell me you don't feel this, and I will back off. Tell me you might want this, and I will wait as long as you need." He lowered his head, his lips grazing my cheek, "Or tell me you feel this as strongly as I do, and I'll take you upstairs right now."

My armor was on the floor.

I opened my mouth to speak, but Mr. LeClair called out Griffin's name. We turned our heads and there he was, charging over with another man in tow. "I want you to meet a friend of mine," he said, and Griffin reluctantly extended a hand.

After the introductions, I excused myself and downed a glass of punch. But as the evening went on, the electricity between Griffin and me only grew. When he'd glance in my direction, my skin would come alive. When we'd pass each other in the room, I'd feel his fingers graze the underside of my arm or the tips of my fingers, sending such a spark through me that I might have thought he'd run his hand right up my thigh.

At nine o'clock, he pulled me aside. "Celina is tired. I'm going to drive her and Éloïse back."

"I'll stay and help clean up, then meet you." Celina came over and leaned into me. "We'll relive it all tomorrow," I said.

But after they left, the party did not dissipate. It seemed to kick up a notch. Mr. LeClair began pouring wine, Mrs. LeClair put on French music, and dozens of guests stayed to mingle.

I was picking up empty cups when Griffin returned. He stepped into the corridor in his overcoat, and our eyes met through the glass door. In that split second everything else seemed to disappear. There was no perpetuating loss, no impending performance, no question or fear to entertain, no emotion to hide. I opened the door and moved toward him, one reflexive step at a time.

"I came back to get you," he said. "I didn't want you to have to walk back. Not in those shoes." When he lifted his gaze, my mouth found his.

It was the kind of kiss that could unravel even the most impervious corners of a girl. He wrapped his arms around my waist, and I breathed in the scent of the cold night air lingering on his skin, wishing I could stretch this moment out into a thousand moments. I was utterly surprised by how fiercely I wanted him. All of him. I took his hand and led him up the stairs.

Under the pitched roof of the LeClairs' upstairs room lay an over-sized rug, two tufted wing chairs, and a roll-back leather chaise lounge. The back window shone brightly with moonlight. Griffin threw his overcoat and jacket on one of the chairs without breaking stride, then pulled me into his crisp shirt and his open mouth. The sounds of muf-fled voices and French music vibrated below us. I backed him toward the chair and pushed him into it. Unfastening the pearl bead at the back of my dress, I let the silk fabric slide off my body. I pulled the pins and flower from my hair, unfastened my bra, and let everything fall to the floor before sliding onto his lap. He brushed my hair away from my face and kissed me, whispering against my lips, "You don't have to perform for me, Gracie Wilder." I kissed him harder.

He ran his hands along my back, traced the contour of my hips with his fingertips, and every cell in my body hummed with life. The tender-ness of his touch melted the frame of my shoulders and neck, liquefied the solid structure of my legs until I was sure I'd never walk again. Then he wrapped me around him, carried me to the leather chaise lounge, and laid me down.

We quickly found our rhythm. He seemed to be exploring me, want-ing to understand me, watching how I responded, and diving deeper when I did. I was blissfully in my body, wanting to feel every detail: his muscular shoulders, the smooth texture of his lips, the weight of his body on mine.

In my past relationships, I had avoided my own pleasure. Ignored my own desire. But not now. Not with Griffin. He placed no demands on my body. There wasn't an ounce of arrogance or selfishness in the way he touched me. He said nothing—not a single perfunctory exclamation—and he missed nothing. When we rolled onto the rug, he landed soundlessly, bringing me down on top of him. As we moved between the shadows, intertwining like the petals of a lotus flower, I could not remember a time when I'd felt freer than I did tangled up in his arms.

Afterward, the floor below buzzed with music as he lay winded against me. "Beau," I whispered. It seemed right to call him Beau then. He lifted his head and gazed back at me. I ran my fingers through his thick hair. "That was an anomaly, right? It couldn't possibly always be like that."

"That sounds like a challenge," he said drolly, his hair brushing my skin as he kissed his way slowly down my chest.

"Éloïse will worry," I finally said, finding that single thought to be my connection to the outside world.

"I told her not to wait up," he murmured, his mouth busy.

I closed my eyes and melted into the floor. Relaxed and unwoven, I whispered, "Oh, you'd be hard to get over."

He looked up, his eyes shining. "Then don't," he said.

29

GRIFFIN

I was caught up in Gracie, unable to focus on anything else. I was also literally caught up in her—her hair, her legs, so much leg. With her audition having been pushed, there seemed less urgency to get back to Chicago. We decided to stay one more day.

Éloïse and Celina went to the shop, and Gracie and I offered to have dinner ready when they returned. We went to the market to buy groceries, then spent hours in bed. By two o'clock, I was worn out. She pulled the yellow quilt over my chest. "Sleep," she said. But as I watched her leave the bed, her skin radiant in the afternoon light, I found that I wasn't ready to have her out of reach.

It was a perfect day that ended with cooking pasta primavera barefoot in the little kitchen, chopping vegetables, and slow dancing while the sauce simmered. I couldn't believe we'd found our way this far.

But in tune with other great things in my life, the joy of that perfect day dissolved by morning. My phone rang at eight. It was Teddy.

I sat up from where I was lying on the pullout sofa and answered.

"You getting close?" he asked.

"Close to what?"

"*Home.* You're supposed to be back today."

"Oh. We delayed a day."

Teddy countered my nonchalance with "Shit!"

"What is it?"

"She's asking for you."

"Who?"

"Mom."

I might have laughed. "You're pulling my leg."

"Beau, I'm serious. They adjusted her meds, and she's been lucid a few times in the last two days, talking with us for a couple of minutes at a time before she gets confused again. And she keeps saying, 'Where's Beau?'"

I was on my feet then. The blood drained from my face.

"Pop keeps asking me if you're on your way." He added tentatively, "And he keeps asking about the car."

"The car's fine. Tell him it's fine. Do you think you could put her on the phone?"

"That hasn't worked in years. She gets confused and agitated." I knew he was right. She would need to see my face, touch it even, to know I was who she thought I might be. "What should I do?" Teddy asked. "Pop says not to talk about you. Not to make her sad. You want me to tell her you're coming?"

I sighed. "Maybe you should listen to Pop."

"Beau, come on, man. Your opinion is the one that counts. I don't know if you remember, but you pretty much raised me. You want me to tell her you're coming?"

"Tell her I'm on my way. I'll drive through." I imagined Gracie could take a couple of driving shifts and we could load up on coffee.

"It's like a twelve-hour drive, right? She'd be asleep by the time you got here."

"Then I'll be there when she wakes up in the morning. Tell her just one more day."

"Okay, but don't kill yourself getting here," he said.

When he hung up, my mind was racing, but my feet were cemented to the floor. Gracie found me like that, and when I told her, she said, "We'll leave right away."

———

Gracie packed her things while Éloïse fixed me a large coffee in the kitchen. I paced.

"It's not easy to go back," Éloïse noted.

"And yet I need to get there as soon as possible."

"You'll find a way," she said.

I hoped so. I fixed my eyes on the half a dozen glazed terra-cotta plates that hung on the wall beside the refrigerator. "What are these?"

"Pieces of stories," she said, glancing over.

I studied them closer. They each had a glossy image like a bear, an eagle, or a dancing flame. And underneath the images in small letters were words: *Bear cried out. Eagle was impatient. The fire grew until it reached the sky.*

"You made them?"

She handed me a travel mug of steaming coffee. "Yes, when my mother was dying. She gave me the stories, and I made these so that I'd see them every day. So that I'd remember."

"They must be sad stories, but you made them beautiful."

I watched the lines around her mouth deepen. "Thank you," she said.

Celina trudged into the kitchen with a pout on her face. "If I were glue, I'd stick to you and keep you here," she said, wrapping her arms around me.

"Keep imagining things even better than they are," I whispered into the top of her head.

Éloïse took a turn pulling me into a hug and then pointed me toward the door. "And you're off."

PART THREE

You are what you believe yourself to be.

—PAULO COELHO

Many men go fishing all their lives without
knowing it is not fish they are after.

—HENRY DAVID THOREAU

30

GRACIE

Our bags filled the trunk, the blackbird hung from the rearview mirror, and the mysterious key still rested against my chest, as Griffin drove us away from Old Montreal. Our plan was to get as close to Chicago as we could and then check into a motel for the night, making the rest of the distance a quick trip the following morning. We made good time rumbling down the highway, talking and listening to music. It was hard not to want to always be touching him—his knee or his hair—as if the nerve endings in my fingertips were trying to confirm that he was molecularly there. I'd never had a burning desire to want to reach another person in this way. It was thrilling and intoxicating.

I dozed for an hour and awoke to a fresh flurry of snow. We stopped at a gas station, where I stood in the parking lot watching large, beautiful snowflakes land on my palms and quickly vanish. The snowmelt lingered like a damp kiss.

I took the next shift driving while Griffin slept. I kept the radio off, enjoying the way his breath rolled in and out like a wave. I pictured the dance I would perform in two days' time. I painted each detail in my mind and watched it play out in vivid color. The way Celina had taught me.

———

The night before we left Montreal, I had cuddled next to Celina on her bed admiring the paper stars that hung from her ceiling. "When will you be back?" she asked.

"I won't stay away long," I promised.

She scooted down under her covers and pulled them up to her chin.

"What will you dream?" The question lifted out of one of the oldest rooms in my heart.

"I don't know," she said.

"What if you dreamed of discovering the key to a secret garden—a beautiful place with flowering trees and white rabbits and silver swans in a small pond. And you can bring anyone you like there." It filled me with joy to be able to share the very dream that had comforted me so many nights as a child.

"I'll bring you," she said.

"I'll be there."

She took a long breath and returned the question. "What will *you* dream?"

"I don't know," I realized.

"Maybe you could dream that you're on a beautiful stage, and a girl—a lot like me—asks you to teach her to dance. And so you do. And it makes you both so happy."

"I love it," I told her.

I would dream of the child I once was, bring her home, and teach her to again dance with her whole heart.

———

Griffin was behind the wheel by the time the sun lowered over tall stalks of pale wheat on a snow-dusted farm. We decided it was the most beautiful golden hour we'd ever seen. We checked into a modest motel just outside Kalamazoo, warming each other under a single sheet.

By six the next morning, we were back on the road. But the mood changed when smoke seeped out from under the hood of the Falcon. We pulled over on a country road and got out to survey the situation. A thick fog enveloped Griffin when he opened the hood. It rose and pillowed into the sky. Watching him tread the pavement, I felt as sick as the car.

A quick search showed us to a service station less than a mile off the main road, where a man in grease-stained jeans and a shirt embroidered with the name *Norton* examined the car and told Griffin, "It looks like it's the carburetor. Won't be an easy fix on this old thing. I'm going to need a few days."

"Days?" Griffin was dumbfounded.

"This ain't an oil change, buddy. I'll get you the number for the rental place."

While Norton walked inside, we lingered in the garage standing over the car like one might a dear friend in a hospital bed. Griffin wiped some moisture off the canvas top with his bare hand and only sighed. I carefully took the blackbird down off the rearview mirror and held it with both hands.

We sat on a pleather sofa in the service station waiting for our rental car to be delivered. The smell of vanilla air freshener wafted through the waiting room. A young woman sat across from us, bouncing her small child in her lap, while her husband watched football highlights on a large flat-screen TV. The sounds of sports commentators squawked into the room. Griffin sat soundlessly beside me, watching the TV and the little family for a long time. Then he said, "There was a baby."

I wasn't sure I'd heard him correctly at first. "There was a baby where?"

"Keira. I lost them both."

I wished someone would switch off the damn TV. I couldn't get my thoughts together with all the noise.

"Maybe it's karma," he said.

I took one of his hands in mine and searched his face. His gaze was pointed at the floor. "Why is it karma, Beau?"

"Because I stole a prayer once. A woman who couldn't have a child was grieving, and I took her paper from the stone arch of Fidelis when I was eleven."

"That's just a coincidence."

He stared at me. "You believe that coincidences can have meaning."

"But not *everything* is meant to be." I squeezed his hand tighter. "Life only gets better from here. You hear me?"

He nodded agreeably, but still his head and shoulders slumped forward. "What if I'm too late and I've missed her? I'll get back and my mom won't know me. I'll have missed my chance."

"We have to stay positive," I tried.

"I'm not sure that's enough."

His vulnerability was so beautiful that I found myself leaning my body into his, wanting to absorb this beauty and his pain with it. "Things are going to change for the better," I said. "You're going to get your company back up and running, and I'm going to get Olivia Garza to accept me into her dance company. We'll be on another adventure in no time. Maybe we'll go to New York."

"Why New York?"

"Well, Garza's spring dance tour will perform there. And it might be fun to see the city together."

"There's a tour?" He sat up a little straighter, and it prompted me to do the same.

"Eight cities in four months or something like that."

"You'll be on the road for four months?" His questions just kept coming, and I realized how much we still had to discuss.

"*If* I get the position."

"Gracie, I can't just be your sidekick. It's one thing to have done it for the past week, but it can't be my new full-time job."

"I know that," I said defensively. "And I never asked you to be my sidekick."

"You just asked me to drive you to Canada."

The little family was watching us now. Even the child appeared curious about our argument.

Maybe Dr. Peck had been right. Maybe growth was not a linear process. It felt more like a dance of letting in and letting go. Griffin and I would have to learn the dance.

"I'm sorry," he said after a moment.

"We're just tired," I said, hoping.

"I love your optimism. But I can't go to New York, because I have to deal with my aging parents and my mortgage and whatever else gets thrown my way." He inhaled sharply and sighed. "And I won't hold you back. I won't have you looking over your shoulder for me when you should be going after what you want. I won't get in the way of everything you've worked for."

"What are you saying?" Anxiety pulsated through me in a dreadful and familiar tempo. "Are you trying to cut your losses?"

"No. I just can't be the reason why someone else doesn't have the life they want."

"You already have an exit plan," I accused.

"Of course I don't. I just don't want to let you down."

I waited for him to say something that would turn everything right around, but instead all I could hear were football highlights in the background. My breath felt tight in my chest, and I feared I might spiral into a classic panic attack. I got up and walked outside.

The strip mall was covered in a slip of clean snow, but my blood surged hot as my primal fight or flight threatened to make me run from the man I loved as if he were a threat. Thankfully, it seemed my heart had become tethered to his. I stood as still as the night, allowing myself to feel. Allowing myself to remember.

———

She had woken me early before I had time to clear the scattered thoughts of dreams. When I came out of the haze of sleep, feeling her kiss my cheek, hearing her light voice whisper, "*Je t'aime.* I love you," I knew by the tone of Madame Bisset's voice that she was saying goodbye. I went into a panic. I seized up, my arms clutching her neck. I wailed, "Don't go" between deep sobs. She tried to calm me, tried to quiet me, but all I could do was fall apart. She was leaving, and my heart was breaking, and it was all my fault.

My father was in the stairwell waiting for the goodbye to end. He opened my bedroom door wider, and Madame Bisset took the cue. She rose to leave, and I followed, still with one arm tightly around her narrow shoulders, still shaking and crying. My father tried to pry me from her, saying, "We will forward her our new address when we move." But this was a statement he had no intention of following through on. He was after a clean slate.

At the front door, Madame Bisset's eyes were like quiet storms. She pulled my head into her soft chest, kissed the top of my head, and said into my ear, "*Petit à petit, l'oiseau fait son nid.*" Little by little, a bird makes its nest. She'd spoken this proverb to me before when I was feeling impatient. But I knew it was more than patience she wanted me to have in that moment; it was hope. She set me in front of her so she could look me in the eye and said, "You will always live in my heart, *ma chérie*, but now you must go and create your beautiful world without me. It is yours to create. Do you understand?" I managed to nod my head. "Follow your heart and never stop making magic. Promise me." She kissed me quickly before the storms in her eyes could be released, and with her avocado-green case in hand, she hurried out the door, unknowingly taking part of me with her.

———

I folded forward over my legs in the parking lot to try to slow everything down—my thoughts, my breath, the tears streaming down my face, the snow falling around me. Then I felt his hand on my back and stood.

"I'm not a regular person," I told Griffin, and he wrapped his arms around me.

When Norton interrupted with news that the rental car had arrived, we gravely pulled our things from the Falcon and piled them into a Toyota Highlander. The rest of the drive was fraught with silence as we both tried to imagine a way forward.

Griffin offered to help me up to my flat with my things, but I told him he should get to his mom straightaway. It was already ten o'clock. "I'll come by later," he said.

"I might need the day," I told him.

He solemnly agreed and drove away.

Joel, my building concierge, helped me get my things into the elevator. He wanted to tell me about my pile of mail and who'd come and gone while I was away. But I wasn't ready. "I'll come down later, and you can give me the full report," I told him. "Right now I need to go figure out how a person can feel rapture, anger, and loss, all in a day's time and still," I sniffled, "well, survive." Poor Joel. He smiled politely as the elevator doors closed with me inside.

I was welcomed by the comforting sight of my petite flat. My favorite wool blanket was folded at the end of the couch; my teacups were all lined up on little hooks underneath the cupboards. But when I peered into Ana's room and saw that she'd already packed up and moved her things, I sank into the couch. My joints ached, and my jaw was sore with an arthritic kind of sadness that sits deep in the bones. I numbed my inflamed feelings on daytime television, and eventually toast with jam, which was all I could find to eat in my sparse kitchen cabinets. Then I pulled the wool blanket over me and fell asleep.

When I woke, the light was low in the sky and the clock read 5:06 p.m. That was the moment—fresh from sleep—that I felt my love for Griffin eclipse my uncertainties. I reached for my phone to ring him, to tell him that I couldn't imagine my life now without him in it, that I believed we could overcome anything together. But when I picked up my phone, I saw that I'd missed a call. I casually played the message.

Gracie, this is Linda in Olivia Garza's office. It's four thirty.
We've been waiting thirty minutes and you're not here. We hope
you're still coming in today for your audition, but we will be
wrapping up in an hour so . . . okay. Take care.

"Noooooo!" I screamed at my phone. "No, no, no, no, no!"

How could this be? They'd changed the date. Just yesterday I had done the math. Three more rehearsals, two more days, one more chance.

But this was not a sum that could be counted. Some things just don't add up.

31

COOPER

The difference between patterns in human behavior and patterns in the natural world is that nature relentlessly adapts to its conditions. You can watch a sunflower turn its head toward the sun in an afternoon. People take longer. A person might stare into the darkest part of their life, day after day, before learning how to shift their view.

Because of a supernova explosion, and the culmination of stardust the perfect distance from the sun, we got ourselves a planet formed by carbon, nitrogen, and oxygen. And when you burn something that was alive, you get billions of carbon atoms that create DNA. Something new grows from the ashes. Human behavior mimics this evolution, but with resistance. Why? Because unlike the natural world, a person can question whether they are capable or worthy of creating something new. They might make the same pattern of decisions, over and over, before realizing they can turn in a new direction.

I met Griffin at Oakview when he got back into town. I arrived early and spent ten minutes talking with his pop about sports and the upcoming holidays. Griffin's knock hit the door with insistence.

"How's the car?" Owen asked right away.

"A little carburetor issue at the end, but she's fine. She'll be fine," Griffin said.

Owen only sighed.

"How's Mom?"

"Not a great day, I'm afraid."

Griffin sat next to Lara in a stiff chair, in a stiff position. "It's Beau," he said gently, but she did not respond. He let his head fall into his hands.

"Maybe tomorrow will be better," Owen told him. "Tomorrow she'll be glad to see you." But there wasn't a damn one of us who believed it.

I tried to take Griffin out for a beer, but he insisted on coffee. We went to Joe's Café and got a couple of bowls of chili and corn bread. He spent more time staring out the window at the steeple of Fidelis than he did eating his lunch. He looked like shit.

"I have that meeting at the *Tribune* tomorrow," he said.

I bobbed my head and wondered if his plan to save Fidelis was just another futile attempt to save himself. "So, we're all going to go to the Ale House tonight," I said, changing the subject. "You in?"

"I'm going to sit that one out."

I almost laughed. "What are you talking about, you're going to sit that one out? You love the Ale House."

"I need to get my shit together." It was as clear as the grip on his coffee cup that he wasn't sure what that meant. "I can't just spend my time at your house and P.J.'s house and the Ale House."

"Okay," I said, a little defensive. "Well, what are you after? 'Cause whatever it is, just fucking get after it, will ya?"

He gave me a hard look.

I had grown impatient. "Okay, I know I blew up your life."

"It wasn't just you," he mumbled.

"It wasn't my place to get involved, and I handled things badly. I'm sorry. But you can't just sit on the sidelines from now on."

"You think that's what I'm doing?"

"I think you're dropping the ball."

"What the fuck are you talking about?"

"You like Gracie?"

The answer was all over his face.

"Then why are you sitting here with me, eating bad chili?"

"I don't know if it's going to work," he said grimly.

"There's things you can't fix."

"You think I don't know that?"

He hadn't let me finish. "But there's things you *can* fix."

He took a bite of corn bread, maybe hoping I'd do the same and shut up.

"It's self-sabotage, man. You sitting here like this. I can handle you being pissed at me. But stop punishing yourself."

He shook his head. "I let everybody down."

"No, you don't."

"I never go anywhere, but the one time I leave town, that's the time Mom decides she wants to have a chat. Been waiting around for years, and I fucking missed it."

"Yeah, you did. You missed it. But you had no control over that."

He got up from the booth.

"Where you going?"

"Back over to Oakview."

"She's not going to know you're there."

"I know. But it's just what I do."

He was back in town only a few hours and already back to his sad routine.

———

When I left Joe's, I headed for the Ivy. I'd been hoping to hear back from Bisset, but people staying in hotels have a habit of not checking their messages. Maybe she'd seen the phone's flashing light and thought it was just the front desk asking if she wanted turndown service. I still had the note she'd left for Gracie, and Gracie was already back in town. I was getting antsy.

I walked into the elegant lobby of the boutique hotel and asked the guy behind the reception desk if he'd mind calling Bisset's room. He tapped his finger on his chin as he checked the computer and then squint over the rim of his wire glasses. "She's checked out," he said. Suddenly my chili wasn't settling so well.

"Look, I know it's probably not your policy to share personal information, but is there any chance you'd be willing to get a message to her?"

The man turned up his nose. "She's no longer our guest."

"But she was a few hours ago, and she had to have left a phone number." I leaned in. "She's just missed the opportunity to connect with the very person she came to town to see. What do you say? Will you give her a call?" I slid my business card across the counter, and he picked it up with two careful fingers.

"I'll discuss it with my manager," he said, before directing his attention to a woman waiting to check in.

I backed out of the way and then out of the hotel. I hit a nearby convenience store and dropped an Alka-Seltzer into a bottle of red Gatorade. I downed the frothing red liquid, thinking I'd let my stomach settle, and the day, then see where the chips fell. If I didn't have anything of substance by morning, I'd come clean to Gracie.

32

GRACIE

Ana sat at the end of the couch with my feet in her lap. I was in yesterday's clothes, and worse, yesterday's makeup. "Have you heard the one about the guy who goes to the doctor?" she asked.

I looked at her through puffy eyes and smudged mascara and shook my head.

"Well, this guy goes to the doctor and the doctor says, 'I'm so sorry, but I have bad news and even worse news.' The guy says, 'What's the bad news?' and the doctor says, 'You only have twenty-four hours to live.' The guy gasps and says, 'That's awful! How could there be news worse than that?' And the doctor says, 'I've been trying to get ahold of you since yesterday.'"

I felt the muscles in my face break into a smile, but when I tried to laugh, my head throbbed. "Is this what a hangover feels like?"

"You could use some sleep. And a shower would do you wonders."

I swung my feet onto the floor and sat up, a little dizzy. "What time is it?"

"Eight thirty in the morning," she said, yawning. "And you're out of coffee."

I stood and heard my back crack.

"Are you going to be okay on your own? I mean, for the weekend. Obviously, I don't mean like in general. 'Cause I could come back for a while and—"

"No," I cut her off. "I'll be fine. Don't I look like I'll be fine?" I said, throwing clumps of thick tangled hair off my shoulders ironically.

She couldn't keep a straight face.

I stayed under the hot water in the shower until my skin became an unnatural shade of pink. I dressed in black leggings, a warm black top, and my Converse low-tops, then wrapped my heavy red scarf around my neck and headed out toward the Harris Theater.

Traffic was a bear, and at ten o'clock, cabs were still scarce. I punched the ride app on my phone, and ten minutes later, a nice lady in a white Honda Civic picked me up.

When I stepped out of the car, I saw Myla Jane strumming away on her guitar. I nodded in her direction, and she nodded in mine as I hurried to the entrance of the theater.

I found the doors locked, but a woman in a slick ponytail saw me at the glass. She crossed the lobby with a no-nonsense expression and opened the door about six inches. "Crew members enter on the other side," she said.

"Oh, I'm not crew. I'm Gracie Wilder. I was scheduled to see Ms. Garza today."

"Yesterday," she corrected. "You're a day late. We waited. But not this long."

"There's been a mistake," I tried. Ponytail girl held the door firm. "I received a call saying my appointment had changed from Thursday to Friday at four."

She cocked her head and narrowed her gaze. "Your appointment didn't change."

"Can I please speak with Ms. Garza? If I could just explain to her—"

"You had your chance, and you should know by now, they don't come along every day." With that, she closed the door and spun on her heels. I stood frozen at the glass, watching her walk away.

Somewhere between five and twenty-five minutes later, I heard Myla ask, "You going to stand there all day?"

I turned. She was holding her guitar silently across her body.

"Why so blue?"

"That dream of mine isn't going to happen."

"You sure about that?" she asked.

"Quite sure. I'm a dancer without a stage."

Myla flinched with surprise. "That's the stupidest thing I ever heard. The world's your stage, young lady. You're knockin' on the door, lookin' for someone to give you something. *Shit.* Don't wait for someone to give you permission to do what you want to do. You a dancer? Then go dance!"

"It's not like that," I said. "I mean, it was going to be so much more than that. I had plans to really do things, create things, change things." Even to my own ears it sounded stupid.

"You want to change things, then go change them. You down on your luck? Then you get your ass back up."

I shook my head with a feeling of powerlessness.

"There's more than one way to skin a cat," Myla said. "Now, are you going to buy a song?"

I lazily pulled a couple of dollars out of my bag and attempted to hand them to her.

"You got anything more in there?"

I was both annoyed and a little charmed by Myla's ability to say what she thought and ask for what she wanted. I dug into my bag and this time pulled up a loose twenty-dollar bill. She took it from my hand and said, "I got an idea. Follow me."

I found myself blindly following Myla and my twenty-dollar bill. "What's this all about?" I finally asked.

"We're going to the pavilion," she said.

"The Pritzker Pavilion?" It was the outdoor music arena that sat right behind the Harris Theater. It had been designed by the architect Frank Gehry and had a modern crown with giant stainless-steel petals peeling away from center stage.

"No performances there this time of year. Until now." She was laughing.

"Myla, is that even allowed? Can't you just play here? Or by the park?"

"I'm getting you a stage, baby girl."

I reeled back, my feet taking me several steps in reverse. "Oh no—"

"You just got to put it all out there. Then you'll feel better." She grabbed my hand and pulled me onward.

"But there's no point. It's not like anyone is going to notice."

We were nearly there now. She glanced back at me. "*You'll* notice. And I'll have twenty dollars."

Myla walked onto the stage and disappeared from my sight. When she reemerged a moment later, she was accompanied by a tall, lanky man with thick gray eyebrows and a mustache. "This is Mel. He owes me a favor," Myla said with a grin.

"You have five minutes," Mel explained.

"Is this going to get us arrested?" I had no interest in humiliating myself or ending up in the city jail.

"Not if you're any good," Myla noted with a hint of comedy. "So, what's your song? I know all the classics."

"I don't know." It was too much pressure. "Maybe you just play, and I listen."

"Maybe I just play—you know, write you a little something—and you just follow the music. Can you do that?"

"Fine," I told Myla, thinking I should just get the spectacle over with. "But not too loud, okay?"

"Loud is the point. Go on and be big and loud," she said, pointing for me to stand center stage while she positioned herself on the apron.

"This is stupid," I called back to her.

"We'll see."

I unwound my scarf and took off my shoes before facing four thousand empty seats and a dozen pedestrians walking the perimeter. I was cold, but I figured I would soon be hot with humiliation.

I took a deep breath and watched as Myla scanned the sky, searching for inspiration. Then, pausing with a smile, she plucked the first few notes. They reverberated through the brilliant acoustics of the pavilion and traveled down my spine, raising the hair on my arms. She sang:

> *Like powerful notes from an old guitar, or a weary girl, made to be a star. There's something here; come on 'n see. Come on, it's time to fall free.*

I vacillated, but after a few more lines of music, I let Myla's voice guide the lift of my arms and my legs, dictate the movement of my body. I turned on the soles of my bare feet to a beautiful melody made with powerful resonance. This wasn't the blues. This was more like Myla's gospel. Her tone was rich; her notes were whole; her intonation was melancholy.

The tempo picked up and the song elevated to another level, sending me across the stage like my life depended on it. I could no longer make out the words, but I could feel them. The vibrations of the music and the energy coursing through me became one. I could no longer sense where I was, let alone fixate on a possible audience.

I found a cadence of breath and heartbeat. I split air and time with movement, sweat bursting from every pore and evaporating into the atmosphere. My body was light, honest, raw, strong, playful—fully alive. I reached and lifted and landed and soon encountered a joy so great that I could not contain it; I could only release it with every turn. The vibration inside me grew, an instrument all its own. It was like dark matter. It was like the universe. It was like the soul. Millions of life-changing moments fueled me into flight, and when I settled into the last note from Myla's guitar, all I could hear was the sound of my own pulse. All I could feel was the rhythm of the earth and the vibrato of everything.

I stood there dripping with sweat and emotion, watching swirls of colors solidify into shapes, then become people. Vibrations vaguely collected like distant echoes and became recognizable sounds.

Crowds had formed on either side of the pavilion perimeter. People were cheering and clapping. Myla looked at me from over one shoulder, winked, and said, "Now *that's* what I call putting it all out there."

33

ÉLOÏSE

Celina had slept in like a teenager. I was putting dishes away in the kitchen when Gracie called. "Is everything okay?" I asked right away.

"Yes," she said, nearly breathless. "I understand it now. Why your mother chose to give me the story of the blackbird."

"She said it chose *you*," I told her.

Sounds of car horns and truck brakes screeched in the background. "I wouldn't have understood it if she had just said to me all those years ago, *Hey, kid, you will fall on dark times. But if you listen, you will find the one person who can lead you out. You will find yourself.*"

I stood frozen at the kitchen sink, flooded with feelings of sorrow and joy and certainty.

"That's what it's about, right? The story?" Gracie asked.

"Yes," I managed. "It's a story of finding your true spirit. That insight and spark woven within yourself."

"Thank you, Éloïse," she said, city sounds swelling around her.

"Celina and I send our love," I whispered, not wanting my voice to crack under the weight of emotion.

She promised she'd call again soon and then said goodbye.

I stood in the silence for a long time, a smile lifting my face like the soft rising of a crescent moon.

———

I was sitting with a mug of coffee, admiring the terra-cotta plate in the middle of my kitchen table, when I heard Celina coming down the hall. I pushed my chair back with the instinct to assist her. But she was so strong now, so capable. She came into the room in her pink pajamas, one supported step at a time. "I hate that they're gone," she said.

"The house is quieter now," I admitted. Maybe quieter than it had ever been.

"Will she really come back?"

"Yes. And we can go visit."

Celina came closer and hovered over the table to see what had been holding my attention.

For the past two days I had worked with small, colorful pieces of glass to make a mosaic. I had paced through fragments of a story in my mind and transformed the persimmon-colored clay into a floral landscape. I was rather proud of the result. A red poppy burst brightly against pinks, yellows, and greens. It wasn't perfect, but I had made it more beautiful than it had asked to be.

Celina touched one finger to the words I'd inscribed at the bottom: *Eternal Spring.* "What's it for?" she asked.

"The wall." I gestured to where the other plates sat on hooks in neat rows. "I felt it was time for a new story."

She raised an eyebrow. "There's a story in the plate?"

"Sit down," I said, "and I'll tell you. You're not too old for stories, are you?"

She shrugged and settled in beside me. "What's it about?"

"Well," I paused to consider, "it's about the most wonderful season of my life." I leaned back in my chair. "It's about *you*."

And just as my mother had done with me, I sat at the kitchen table and told my daughter a story.

34

COOPER

Gracie was out when I arrived. I'd finally gotten the nerve to tell her about Jackie Marley and return the note from Michelle Bisset, but when Joel greeted me in the lobby of her building, he said, "Your cousin left about thirty minutes ago." Part of me was relieved. I thought about coming clean to Joel. I needed to clear my conscience. But I wasn't sure how that story would sound coming out of my mouth: *I'm actually not her cousin. I stole that note hoping it would lead me to some information, make me a hero in Gracie's story, and put me back in the good graces of my best friend.*

I decided to skip that speech and instead just told Joel, "Tell her Daryl dropped by."

Twenty minutes later, I had burned through three and a half cigarettes and walked ten city blocks. When my phone rang, I stopped in my tracks. It was Geneva Wilks, Mr. Wilder's former assistant. I stamped my cigarette out on the sidewalk and ducked into a Starbucks to escape the howl of the wind.

"Is this Daryl Cooper?" she asked when I said hello.

I had to raise my voice to be heard over the screech of the espresso machine. "This is Cooper. What's up, Geneva?"

"Can you come into the office?"

"Sure."

"Like, right now?"

"I'm on my way."

I hailed a cab, paid the cabbie too much money, and was there in ten minutes.

I was winded when the woman at reception greeted me. "Will you let Geneva know Daryl Cooper is here," I said, trying not to pant. But Geneva was out at reception before the call was made. I followed her down the hall, her patent leather heels only two quick clicks in front of my long strides. Her stacked gold and gemstone bracelets jingled with persistence.

She halted our march at her desk and spoke to me in a hushed voice. "It just arrived. I haven't alerted anyone yet. You have ten minutes to talk me through this, and then I'm sending it to IT."

I was a thrill of nerves. She motioned for me to sit in the chair opposite her. I cracked my knuckles and complied. She closed her personal laptop, put it on a shelf under her desk, pulled out another laptop—David Wilder's—and powered it on. We waited in uncomfortable silence while it slowly glowed to life. I glanced around at the fine artwork on the wall behind her and the large magnet board beside her desk that neatly held dozens of memos and notes. "Beautiful fall day, isn't it?" I said, a poor attempt at charming conversation. Her reticent glare told me that she was in no mood for small talk.

"Okay. What now?" she asked. I quietly talked her through a soft boot and a password change, but when we hit a roadblock, I had to try to explain an override. After the whole of ten minutes, she slumped back into her chair with defeat. "This was a bad idea," she said. But I wasn't ready to give up. I got to my feet and started pacing the space behind her desk. I tried to describe a more complicated approach, but Geneva's co-workers were starting to get curious, and Geneva was growing more uncomfortable. "This isn't working," she moaned, throwing up a hand in frustration. Her bracelets clanged and then fell silent.

"I just need to think."

"Should I try logging in with words like *Grace Marie* or *The Three Lions?*"

"What's The Three Lions?"

"The nickname for England's football team. He was a devout fan."

The login was set up to allow only three tries at a password before locking. "Yeah, okay. Try that one," I decided. It was a weak attempt and it failed.

Geneva shook her head. "You should go. I'm sorry. Please tell Gracie I tried."

My blood pressure was up. I didn't like dead ends. "Five more minutes," I urged. "I have another idea." But Geneva was resolute. She was done. I wanted to argue, to convince her that we were almost in, but her lips were drawn tight with stress. "Okay," I surrendered. Her expression was sympathetic then. I was aware of my failure, and I avoided her pitying look. My eyes landed instead on a flyer tucked into a neat row of papers on the magnet board. It was one of the notices postponing the 150th anniversary celebration of the Abrams Building, a storyline that seemed to follow me everywhere I went. "Do you know the building?" I asked.

She followed my gaze to the flyer. "Yeah. Mr. Wilder loved it and went there a lot before it closed down. It's right around the corner from his favorite café."

"Joe's?"

"That's the one." She reached for the flyer. "I suppose I can take this down now."

A thought came at me like a bullet. I straightened my shirt and took a couple of steps back. "Geneva," I said quietly, "try typing in the password *Fidelis*."

"What's that?"

"A name that might have meant something to Mr. Wilder." I spelled it for her, and she carefully punched in the letters. Then I watched her lips part with astonishment. We were in.

35

GRIFFIN

Mom was napping in her wheelchair by the window when I arrived on Friday. I took the chair that was typically Pop's and pulled it into a spot adjacent to her. I would be there when she woke.

It was an hour before her eyes fluttered open. "Hey there. How you doing?" I asked tenderly, wondering if she even assessed these things.

Her face lifted at the sight of me. "Beau?"

My heart stopped. "Yes, Mom, it's me. It's Beau." I reached over and rested my hand on hers. "I'm here."

She smiled and whispered, "The stairs."

"The stairs?"

Her words were slow as if she was selecting each one with care. "You came running up the stairs. To the door."

I felt a deep ache in my chest. As a kid I always ran the last block home from school, and when I saw the steps up to the front door of my house, I ran even faster. "I'd run into the house," I said.

She nodded. "You'd sing, *It's me.*" Her voice crackled as it lifted.

"Yes." I swallowed back tears. "And you would call out, *Hi me.*"

"I've been gone."

"But you haven't been alone," I told her. "And I'll stay with you."

She patted my hand, and her eyes drifted to the window. "You wanted to build things. Like Fidelis."

Once, a long time ago, she had known the boy who bounded up the steps to her home. She had asked me where I was going each time I left. She had known what I loved and what I dreamed. "Yes, it was my favorite. And you knew it when it was still a church."

"The businessman," she said, returning my gaze.

"Yes, the businessman. He changed it, didn't he? Mr. Abrams."

Her eyes searched mine. She reached up and touched my cheek with her cool, frail hand. "My boy," she said, soothing years of sadness. "It hasn't been easy for you."

I shook a little as I struggled not to cry.

"But there is always a gift." She withdrew her hand, still I could feel its imprint on my face.

"I love you, Mom."

"I love you," she said. "Now, go be happy."

It was only a moment later when her face became agitated, and she tried to stand. I told her that she was okay—that we could just sit together a while longer. But she said that she had to go to work. The nurse hurried in to calm her while I stood by wiping my face on my sleeves.

———

I was in the hallway when I heard Pop walking up.

"Beaumont, I thought you were at home. Gracie was just downstairs hoping to find you. I'm sorry. I didn't know." He took a closer look at me. "You okay?"

"She knew me, Pop." His face softened into a smile I rarely saw anymore. "It was great, and then . . . then she had to go to work."

Pop pulled me in for a hug. "She's been wanting to go to Marshall Field's to work the sales counter again for a couple of days. In her mind, she's still twenty-five." His expression was bittersweet when he pulled away. "I'm so glad you had a moment with her. What else did she say?"

"She mentioned Fidelis. How I'd always wanted to build things. Oh, and *the businessman*," I said, still processing those two treasured minutes.

"The businessman? You mean the interview you were supposed to have before you left town?"

I shook my head. "No, not David Wilder." She couldn't have remembered that. But my mind was racing. "Pop . . . you know, I gotta get going."

"Go ahead, son. Go find Gracie."

I walked down the hall toward the elevator, passing folks in wheel-chairs and on walkers. Everywhere I looked, stories sat in silent mouths and hearts beat wildly with questions. That place was the whole damn world. Hand to God. It was unmistakable. And it was in that place that I finally heard what my life had been telling me.

36

COOPER

Michigan Avenue was a rush of parkas, so I cut over to Lakefront Trail with the joggers and parents pushing strollers. There was a couple at the waterfront holding hands as if it were July, and an older man in a fedora walked the path with his hands clasped behind his back.

When I was a good distance from all the foot traffic, I called Griffin. "Where you at?" I asked as the wind threatened to lift my Hawks cap right off my head.

"Just left Oakview. Getting off the El at Sedgwick. What's up?"

He sounded rushed, so I cut to the chase. "I was able to access Wilder's account. Gracie will be getting her father's letter after all."

I could only hear a train thundering distantly on the other end of the line. "She has a sister," he finally said. "Family she didn't know about. That's probably what it says."

"Also . . . about the outfit that bought Fidelis . . ."

"Let me guess," he said. "It's owned by David Wilder?"

That stopped me. "Close." I stepped off the trail and used a wide tree as a windshield. "David Wilder's personal attorney, George Brockwell, helped him solidify the Abrams deal out of the way of the news spotlight.

Kept it a secret under the name Garden Group. But Brockwell only just discovered that Wilder signed the deed and permits over to *Gracie*. Can you even believe it?" There was a gap of silence. "Griffin?"

"A stage," he finally said, with a shudder of awareness. "*That*'s why he called me. He'd have wanted me to build her a stage."

"A stage?" I was still putting it together.

"A theater for the community. I always did say that the acoustics in there are incredible."

I was dumbfounded. Mr. Wilder had called the man who broke the facade of Fidelis, to ask him to restore its soul. "But how'd you figure it out?"

He took his time answering. "I'm not sure. I think it was something my mom said that helped me put it together. Yeah . . . she's the one who helped me figure it out."

We were both quiet for a moment so that our voices wouldn't break under the weight of what he'd just said. After all these years, Griffin had gotten a moment with his mom. I didn't understand it, but for once it didn't matter. "Well, Beau Griffin," I said, swallowing the lump in my throat, "it sounds like you can finally go get after it."

I could hear him smiling through the phone. "See you at flag football at four?"

He was back. "Yeah, don't be late. We're gonna be the team to beat this year."

———

I stayed by the lake trail long after the call. I found an empty bench and a break in the wind long enough to light a cigarette. I tried to grasp how Griffin's mom had helped him make sense of Fidelis. And how Gracie had arrived at the answers she needed without knowing why her father had been in the streets of Manhattan that night, without knowing who had typed the letter or where it had ultimately been sent.

I was always going to be your number one guy for tangible evidence and calling a spade a spade. We have to trace a line back through history to garner the facts. But as the nicotine buzzed in my bloodstream, I started to wonder if there was something outside the concrete causal chain that a man just can't get his fingers on. Some kind of element beyond nitrogen and carbon that permeates our lives.

It's enough to make a guy like me crazy, but maybe there *is* something like thread, connecting all of us to everything. Tugging at a woman void of memories and her son's ability to rebuild. Uplifting a man in his final hours with the notion that *it's not too late* and leading his daughter to understanding. Who knows, maybe it's even what gets the old man to his feet for his afternoon walk by the lake.

Of course, it's not tracible. But I could probably produce evidence. You know I could. Just don't ask me to define it. I'd rather just tip my cap.

37

GRIFFIN

I waited for the light to change at the underpass and crossed the street in front of Fidelis. Aside from the boarded-up windows, it looked no different from when I was a kid, and it felt like my whole life had been pointing me toward that moment.

Gracie was standing near the entrance and whirled around when she heard my footsteps. "Griffin, I've been looking all over for you."

"Aren't you supposed to be dancing for Olivia Garza today?"

She exhaled. "No. That's not going to happen now. Seems I'm not meant to dance with the best. But I think I've worked out how to dance with the best of myself." She cringed. "That must sound stupid."

It sounded like a gift. I took both of her hands in mine and bent my forehead to hers. "I'd go anywhere with you. Any adventure. I'd find a way."

"Me too," she said. "Anywhere!"

The gold chain around her neck glinted in the sunlight. I traced it with a finger and pulled up the key from where it had been tucked away. "I think there's one more lock to try."

She looked confused, but before I could say anything more, she pulled the chain from around her neck and walked to the entrance. She stood there for a moment looking up at the spire towering overhead. Her back was still to me when I heard the lock click and release. The door swung open, and she turned around, mirroring my amazement. "But why?"

"He didn't want it to be torn down."

She swayed on her feet. "But what am I supposed to do with it?"

I stepped closer and held her shoulders, steadying her as best I could. "Well . . . it would make a *great* theater."

"A theater?"

"A place to come together and be inspired. Just like you said."

Tears filled her eyes. "That was his idea, wasn't it? The Fidelis Theater." Her gaze lifted and her face brightened as if she could envision it.

"It would be a big job. But, if you need a contractor . . ."

She laughed, then buried her face in my chest and cried.

———

Stepping into the atrium that afternoon, seeing the grand arch of Fidelis with all its heartache and hope surrounding us, felt like a great homecoming. We walked to the center of the building where the office lofts had been erected, almost entirely concealing the building's architectural beauty. I showed Gracie how the lancet window could be freed to direct pools of sunlight at her feet and where a stage could rise from below the engaged column. We talked about bringing artists together—architects and carpenters, dancers and musicians—and bringing the community back into the walls of Fidelis. We walked the marble tile floors and ran our hands along the arc of stone trimmed with bits of paper. Fidelis's history and its heart were palpable, and it was clear she felt it too. Her expression was one of awe when she looked at me with those kaleidoscope eyes and said, "Yes. I want to create something beautiful here. And I want to do it with *you*. What do you say?"

"Wilder," I sighed, "it's like I've been trying to tell you. We're in this together. No matter what it is or what comes our way." And there under the splintered arch of Fidelis, I kissed her.

Later, as we were leaving—idling in the sunlight spilling through the large open door—something small and familiar caught Gracie's eye. "Look," she pointed. There, among thousands of petitions wedged into the arch, was a piece of paper with bright red trim. David Wilder was woven into the stone and into the living, breathing story of Fidelis.

"Do you think it was meant to be?" she asked.

I smiled. "I don't know. But Fidelis would tell you if it could. It knows the whole story."

38

GRACIE

When Griffin and I finally locked the oak door of Fidelis that October day, our hands intertwined like grapevines, my eyes fell from the great blue windswept sky to the woman sitting serenely on the bench just outside. Her head was tilted to the side, her gaze reaching the steeple. Her auburn hair fell in wisps around her face, and her red lips were puckered with interest. I knew her immediately, the way you know your own heart.

She stood from the bench when she saw me, her eyes swimming. I ran to her, a deep cry escaping me as I threw my arms around her neck. Madame Bisset held me like the child I had been, like the woman I'd become. And when she was finally able to pull free of my grasp, she gave me the letter I'd been longing for. But I already knew what it said.

I had found the words my father hadn't spoken in a historic city and a haunting countryside, in treasured photographs, their edges loved away, and in memories made new with contemplation. I had found his words in people I knew and in people I'd never met whom I grew to love. I had found them in what I'd created because of him, and in what he believed I could still do.

I found my father's words inside of me. I found them long before I got his letter.

Dear Grace Marie,

You were a baby when I promised your mother that I would protect you and teach you to love the world. I struggled. It is hard to love the world when your heart is broken, and my heart broke when your mother died. You are the one who saved me from many nights of despair. You would twirl into the room or smile at me from across the table, and I'd see a love so generous that I'm not sure I ever felt worthy of receiving it.

I wasn't able to protect you when you needed me most. I've never known how to speak of my regret. But the miracle is that you showed me that you could still love the world. You have been bold and brave, wiser and more courageous than your father. And you have been brighter than any light in my life.

If you can find it in your heart, I'd like for you to meet a girl named Celina Fournier. I came to know her mother years ago, and though our connection was brief, Celina was born, a child with great vision. I wish I'd known how to introduce the two of you myself. I wish a great many things. My hope is that now you will come to know each other as family.

I will never forget the first time I took you to the ballet. You said that one day you might dance on a big stage too, and later, you asked me to buy you a blackbird. A bird of promise, we were told, that could help you find your way if you got lost. I was never quite sure what would help you find your way, Gracie dear. Remarkably, you went on to perform on many big stages. Still, you dreamed of a place that would feel like home—a stage that would not only elevate you as a dancer, but would elevate joy. I've long wanted to build you that stage, in the same way I suppose every parent wants to hold their child up and say to the world, Look how lovely. But I know that dreams must be built by the dreamers themselves. So, my wonderful, imaginative girl, after all these years, I give you the blackbird, and with it, the key to a place that knows what it means to dream. Fidelis. Dance, my darling. And know that I have always and will always love you.

Oh, and Gracie dear, I'm so sorry I'm late.

—Dad

AUTHOR'S NOTE

ONE THING WE CAN ALL attest to is that there is no love without loss; it is the other side of the same coin. What deeply interests me is how loss impacts our identity. Whether it's the death of a loved one, the end of a relationship, a trauma that steals pieces of us, or intergenerational heartache, these experiences change how we understand who we are. Again and again, I see that we become what we believe ourselves to be. So, it feels important to consider the origins of our beliefs, the stories that were given to us and the narratives born of our own experience. What happens to the girl who swallows a story that says she is unlovable? What happens to the man who carries the myth that he is worthless? How do we make meaning from our sorrow and heal the wounds that we carry? This was my inspiration for *Threads of Us*.

At the start of the novel, Gracie Wilder has buried her history, giving her pain time to embed itself, resulting in shame and anxiety. Beau Griffin is living in his past; he is stagnant in his grief, unable to feel much of anything in the present. I wanted to explore what would happen if these characters stopped being passive in their pain and instead chose a path of presence and action. I gave their inner healing an outward journey, one that could be transformative.

I chose contemporary dance for Gracie Wilder in part because I love dance, but also because I wanted her healing process to permeate the external. She has echoes of trauma in her body that keep her from fully living in her body, and her choreographed life does not have her feeling free. Her need for bodily autonomy and agency drives much of her journey. (One might also go as far as to say that the work of healing is itself a dance—one step backward, two steps forward.)

As I was writing *Threads of Us*, I explored some questions that live at the intersection of my faith and my love of science. Can we distinguish coincidence from synchronicity? What is happenstance, and what is meant to be? How do we make sense of the difficult things that happen to us? The character Daryl Cooper represents hard facts and evidence, whereas Gracie Wilder represents a more intuitive search for the living truth. I entertain the question, *Can love transform our suffering?* My intention is not to alleviate the mystery woven within life, but rather to bring light to the power of love, which is itself a mystery.

The Fidelis building in the novel is fictitious but inspired by real history. Thanks to my father's research, I know that my great-great-great-grandparents, Luke and Nora, settled in Chicago from Ireland in 1867. They lived in the area we now know as Old Town. The only place in that neighborhood where I can be sure they spent time is St. Michael's church. The Great Fire of 1871 took much of the city and left St. Michael's damaged but standing. Years ago, I went to visit the church for the first time, and when I ran my hands along the walls, I couldn't help but wonder if Luke and Nora's prayers were still lingering between those stones along with the hopes of generations. This was my inspiration for Fidelis and its historic arch in *Threads of Us*. It serves as a tangible representation of intergenerational love and pain, as well as the question: *How can we heal our way forward while also healing history backward?*

The novel ends on a note of hope and vision for the future. It ends here because we build life one day at a time, and one thing we can be sure of is that we will persist. We can be sure that we are powerful beyond belief. I'd like to think that we can draw toward us all manner of dreams if our longing is just long enough. If we don't give up. Like Gracie Wilder, we might find that there is music everywhere. We might hear something within ourselves that will empower the narrative. We might find the answer we've been looking for within our very own story—a glimmer of gold, a hidden thread.

———

Thank you to Lisa Fugard, Katie Gilligan, Heather Hach, Kari Estrin, Meta Valentic, Becky Pfordresher, Kim Gruenenfelder, Missy Masters, Jennifer Good, Gaylyn Fraiche, Margaux Froley, Jen Jones Donatelli, Jenny Rieger, Elizabeth Finlay, and Kelley Syverson for offering me feedback and encouragement during different stages of this process.

Thank you to my family of origin: Mom, Dad, Caroline, Andrew, and our whole bighearted clan. What would we do without us? And thank you to my chosen family: incredible friends who are with me on the best days, the worst days, and everything in between. I love you.

My deepest thanks to Kevin, Adeline, Keegan, and Brennan. You are my heart. My very best story. Let's keep dreaming. Together, anything is possible.

ABOUT THE AUTHOR

CHRISTIE HAVEY SMITH'S LOVE FOR story was shaped in the film business, and for over a decade she has been helping people explore their own narratives. She has taught creative and contemplative writing at Loyola Marymount University and the Greenhouse—a local retreat center she founded. She is also the author of the narrative nonfiction work *From Three Feet Off the Ground*.

christiehaveysmith.com